confessions OF A klepto-maniac

JESSICA SORENSEN

Confessions of a Kleptomaniac
All rights reserved.
Copyright © 2015 by Jessica Sorensen

ISBN: 978-1517638306

This is a work of fiction. Any resemblance of characters to actual persons, living or dead, is purely coincidental. The author holds exclusive rights to this work. Unauthorized duplication is prohibited.

No part of this book can be reproduced in any form or by electronic or mechanical means including information storage and retrieval systems, without the permission in writing from author. The only exception is by a reviewer who may quote short excerpts in a review.

Any trademarks, service marks, product names or names featured are assumed to be the property of their respective owners, and are used only for reference. There is no implied endorsement if we use one of these terms.

For information: *jessicasorensen.com*

Cover Design and Photo by Mae I Design
www.maeidesign.com

Interior Design and formatting by:
Christine Borgford, Perfectly Publishable
www.perfectlypublishable.com

Confession

ONE

I'm far from the perfect person everyone thinks I am.

Luna

"I WANT YOU to light it on fire." My mom urges the matches and lighter fluid toward me. "You should be the one to do this. It was your mistake."

I tuck my hands behind my back as I look at my clothes, jewelry, and a few pairs of heels piled on the back lawn. "I can't."

"Luna, this isn't up for debate. You will burn these clothes. They're too immodest. I can't believe you bought them." She points a finger at the pile of clothes. "Those shorts are too short, and don't even get me started on the skirts. They don't even go to your knees. Our rules are no skirts unless they go to your knees. You know that, so why would you wear it? What's wrong with you?" She shakes her head, utterly disgusted with me. "Your father and I taught you to be better than this." She eyes the skinny jeans and black T-shirt I'm wearing. "Maybe we should burn those jeans, too. They look really tight."

"These jeans are fine," I mutter, wishing I could stand

up for myself once in my life.

I wish I could say a lot of things to her: Her standards are too high. I don't think I'll ever be the perfect, proper, church going daughter she wants me to be. I'm nowhere near perfect. Some of the stuff I've done . . . They'd probably lock me up if they knew everything about me.

Just open your mouth and tell her you don't want to burn your clothes, that you like the shorts and skirts.

My mouth opens, but no sound leaves me lips, and I shake my head, disappointed with myself. Even at eighteen years old, I still feel like a child whenever I'm around my parents.

"I'm not going to argue with you." She smooths invisible wrinkles from her turtleneck sweater. It's eighty degrees outside; she has to be sweating to death. But that's how she always dresses, like she's afraid to show even an inch of skin. "After what you did last weekend, you're lucky you're getting off this easy."

Easy? Is she kidding me?

Gritting my teeth, I grab the lighter fluid and box of matches from her hand and turn to the pile of clothes. The smell of the lighter fluid makes me gag as I douse my beautiful skirts and shorts I've secretly been wearing over the last year.

I was always careful not to wear them any place my mom might see me. I'd change into the outfits at school or at one of my friends' houses then change back before I returned home. But last weekend, I was at one of the few parties I've gone to when the cops showed up and forced everyone to call their parents. I didn't have an extra set of clothes with me, so not only did my parents have to come and pick me up from a party, but they saw me in the little black dress I had on.

Burning the clothes is my punishment, and my mom

also put a tracking app on my phone so she can keep tabs on me. It's not the first time she has done this, and I'm guessing it won't be the last.

"Now the match," my mom says after I've soaked the clothes with lighter fluid.

Tears burn my eyes as I pluck a match out of the box, strike the tip against the side, and drop it onto the pile. As the clothes erupt in flames, I have to look away. I stare down at the burn scars on my hands, struggling not to cry.

I got the scars when I was younger and our house caught on fire. I can't remember much about what happened, but sometimes, when I'm dreaming, I see myself in a bedroom, about to be burned alive.

"This is for the best." My mom's expression sharpens when she notes I'm looking at my scars. "Luna, get over it. We're outside, in the backyard. The house isn't going to burn down." She huffs an aggravated breath when I don't look up then cups my chin with her fingers, forcing me to meet her gaze. "This little phase you've been going through is going to end. Fitting in isn't what's important in life. As long as you live under my roof, you will obey our rules. You will wear clothes I pick out for you. You will never, ever wear a dress or any outfit like that again."

I smash my quivering lips together. She doesn't get it. Changing the way I dress isn't about fitting in. It's about being myself.

My parents have always been strict with me. They have hardcore beliefs about how people should behave and dress, and I'm expected to live up to those standards. Their beliefs aren't the only reason they're so strict, though. A lot of it has to do with how they were raised.

My grandparents on both sides are extremely intense. They frequently lecture my mom and dad on ways they need to improve not only themselves, but me, too. My parents act just like their parents do and have similar rules. There is no cursing allowed, only PG movies are permitted, and Sunday's are spent at church. I have to wear clothes my mom picks out, no makeup ever, and no dating unless she approves of the guy. My mom has only ever approved of one guy. He goes to our church and is about as boring as watching paint dry.

I went out on one date with him and was completely miserable. When I came home and told my mom I didn't want to see him again, she said, "You're expecting too much. Dating isn't supposed to be fun. It's supposed to be an opportunity to find a person to marry and start a family with. That's how things worked with your father and me."

I didn't know how to respond to that. I'm only a senior in high school, and marriage and starting a family are the last things on my mind. What about graduating? College? Of course, these were things I thought but didn't dare say aloud. I knew if I did, she'd give me a lecture about how I'm not going away to college, not if they have any part of it. Then I'd be punished—their way of trying to mold my mind to be more like theirs.

Things have been this way for as long as I can remember. I've never had control over my life, never had the chance to be my own person. I've never had the freedom to explore who I am, what I like, what I want.

What I do know about myself is that I sure as hell don't want to stay home after I graduate and wait for a future husband my parents approve of to put a ring on my finger and knock me up. I want to finally be able to explore who I am.

The outfits burning on the lawn are a step in that direction, my way to find out what *I* like. But in the back of my mind when I was wearing each outfit, I heard a voice whispering that what I was doing was wrong. I heard the voice every time I did something rebellious, and the voice sounded like my mother's.

"You don't want to turn out like your aunt Ashlynn, do you?" she asks as the fire simmers and hisses.

Whenever I screw up, she throws Aunt Ashlynn into the mix. She's what the Harveys consider the bad seed of the family. I haven't seen her since I was four years old and hardly remember anything about her, yet I feel like I know her since she's constantly used as an example.

I almost reply yes and tell my mom that I want to be just like Aunt Ashlynn. But the fear of getting kicked out of the house stops me. While I want to move out on my own, my parents won't allow me to get a job, so I have no money, no place to live, no nothing.

"No," I mumble, watching the flames blaze higher.

"Good, because after the stunt you pulled, I was starting to wonder if it was time to give up on you," she says coldly.

Maybe it's because I don't think I can do this anymore.

Silence stretches between us as the fire crackles, singeing the clothes and melting the jewelry.

Again, I look down at the jagged, elevated scars that cover my palms. Considering my history with fires, you'd think my mom would've picked a different punishment. But, no, that's not her style. She likes to punish to the max and make me as uncomfortable as she can.

"I need to go pick up a few things from the store for a school project," I lie, backing away from the fire.

"Take your phone with you so I can see where you are at all times," my mother shouts as I slide open the back door of the house. "You're on thin ice. If you keep heading in this direction, then . . ." She trails off, turning back to the fire. "This punishment will seem like a piece of cake."

I step inside the house and shut the door, wanting to scream until my lungs explode. I want to shout that I'm not a bad person, that I behave better than most of the people I know, and that I'm sorry I'm such a disappointment.

    Instead, I go out to the car and drive to the store, doing exactly what I'm supposed to do.

Confession

TWO

Sometimes, I do bad things just because it makes me feel better.

Luna

BY THE TIME I park in front of Benny and Gale's Corner Store, the sun is setting behind the shallow hills. Soon, the entire town will close up for the evening. That's how things work in Ridgefield. It has a 50s, small town, homey, good neighbor vibe.

Tourists who drive through here during the summer are always raving about what a fantastic town it is and how wonderful the people are. But I've grown up here, and not everything is how it appears. Like every other place in the world, the people who live in Ridgefield have secrets kept hidden behind locked doors. Sometimes, the occasional secret slips out and ends up printed in the news, like the time Mable Marleinton got arrested for drug possession and assault.

I have secrets, too. Mine have remained a secret, though. Thank God.

"Hey, Luna," Benny, the owner, greets me as I enter the store. "What are you doing out this late?"

I contain a sigh. "My mom needs me to pick up some last minute stuff for a brunch party she's having tomorrow," I lie.

His warm smile makes me feel a pang of guilt over what I'm about to do.

"Tell her I said hi, okay?" he says as he punches a few buttons on the register. "I haven't seen her for a couple of weeks."

"I will," I tell him then hurry down the nearest aisle.

I tie my hoodie around my waist and wander up and down the aisles, trying to figure out what I'm going to buy for the fake brunch party. I decide on some paper plates and cups with smiley face hearts on them. Then I veer down the makeup aisle and eye the section of brightly colored nail polish.

My mom would lose her mind if I painted my nails a bold color like luscious purple or seductive red. I don't even like red or purple that much, but just the thought of her telling me I can't paint my nails makes me want to.

What if I did do it? What if I said to hell with her rules and did whatever I wanted? What would she do? Probably get rid of me like she did Mr. Buttons, a puppy I found on my way home from school. My mom thought he was the cutest puppy in the world until he pooped on the carpet and chewed up a favorite pair of shoes after weeks of trying to train him. Then it was bye-bye, Mr. Buttons.

Is that where I'm heading? Is my mom going to kick my ass out the door like she did with Mr. Buttons?

Do I care?

Anger and guilt blaze through me. Why can't she just accept me for who I am? Why can't I act how I want without feeling guilty?

Nearly bursting with frustration, I snatch up some bottles of nail polish and stuff them into the pocket of my hoodie. For a second, I feel calm, like I have control over something. Then the images of my clothes on fire flash through my mind, and those invisible fingers wrap around my neck. Struggling not to scream, I start stuffing random items into my pocket one after the other. I'm not even paying attention to the items I'm picking up. Usually, I'm more careful, but today has been overwhelming, and I can't seem to think about anything except my clothes.

They're just clothes, I keep telling myself. But they weren't just clothes. They represented the time I spent finding my place in the world. And now it's all gone. Where does that leave me? Back to being my mom and dad's puppet? Back to dressing how they want me to, only listening to music they approve of, going to church, spending at least three hours a day working on homework even when I don't have anything to work on?

Sure, I have to do most of those things already, but being able to dress how I want gives me room to breathe. Now the air is gone again, and I'm going to spend every day feeling like I'm slowly drowning.

I add more items into my pocket, growing more furious by the second. But then I freeze mid-pocket stuff, realizing I'm not alone.

Standing down the aisle with his eyes trained on me is Grey Sawyer.

I gape at him with a hand-caught-in-the-cookie-jar look on my face.

Grey is one of those guys who is perfectly put together. His brown hair looks so soft, and he has these incredibly blue eyes. Plus, he's taller than me, which is rare considering I'm almost five-foot-eleven.

I used to have a crush on him—still do when I'm being honest with myself. Normally, I'd dance up and down that he's staring at me so intently. Right now, though, I wish he'd leave.

Instead, he keeps his eyes on me and cocks a brow.

Panic slams through me. How long has he been watching me? Maybe I should ask him. Just say, *Hey, did you just see me jack, like, ten items from sweet old Benny?* On top of that conversation being awkward, Grey and I aren't in the same social circles, and I don't know him well enough to guess how he'd react. All I really know about him, aside from the fact that he was blessed with the gorgeous gene, is he's popular and has a bunch of friends who constantly make fun of people. He sometimes joins in with them and acts like an asshole, but he has been quieter this school year.

It's strange to see him as the more reserved guy he's pretending to be. I've witnessed him be a cocky jerk several times, like during sophomore year when I asked him to go to the Girl's Choice Dance. It took all of my courage to ask him, and all he did was give me a once-over and tell me no fucking way. Then, two days later, he said yes to Cindy Pepperson, a pretty, popular cheerleader. That's when I realized he had a type, and I didn't fit the criteria.

The worst part was he told the entire school about the dorky, prude girl who asked him out, and I was mocked for an entire year. Back then, I was different, though. Back then, I still wore outfits approved by my mom . . . okay, which I guess I kind of do now.

My gut churns. I don't want to go back to being that girl.

I start to back away from Grey, figuring it might be better to make a run for it.

His head slants to the side as a mixture of curiosity and concern rises in his expression.

My heart thuds in my chest. *What the heck is that look for?*

"Did you find everything you needed for your mom's

party?" Benny appears at the end of the aisle.

I swallow the lump wedged in my throat. "Yep, I think so." I hold up the paper cups and plates I'm carrying as I peek over at Grey, wondering if he'll out me to Benny.

Grey's expression is neutral and completely unreadable, and my discomfort amplifies.

"Luna, I need to talk to you." Benny throws a swift glance in Grey's direction, and then his eyes land on me. "Could you come to the front of the store with me, please?"

Oh. My. God. He knows.

God. No. No. No. This can't be happening.

Vomit burns at the back of my throat as I nod.

Benny motions for me to follow him and heads down the aisle.

My adrenaline soars as I trail after him. What am I going to do? My parents are going to kick me to the street if they find out I've been shoplifting. Do I have time to empty out everything from my pocket?

As I squeeze past Grey, he reaches out and discreetly but quickly tugs my jacket off my waist.

"What are you doing?" I hiss as he puts on the oversized grey jacket like it's his own.

Before Grey can answer, Benny twists around with a stern look on his face. "Luna, I need to see you now, please."

Nodding, I hurry away from Grey, but I can feel his eyes boring a hole into the side of my head.

Once we make it up front to the register, Benny instructs me to empty out my pockets, and I do what he asks, taking out my cell phone, a pack of gum, and a ten-dollar bill.

Puzzlement etches his face as he sorts through my stuff then looks down at my waist, his confusion deepening.

I hold my breath, waiting for him to say something.

"I'm so sorry, Luna," he says, running his hand over

his bald head. "I thought maybe . . . You know what, never mind. I think I'm losing my mind in my old age."

"It's okay." I feel sick with guilt.

I hurry and pay for the paper plates and cups then bolt out the door and back to my car. By the time I turn on the engine, my heart is pounding so hard I swear it's going to give out on me.

I'm the worst person in the world. I really am. And now Grey knows it I am. Even my closest friends don't know I've been shoplifting for years. Not because I need the stuff, but because, for some messed up reason, it gives me a sense of control.

I consider waiting until Grey comes out of the store to get my jacket back. I could ask him why he did what he did—why he helped me out—and if he plans on telling anyone about it. But when I see him exit the store with my jacket on, I chicken out and hide in my car.

"This is so messed up. What the hell am I going to do?" I crank up the music. "Breathing Underwater" by Metric blasts through the speakers as I let out a deafening scream.

Confession THREE

> *I don't like geese.*
>
> Luna

FLAMES BLAZE AGAINST the walls, melting the paint and wallpaper. Smoke funnels through the air so thickly I can't see. I gasp for air as I roll out of bed and get down on all fours. The floor is hot against my palms as I crawl in the direction of my bedroom door.

"Mommy!" I cry as I blindly try to find my way out of my room. "Mommy, help me!"

The fire crackles and sweeps across the room, singeing the floor, the ceiling, everywhere. My eyes burn against the brightness, and my skin feels like melting wax.

"Mommy!" I shout and am turning in the opposite direction when the fire blocks my path.

So much smoke. I can't breathe.

No one is coming for me because I'm a bad girl. No one helps bad girls. My mom's words echo in my head, and I realize in horror that it must be true. No one is going to rescue me. The fire is going to kill me.

I fall flat on the floor as smoke circles me. I gasp for air, but with every breath, my lungs feel smaller, like they're shrinking.

"I can't breathe . . ." I choke out as my eyelids drift shut.

Pain, so much pain. Just let me die.

Suddenly, I'm lifted from the floor.

"Hang on, Luna. I'm going to get you out of here." The voice is so familiar, so comforting.

I open my eyes as I'm carried away and search through the smoke, trying to see their face, but all I see are smoke and flames.

Everywhere.

My eyes snap open, and I bolt upright in bed, dripping with sweat. It takes me a second to process that my room isn't on fire, that I'm safe.

I flop back down in my bed and stare up at my ceiling. I haven't dreamt about the fire in a while. I hate that it resurfaced. I don't like being reminded of that night almost fourteen years ago when I thought I was going to die until a fireman carried me out of the house. Or, at least that's what my parents tell me. I'm not so sure. Whenever I dream about what happened, it feels like I knew the person who rescued me. I have no clue why my parents would lie about something like that, though.

I try to go back to sleep, but my mind is too wired, and I end up lying in bed awake until the sun rises.

It's fall break, so I don't have school for an entire week. I hate when we get long breaks, because it means staying home with my mom. She won't let me out of the house, and I have no choice but to spend time with her, cooking, cleaning, and listening to her lectures on why I need to be a better person and how disappointed she is that she even has to tell me this, because I should just *know*. She won't let me have my phone, either, so I lose all communication with my friends. Thankfully, I managed to send them a text before I handed the phone over, so at least they know what's up.

Toward the weekend, she brings out the photos of her

sister, Aunt Ashlynn. In most of them, she looks around the same age as I am and resembles a younger version of my mom. She has freckles on her nose like I do, and for some crazy reason, I find comfort in the fact that I share a trait with the rebel of our extended family.

"See these, Luna?" My mom sits down beside me on the sofa and starts flipping through the photo album. "Look at how she's dressed. Look at the people she's hanging out with. Don't they look horrible? Doesn't she look miserable?"

I nod, but I don't agree at all. If you ask me, Aunt Ashlynn looks pretty damn happy in most of the photos, smiling and laughing with people I assume are her friends. I wonder if she's still happy now or happier even.

"What happened to her?" I stare at a photo of her on the beach with a group of friends. She's wearing cutoffs and a bikini top, and her eyes are lit up like she's happy. She looks so carefree, like she's saying to hell with her parents and their rules.

My mom's jaw ticks as she slams the album shut. "How would I know? I haven't spoken to her for almost fourteen years."

"Don't you miss her?" I ask. "Don't you want to know if she's okay?"

"No one misses Ashlynn." She rises to her feet and shoves the album back onto the shelf beside the mantle. "I'm going to cook dinner. Go and work on your homework until it's time to set the table."

"But I already did my homework."

"Well, do extra credit, then," she snaps then leaves the room.

I steal the album off the shelf, take it to my room, and spend the rest of the night pretending to do my homework while flipping through the album some more.

I've never had a chance to look at it alone. Usually, it's

a punishment tool to show me what I'm never supposed to become. Being by myself with plenty of time to absorb each moment, I get a sense of peace looking at the photos.

Right before I put the album back on the shelf, I remove a photo of my aunt Ashlynn at the beach and hide it under my mattress. As I fall asleep, I vow to myself that I'll one day get over my fear of my parents and live my life the way I want to. I'll be as happy as Aunt Ashlynn was in the photos.

The next day, I attend church with my family then return home and help my dad clean the garage. We don't talk. My father and I rarely do. I used to think it was because he was a man of few words, but when he's around other adults, he can be quite chatty.

The lengthy, dragged-out week gives me plenty of time to overanalyze what's going to happen with Grey when school starts again. What will he say to me about what happened? Maybe I will luck out, and he won't say anything at all.

By the time Monday rolls around, I'm forced to face the inevitable. I have to go to school and face Grey, and I have to do it while I'm wearing an outfit pre-selected by my mom.

When the sun comes up, she bursts into my room and picks out a pair of tan slacks two sizes too big along with a cardigan that buttons up to the neck. She even searches my bag to make sure I'm not trying to sneak any clothes out with me.

"Remember to come straight home after school," she reminds me as I grab the car keys from the wall hook. "And don't leave the campus until school gets out, even for lunch. I'll be checking your phone to make sure you don't. And I'm going to call the principal to let him know you're not allowed off campus."

I grind my teeth until my jaw aches.

"You did this to yourself." She stops stirring the pot to

yank on my sleeves and unroll them. "I don't even want to think about how you got ahold of clothes like that. I bet it was from one of those friends of yours."

Lately, she has been putting the blame on my friends whenever I do something wrong, like I've recently fallen in with the wrong crowd. But I've been friends with the same people since elementary school, and she knows this.

"It wasn't my friends." I grab a granola bar and a bottle of juice to take with me so I don't have to stick around and eat breakfast with her. "I bought those clothes myself."

"That makes it worse." She crosses her arms and stares me down. "That means you made bad choices on your own. You can't blame that on anyone else."

"I don't," I mutter quietly enough that she can't hear me.

"What did you say?" she asks as she reaches into the pocket of her apron.

"I said I'm going to be late for school if I don't get going."

"Fine." She withdraws her hand from her pocket, her fingers enclosed around my phone. "I'm only giving this to you so we can keep an eye on you. If it weren't for the tracking app, I wouldn't let you have it."

"Thanks." I snatch the phone from her and make my escape for the door.

"Remember who you are, Luna!" she shouts.

She has said the same thing to me every day for the last five years. I want to tell her that I don't know who I am, but that I'm definitely not the daughter she wants. Like always, though, I remain silent and nod before I close the front door.

Once I climb into the car, I text Wynter, one of my best friends on the planet since second grade. We were the first two members of our group of five friends. It all started with us, a bottle of nail polish, and Wynter coaxing me into rebelling for the day, although it didn't take that much effort to convince me.

"We can use fingernail polish remover before you go home," she said as she painted my nails a bright pink shade.

I was awestruck by the color. It was the first time I'd ever felt pretty in my life.

"This is fun. And it looks so pretty. Like princess-worthy pretty."

"It's totally princess-worthy," she said with a huge grin on her face.

I smiled, but then my happiness faltered. "I just wish my clothes matched."

"One day, they will," she promised.

And she made good on that promise the day I turned seventeen, and she bought me a new wardrobe, which now is nothing but ashes.

Me: Can u bring me some clothes please?

Wynter: OMG! She gave u your phone back!

Me: Yep. But only so she could keep track of me.

Wynter: She's so crazy. And FYI, I was already planning on bringing u some clothes.

Me: Ur the best. I feel so bad that u gave me all those nice clothes and now they're gone. It's such a waste.

Wynter: It's not your fault your parents are cray-cray.

Me: I know, but I wish they weren't. Their punishments aren't even in the realm of normalcy.

Wynter: Ur telling me. Remember that one time they made you write I Will Not Color On My Walls a thousand times?

Me: That one was pretty bad . . . I hated that u were there and had to see me do it.

Wynter: I felt so bad for you. And it never made any sense to me. I mean, they made you write it on the wall and then paint over it. I was like, seriously, wth? Why would u have her write on the wall about not writing on the wall?

Me: I never understood it, either. But I still don't think it's as bad as burning an entire wardrobe. And now she's got that stupid tracking app on my phone.

Wynter: Ari's on that. Give him a few days, and I'm sure he'll find some kind of way to get around it.

I smile for the first time in three days.

Ari has been one of my closest friends since sixth grade after his family moved to Ridgefield. Since his family didn't grow up here, a lot of people treated him like an outsider. My friends and I, being outsiders ourselves, took him under our wing and showed him the inner workings of our middle school.

I actually have four people I consider my best friends. Together, we make up a group of five very different people who somehow work together. Ari is our computer genius who's really into school and getting good grades. Whenever we have a computer crisis, he's there to hack into whatever we need. He once even changed Wynter's math grade from a D to a C so she'd pass Algebra.

Me: Tell him that he's the bestest, bestest.

Wynter: I thought I was the bestest, bestest. :(

Me: No, you're the bestest, bestest, bestest. But don't tell the others.

Wynter: It's our little secret. ;)

I set the phone on the console and back the car onto the road. The drive to school takes me about ten minutes, and I dread every second, knowing I'm going to have to see Grey when I get there.

After parking the car, I collect my bag, get out, and take a seat on a bench in the campus yard. I put my backpack on my lap, trying to hide my clothes as best as I can. As I'm digging in my bag for a stick of gum, I come across a few items I stole a couple of weeks ago. Normally, I hide everything under a floorboard in my closet, but Mom knocked on the door while I was emptying my pockets, and I panicked, stuffing them into my bag.

I pull out one of the items and frown. A ceramic statue of a goose? I hate geese. I really do. They're so mean and noisy. So why did I jack this statue of all things? I don't even need it. What kind of person does that make me?

A terrible one who hates geese for no reason other than they're noisy and mean.

"Dude, what's up with the creepy-ass bird?" Beckett asks as he squints at the figurine in my hand.

Beckett is what most people call the preppy, rich kid of our group. They think he's shallow and spoiled because his parents buy him everything. That's just the surface of Beckett, though. There's way more going on underneath his nice clothes and good looks.

"It's a present for my gran's b-day," I lie, too afraid to tell him the truth.

He slides onto the bench beside me. "I hate to break it to you, Lu, but your present sucks. It'll seriously give your gran fucking nightmares. It's freaking me out now. I bet it comes to life at night and eats peoples' faces off."

"Okay, first off, gross, and second, you know I suck at picking out presents."

Not wanting to talk about the bird anymore, I shove it into my bag. Out of sight, out of mind, right? Nope. Not even close.

To distract myself from my terribleness, I skim the crowd forming in front of our school. "Where's Wynter?"

He slumps back in the seat, his mood deflating. "She didn't come out of her house this morning when I honked the horn, and she hasn't answered any of my texts."

"Are you two still fighting?" I ask, pulling out my phone.

He props his foot up on his knee and rakes his fingers through his messy, blond hair. "We were never fighting. We just had a mild disagreement." When I elevate my brows at him, his lips quirk. "What? It wasn't a fight. We didn't yell at each other."

"Yeah, because she threw her drink in your face then left your house before you could yell at her. If she had stuck around, you two definitely would've started yelling." I swipe my finger across the screen of my phone.

Me: Where r u?

Wynter: By my locker, waiting for you with some killa clothes.

Me: Awesome. But just an FYI, I'm with Beckett. He seems upset because you blew him off this morning.

Wynter: He totally deserves it. He called me a drama queen

and a spoiled brat in front of the entire school, and he didn't even apologize!

I sigh. Wynter is so about the drama. But Wynter and Beckett didn't used to fight. Back in second grade, Beckett used to have a crush on Wynter and would follow her around like a lovesick puppy. Thankfully, he stopped doing that around fourth grade and decided he just wanted to be friends with her.

Me: He just told me to say he was sorry.

"I didn't do anything that I need to say sorry for," Beckett says as he reads the message from over my shoulder.

"You called her a spoiled brat. You know she hates that, Beck." I shoo him away.

"But she *is* a drama queen and a spoiled brat. So am I. She should just own it." He bounces his knee up and down, growing frustrated. "She always acts like a princess in front of everyone when she's drunk. I'm not going to just sit there and put up with her shit."

I push to my feet. "I know you're trying to look out for her, but maybe next time, you should just take her aside and talk to her instead of yelling at her in front of everyone."

"Maybe there won't be a next time," he says. "Maybe I'll finally get sick of her shit and stop apologizing for stuff I don't need to apologize for."

"You know you're not going to do that. She may be a pain in the ass, but she's still your friend."

"I guess so. I just wish she was nicer and would quit freaking out over nothing."

"She's nice when she's sober, just like you're more serious when you are." I sling the handle of my bag over my shoulder. "I'm headed inside. You coming?"

He shakes his head, staring at the parking lot. "I'm

waiting for Ari. I'll catch up you with you later."

Waiting for Ari is code for he's avoiding Wynter and will probably have a guy bitch-fest with Ari. Poor Ari. He's too nice, and he won't say anything to Beckett, even if he doesn't want to listen to him complain.

I decide to do Ari a solid and send him a text, warning him about Beckett's pissy mood so he'll at least have a choice whether he wants to listen.

After I send the message, I wave good-bye to Beckett then weave through the crowd and head toward the school. With the morning sunlight beaming down on me and all the layers I'm wearing, I feel my skin dampening. It's late September, but since we live in a fairly dry and sandy place, the temperatures are still in the high seventies.

I miss my shorts and skirts. I miss the fresh air on my long legs, which are going to get super pasty hidden beneath the god-awful pants my mom is going to make me wear for the rest of my existence.

When I finally make it to Wynter's locker, I'm relieved to see her waiting for me.

"Whoa, she must really be mad at you." Her face pinches with disgust at the sight of my outfit, just like everyone else who has seen me.

I'm jealous of the cut-offs, silk kimono, and platforms she's wearing. On top of being a diva, Wynter is really into clothes and completely obsessed with shoes to the point where we've all questioned if we should give her an intervention about her shoe addiction.

She closes her locker and sits down on the floor, opening a bag of chips. "You should've stopped by my house and changed before you came to school."

"I didn't have time." I sink down on the floor beside her and slump back against the locker. "I don't want to hate my mom, but sometimes, I really do. I'm such a bad person."

"You're not a bad person. I hate my parents sometimes, too," she says, munching on a chip. "And your parents are freakin' psychos, making you burn all those pretty clothes like that. You seriously need to tell them to fuck off."

A stressed breath eases from my lips. Just thinking about telling them off makes me sick to my stomach. "I'll think about it."

"Don't think about it. Just do it." She offers me some chips, and I grab a handful. "You're already eighteen, for God's sake. They need to realize they can't control you anymore."

Easy for her to say. Wynter's parents are completely the opposite of mine. They pretty much ignore her and let her do anything she wants. Then again, while she pretends her life is fun, I can tell she gets lonely sometimes.

"I've been trying to say something, but I feel like I'm never heard." I look down at my hideous sweater. "And now I feel like I'm starting all over again."

"You're not starting over. Your mom can't burn all those parties and fun things we've been doing." Wynter evaluates my outfit again before springing to her feet. "But we do need to get you out of those clothes like ASAP, or I'm going to have to disown you." She smiles so I know she's kidding.

She'd never disown me over clothes and will always be my friend no matter what. Even if she found out about my klepto habit, she'd probably still love me. Still, I'd rather her not know. I'd rather no one knows about that horrible side of me.

But now Grey Sawyer knows, and I'm going to cross paths with him multiple times today.

"Are you okay?" Wynter asks as she opens her locker and picks up a small stack of folded clothes from the top shelf. "You look like you're sick."

"I'm good." I stand up and stretch out my legs. "I'm

just ready to get out of this outfit."

She gives me *the look* as she hands me the clothes. That look always makes me uncomfortable, as if she can see right through me, and it usually leads to her prying.

"You sure? Because you can always talk to me about anything." Her eyes light up as she claps her hands together. "You know what we should do? We should track down Willow and the three of us ditch today. We can have a girls' day out and binge on ice cream. We haven't done that in forever."

The idea sounds great, but then she'll hold to her word and make me tell her what's bothering me. While I hate keeping stuff from her, confessing my worries with Grey discovering my klepto side means confessing things I'm ashamed of. Hopefully, Grey will keep his mouth shut; otherwise, the rumors will spread through the school like a wildfire.

"I can't ditch today. I have a test in math. Plus, my mom's got the principal on Luna watch." I take the clothes from her and head toward the bathroom. "How about a rain check? Maybe next week sometime?"

"Okay." She keeps giving me *the look* as I wave good-bye then duck into the bathroom.

I peel off the heavy sweater and slacks then put on the black tank top and plaid shorts Wynter brought me. We don't wear the same size shoes, so I'm stuck wearing my tattered sneakers, but they look okay with the outfit.

I stuff the sweater and jeans into my backpack so I can put them back on after school. Then I pop my headphones in and crank up a song. School is one of the few places where I can actually listen to music I like. The rhythm soothes me as I head to my first class, even though school doesn't start for another fifteen minutes.

Since it's a little early, I expect the classroom to be

empty, but when I walk in, Grey Sawyer is sitting at one of the desks. He's wearing a faded black Henley and a pair of worn jeans, his brown hair scraggly but sexy, looking perfectly put together like he did the other day when he saw who I really am.

I start to back out of the room, but he looks up at me before I can make my escape. For a split second, his blue eyes widen, but then he gives me that lazy, I'm-the-shit smile. Even after everything that has happened, the look makes my heart go all kinds of crazy in my chest.

His lips suddenly move as he says something to me.

I tug on the cords of the headphones and pull them out of my ears. "What? I couldn't hear you."

A sparkle of amusement dances in his eyes. "I said, hey, how's it going?"

"Good," I reply, hitching my thumb under the handle of my bag. "How's stuff going with you?"

"The same. You know, just living life and all that shit." He briefly studies me before he returns to scribbling in his notebook.

That's it? No, "Hey, crazy shoplifting girl"? No, "I saw you the other day stealing from Benny, the nicest old man on the planet"? No, "Here's your jacket back, you dirty little thief"?

I reluctantly sit down at a desk across from him. The room is so quiet I can hear the sound of his pencil scratching across the paper. I retrieve my phone and check my messages to kill time, but no one has responded, and I'm left feeling hyperaware that Grey is right there. Usually, that alone makes me a little bit nervous, but now my nerves are even more jumbled. I feel exposed and very uncomfortable in my own skin.

"Have you talked to Beckett this morning?" Grey abruptly asks, startling the living daylights out of me.

I have to catch my breath before I speak. "Yeah, I saw him, like, fifteen minutes ago. Why? Did you need to talk to him or something?"

"I just needed to get something from him but haven't had time to track him down."

"Just send him a text and tell him to bring it to you." I force myself to meet his gaze and point at the window. "Or you can just go outside and search the quad. I'm sure he's still out there." *Bitching Ari's ear off about Wynter.*

"I would, but I can't leave the classroom." When I stare at him in confusion, he looks down at the notebook on his desk, his cheeks reddening with embarrassment. "I'm on academic probation, and I'm trying to get caught up on some assignments so I won't miss Friday's game. And I know if I walk out of here, I'll get caught up with other shit and won't come back. Being in a classroom . . . There are less distractions." He lifts his gaze back to me and shrugs.

He's acting so casual. Maybe he's going to let the stealing thing go. I sure hope so.

I feel a small weight lift from my shoulders at that thought.

"Just text Beckett, then. I'm sure he'll bring you . . . whatever you need."

"I would, but I . . . I didn't bring my phone." He stares at the trees, avoiding my gaze, seeming less confident than he normally is.

Weird. But then again, this whole exchange is weird since the two of us have barely spoken since the dance invite fiasco.

"Another distraction?" I wonder.

He nods, turning his head toward me. For some reason, I feel like he's lying. I don't know why or why it even matters, but I don't understand why someone would lie about not having their phone with them.

"I can text him for you," I offer.

He exhales audibly. "Thanks, Luna. That'd be awesome."

"It's not that big of a deal," I say as I type Beckett a message.

Me: Hey! U need to hit up Mr. Gartying's classroom. Grey's stuck in here and says ur supposed to bring him something. I'm hoping it's not what I think it is, though, because now I feel like an accomplice. ;)

Beckett: Nope, it's exactly what u think it is. Don't worry, though. I'm sure you look hot in handcuffs.

I roll my eyes. Well, at least he's in a better mood.

Beckett: Tell Grey I'm on my way . . . Although, I didn't know u two hung out.

Me: We don't. We're both just stuck in the classroom together.

Beckett: Why r u stuck there?

I consider telling him it's because I'm avoiding Wynter, but that would give him an open invitation to complain about her.

Me: I needed to get an assignment sheet I lost.

Beckett: Gotcha. Tell Grey I'll be there in a min.

"He says he's on his way," I tell Grey as I set my phone down on the desk. I slant to the side to dig out my book from my bag, figuring that's the end of our conversation. But when I straighten back up, he's staring at me with hesitancy written all over his face.

"Can I ask you a question?" he asks cautiously.

I stiffen. *Oh, great, here it comes.*

"Um . . . Yeah . . . I guess so."

"I don't want you to feel uncomfortable or anything, but if I don't ask, I'm not going to be able to stop thinking about it." He fiddles with a button on the sleeve of his shirt. "Is everything okay with you?"

"What do you mean?"

"The store the other day . . ." He scoops up his bag from the floor and sets it on the desk. "When I saw you stealing"—he unzips the bag, retrieves my jacket, and hands it to me—"I just wanted to make sure you were doing okay."

My palms sweat as I take the jacket from him. "I don't . . . I didn't mean . . . I can't . . ."

How am I supposed to explain why I stole some of the stuff that was in the pocket of the jacket? How am I supposed to explain why I steal? I wish I was more like Wynter. If she was in this position, she'd just play it off as being a badass rebel. But I always feel so guilty and ashamed when I get caught doing something wrong, and I'm sure it shows on my face.

"I'm fine . . . Thanks . . . for helping me," I manage to get out.

"Don't worry about it," Grey says. "I get it."

"Get what?"

He offers me a sympathetic smile that only puzzles me more. "That sometimes people have to do extreme things to survive."

I'm even more confounded. Does he think I was shoplifting because I have to? Like I need all those things I stole? Is that why he helped me out?

I should correct him, tell him I wasn't surviving anything except the frustrations in my life. I just have issues, and I'm a terrible, messed up person. But before I get the chance, Beckett strolls into the classroom.

"Aw, look at this. My two favorite people in the whole, wide world hanging out." Beckett plants his ass on my desk. "What a great way to start the day."

I note his bloodshot eyes. *"You're high already,"* I mouth.

He grins goofily and mouths, *"I needed cheering up."*

I bite back a smile. When Beckett's in a good mood, he can be quite charming, but I don't want to encourage him.

He winks at me before turning to Grey. "So you're still on academic probation, huh? That sucks."

"Yeah, I'm hoping I'll catch up by the end of the week so I can play in Friday's game," he grumbles in frustration. "But I'm not sure if I'll be able to pull it off. I suck at this class."

Beckett deliberates something before his gaze glides to me. "Luna's pretty good. Maybe she can help you."

"Willow is better than I am." I give him a pleading look not to push this. Even before Grey found out I'm a klepto, I don't think I could've handle being alone with him. "You should ask her to do it."

Beckett dismisses me with a wave of his hand. "Don't listen to Luna," he tells Grey. "She's just shy."

"No, I'm not." I blast Beckett with a look. "I'm being honest. I'm not as good at this class as Willow is, and she's a way better tutor."

"I'd love it if you would, but it's okay if you don't want to," Grey says, but he seems disappointed.

Beckett gives me a what's-wrong-with-you look that makes me feel like the biggest jerk ever. I'm being rude after Grey saved my butt from getting busted at Benny's. I kind of owe him.

"No, it's okay," I tell Grey. "If you want me to tutor you, I will."

Grey smiles a full-on, genuine smile. "Thanks. I really

appreciate it, and I promise I'll be the best student ever."

I return his smile, but on the inside, I'm a wreck. Why the heck did I just agree to tutor him? Grey freakin' Sawyer. The guy who made me feel like a loser. The guy who knows my dirty, little secret. And now I'm just going to, what? Spend hours with him, trying to help him get better with English class, and hope he doesn't want to talk about what I did?

Then there's my mom. She's going to freak if she finds out I'm hanging out with a guy, even if it's just to study. She always gets that way when I try to spend time with guys she doesn't know. She still acts like a weirdo whenever I mention Ari and Beckett.

Reality sets in, and I open my mouth to retract my offer and tell Grey I have something else I need to do, but the bell rings, and people come pouring into the classroom.

While there's a distraction, Beckett pulls a crinkled envelope from his pocket and lays it on Grey's desk.

"Thanks, man." Grey doesn't appear very happy about the envelope as he picks it up and stuffs it into his backpack. Then he collects a small box from his backpack, and with his fingers gripping it tightly, he hands it to Beck. "Here you go."

"Thanks, man," Beckett says, taking the box from him. "And let me know what you decide."

Grey bobs his head up and down, shoving the envelope into his bag.

Curious about what's going on, I attempt to capture Beck's gaze, but he refuses to make eye contact with me.

"I should probably bounce. I do have class," Beck says to no one in particular.

Just then, Logan, one of Grey's friends, drops his books on the desk in front of mine. "What's up, fuckheads?" he greets Grey and Beckett. Then his gaze lands on me, and a grin plasters across his face. "Hey, what happened to the grandma outfit you were wearing this morning?"

"I ditched it," I mutter, opening up my textbook.

"Smart move," he sneers. "You looked like a hideous beast."

"Dude, shut up." Beckett rises to his feet and gets in Logan's face. "Don't talk to her like that."

"Beck, it's fine." I snag his sleeve and haul him back, not wanting him to get in a fight. "He's right. I did look like a hideous beast."

"See? She agrees with me." Logan flashes me what he probably thinks is a charming grin.

I stare at him, unimpressed. *Gag me.*

"I thought I was having flashbacks from last year," Logan rambles on, "when you used to dress like a homeless person. Glad you weren't stupid enough to go back to that look."

"Just say the word, and I'll punch him in the face," Beckett says to me, looking eager to please.

I'm not about to get Beck into trouble. "Beck, I said it's—"

"Quit being an asshole, Logan," Grey interrupts in a harsh tone. He keeps his gaze fixed on his book, flipping through the pages. "Not everyone has the privilege of being a spoiled, rich kid who never has to worry about money."

Beckett gives me a questioning glance then leans in and puts his lips beside my ear. "Why is Grey Sawyer standing up for you? I love you to death, Lu, and I think you're fucking amazing, but Grey doesn't get involved with other people's drama." He moves back, raising his voice. "That's my thing."

"Yes, it is." I stress each syllable. "And maybe you should really think about what you just said, considering you're always chewing out Wynter for being a drama queen."

His brows furrow as if he's just realizing they both share the same trait. "Interesting thought process." He rubs his jawline. "I'm going to have to think about that one for a while."

"Maybe you should do that when you've done a little less . . ." I put two fingers up to my lips and suck in a breath.

He aims a finger at me as he backs down the aisle. "Good idea. Although, I'll probably forget about this conversation by the time that happens."

"Beckett Vincent, get to class," Mr. Gartying barks as he strides into the classroom, carrying a stack of papers.

"Yes, sir." Beckett salutes the teacher before spinning on his heels and disappearing into the hallway.

Mr. Gartying shakes his head as he sets the papers down on his desk. "Everyone, take a seat and turn to the page written on the board while I take roll."

As I open my book to the correct page, I rack my mind for an excuse to give Grey that will get me out of tutoring him. But everything I come up with seems lame and rude.

"You okay?" Grey whispers to me from across the aisle. "I know Logan can be a dick sometimes."

"Yeah, I'm fine," I reply. "And it's not that big of a deal. He was right about my outfit."

"It doesn't matter if he was right." He keeps his voice low. "He shouldn't be an asshole just because he's rich and doesn't know what it's like to struggle."

My gut twists again. "Grey, I wasn't stealing because of . . ." I trail off, fearing what everyone will find out if I say it aloud. I'm scared they'll find out I'm not as good of a person as people think. And most of all, I'm afraid of what will happen if word somehow gets back to my parents.

"Don't worry; I won't tell anyone." He pauses, looking as though he's having a mental tug-of-war with himself. "Luna, I'm here if you need to talk. I know you have friends, but I just wanted you to know that." He smiles at me as he sits back in his seat.

"Okay . . . thanks . . ."

I feel so lost. Why is he being nice to me? Does he feel sorry for me because he thinks I'm poor? Or is it simply because he's trying to be a nicer person now?

As class begins, I'm left with a handful of unanswered questions and stewing in my own guilt.

Confession

FOUR

I suck at telling the truth.

Luna

BY LUNCHTIME, MY brain is drained. I spent half the day obsessing over why Grey was so nice to me and whether he'll keep his promise. I haven't heard any rumors in the hallways, so that has to be a good sign.

After I grab some snacks and a soda from the vending machines, I join Ari, Beckett, and Wynter outside, under the trees. We sometimes leave campus to eat, but my friends always stick around with me and offer moral support when I have to ride out my mother's punishments.

"This is the worst idea ever." Wynter playfully whacks Beckett in the back of the head as she sits down on the grass beside me, and he blasts her with a nasty look. "Why would you get Luna into this kind of situation? Why, Beckett? Why? You know how much she hates Grey Sawyer."

"I don't hate him." I rip open a bag of cheese crackers.

"That's because you're too nice." Wynter steals a cracker from my bag and pops it into her mouth. "But deep down, you kinda, sorta hate him, even if you won't admit it.

You have since sophomore year."

"Hey, I never made Grey pay for spreading that rumor about you back in tenth grade, did I?" Beckett slides on his sunglasses. "I should probably do something about that."

"You mean, like manipulating Luna into tutoring him?" Wynter asks, rummaging through her purse. "Because that's a great freakin' way to make him pay. He ends up with good grades, and Luna ends up traumatized from his douche-baggery."

"Luna didn't have to agree to tutor him," Ari says, picking the crust off his sandwich. "She could've said no if she didn't want to do it."

"Don't be a traitor, Ari. Remember who loves you more." Wynter points a finger at him.

Ari adjusts his square-frame glasses and brushes his shaggy, brown hair out of his eyes. "Since when do you love me more? Because Beckett wasn't the one who yelled at me for spilling his beer at the party the other night."

"Hate to break it to you, dude, but when it comes to loving you more, I think Wynter's the better choice," Beck says as he scrolls through his phone. "I mean, I'm all for an occasional bromance here and there, but love really isn't my thing."

Ari rolls his eyes. "You know that's not what I meant. I just meant that most of the time, you're nicer than she is, but now I'm going to take it back."

Wynter grins smugly at Beckett. "See. I'm the nicer one."

Beckett snorts a laugh. "Yeah, okay."

Wynter lightly smacks Beckett's arm, but he ignores her, which seems to irritate her more. She places her hands on her hips and starts teasing him about being a pothead until Beckett finally scowls at her. Then she smiles, satisfied with herself.

Ari and I exchange a look. We had a conversation once about the two of them probably secretly being in love, and all the fighting is just sexual tension. That's Ari's theory, anyway. I'm not really buying into it just yet. I wonder if they've known each other for so long they have more of a sibling relationship than anything.

"So, are you really going to tutor Grey Sawyer?" Ari asks me over Beckett and Wynter's bickering.

"I don't want to, but I already told him I would." I stuff a cracker into my mouth. "And I can't think of an excuse to get out of it without sounding like a jerk."

Ari bites into his sandwich. "You're allowed to be a jerk every once in a while. You don't have to be so nice all the time."

"I could say the same thing to you." And I'm not nice all the time, not even close. I just keep my dirty, little secrets hidden because the Harveys aren't supposed to be bad or mean or improper.

"Hey, I can be mean sometimes," Ari tries to argue, peeling more crust off his bread.

I laugh. "You *so* cannot. You're, like, the nicest guy ever."

"No way," he insists. "Everyone can be mean sometimes."

"Okay, but still—"

"God, I'm so tired I can't even see straight." Willow drops her bag next to me then dramatically falls down on the grass and drapes her arm over her head.

"Napping is a great cure for that," Beckett says, stealing the bottle of water from Wynter's hand. "Trust me. I'm an expert."

"I'm sure you are, but I can't take a nap right now." Willow unties the over-shirt that's around her waist, balls it up, and tucks it under her head like a pillow. "My mind won't slow down."

"I have something that can help with that," Beckett offers, reaching for his bag.

"No way." I point a finger at Beck. "I'm not going to let you corrupt Willow."

"I'm just giving her a choice." Beck raises his hands in front of him, surrendering. "Chillax, Lu."

"He's not going to corrupt me," Willow murmurs, her eyelids drifting shut. "I'm already corrupted."

The four of us look at each other then burst into a fit of laughter.

Willow contains a smile. "Mock all you want, but I've done some really bad things. I've even come this close"—she holds up her finger and thumb an inch apart—"to being a bad girl."

"Sticking your gum on the bottom of a desk doesn't count," Beckett says, resting his arms on his knees. "Admit it, Wills, you're too sweet to be bad."

"Yeah, you're probably right." Willow rolls on her side and cranes her neck to look at him. "That's more Wynter's and your thing. Ari, Luna, and I have to be good to make up for all the bad stuff you two do."

I set down the bag of crackers, no longer hungry.

"Oh, you think I'm bad, huh?" Beckett teases as he jumps to his feet. "I'll show you how bad I can be."

Willow's eyes pop open, and she scrambles to get up, but Beck snags her by the back of her shirt, yanks her back against him, and tickles the crap out of her.

"Beck, stop!" Willow begs as she tries to squirm out of his hold. "I take it back. You're good!"

"Say I'm a good boy." Beck tickles her sides. "And that you love me."

"Fine! You're a good boy, and I love you!" she manages to get out through her laughter.

Instead of letting her go, he lies on the ground and brings her with him. Then he rolls on his side and tucks his arm underneath her head. With how close they act, I sometimes wonder if there's something going on between the two of them. If there is, though, no one seems to know about it.

"My arm's a better pillow for napping," Beck insists as he presses his chest against Willow's back.

"No way," Willow says, but she rests her head on his arm, and seconds later, her eyelids lower.

Beck looks proud of himself for getting her to relax. It's a hard thing to do with Willow since she's usually stressed out. She's been since the day we became friends back in third grade. She was the quiet, shy girl who wore old clothes that were a little too big for her. She always spent recess on the swings by herself until the day Wynter announced, "She seems sad. We should make her come play hopscotch." So we marched over there and made her play with us. She didn't seem too reluctant, though. In fact, she seemed grateful someone had made the effort to get to know her.

But Willow has every reason to be stressed. On top of helping her parents out financially by working almost every weekend, she's also trying to get an academic scholarship and spends crazy amounts of hours doing schoolwork.

Beck reaches over with his free hand and steals a handful of crackers from the bag on my lap. "Eat before you sleep," he says to Willow, offering her the crackers. "You're too skinny."

Willow opens her eyes and takes the crackers from Beckett. "Thanks, Beck. I don't know what I'd do without you."

"Probably laugh less." He gently pinches her in the side before nuzzling against her.

"That's not fair," Wynter says to Beck with her lip

jutted out. "You're always nice to Willow and Luna, but all you ever do for me is call me a spoiled brat."

"That's because Will and Lu don't call me a rich douche," Beckett mutters. "Nice people get treated nicely."

I internally grimace. What is with all the nice comments getting thrown in my direction today? My guilt is starting to give me a stomachache.

"Okay, I kind of see your point," Wynter muses thoughtfully, but then her mood fizzles as her gaze darts toward the school. "Oh, boy. Here comes drama."

I track her gaze to see Grey heading in our direction. That lazy smile spreads across his face when he notices me looking at him, and my heart betrays me by fluttering in my chest like a lunatic.

"What a cocky asshole, just like every other damn jock in this school," Wynter mutters, glaring at him. "He sees some girls looking in his direction and automatically thinks we're checking him out."

She might be wrong, considering I was just kinda, sorta ogling him.

"Hey, I'm a jock," Beck says. "And I don't think that."

"You're not a jock," Wynter insists. "You just play sports."

Beck tips his head, slides his sunglasses down, and looks at Wynter. "What's the difference?"

"Jocks are sports guys who hang out with other sports guys and obsess about sports and think they're so awesome because they can throw and kick a ball," Wynter explains. "You hang out with a bunch of weirdoes who don't ever want to talk about sports. See? That's how much we love you, enough that we haven't let you fall into the jock mold."

"Gee, thanks." Beck shakes his head in disbelief.

"You're welcome," Wynter replies, beaming. "And you say I never compliment you."

"Hey," Grey greets me.

Ari, Wynter, Beck, and I all look up at him, while Willow remains lying on Beck's arm with her eyes closed. Some of Grey's confidence diminishes from our scrutinizing gazes.

"Are you lost or something?" Wynter points at the school. "The gym's that way."

"I know where the gym is." Grey shoots me a quizzical glance, and I shrug.

Wynter crisscrosses her legs then rests back on her hands. "So why aren't you there? That is where all you jockheads hang out all the time, right?"

"Be nice," I beg Wynter. "Please."

"Why? He and his steroid friends aren't nice to anyone other than Dixie, Mixie, and the ditz squad." Wynter looks at Grey with her brows raised, challenging him to argue with her.

Grey seems the slightest bit amused, the corners of his lips twitching. "If you're talking about the girls on the cheerleading squad, then I think their names are Dixie and Pixie, not Dixie and Mixie."

"You'd know better than I would"—Wynter folds her arms across her chest and pins him with her best sassy smirk—"since you've probably screwed every single one of them."

Ari chokes on a mouthful of food while Beck grumbles, and Willow bites down on her bottom lip to restrain a smile while keeping her eyes closed.

Grey lifts a shoulder. "I guess you'd know better than I do since you seem to know everything about me."

Okay, time to interrupt.

"You said you needed to talk to me?" I say to Grey, leaping to my feet.

His gaze sweeps across my friends then lands back on

me. "Can we talk somewhere more private?"

Wynter mouths, "*Privately? No way.*"

I turn my back on Wynter and nod. "Yeah, sure."

"Be careful, Lu!" Wynter hollers as Grey and I start across the grass toward the center of the quad. "Remember tenth grade."

My cheeks heat. I love Wynter to death, but she really needs to stop saying every single thing that pops into her head.

Grey remains silent as we make our way around the people eating lunch on the grass. I catch people gawking at us and cringe when we pass by Piper Talperson, Grey's girlfriend for the last year.

Grey has stuck to his type over the years, and Piper fits it impeccably: a popular cheerleader with curves. Her hair and makeup are always flawlessly done, and she wears the latest fashions. Honestly, she reminds me a lot of Wynter. Only, Wynter has more of an edge to her style and is a hell of a lot nicer.

Looking annoyed, Piper stands up from the bench she's sitting on and pushes her way over to us.

"Babe, where are you going?" she asks Grey, snagging the sleeve of his shirt.

Grey stops, casting an uneasy glance at me before facing her. "I just need to talk to Luna about something for class," he explains.

"Oh, hey, is it Luna?" she says like she just noticed me standing there and has never met me before.

"Yeah." I force a smile, even though it's hard.

Piper isn't a very nice person. I've seen her do a lot of cruel things, like openly mocking the other girls in our gym class, calling them fat and ugly and flat chested—yeah, the last one was directed toward me. She also loves to gossip and has destroyed many people's reputations by outing their secrets.

Her lip curls at me before she zeroes in on Grey again. "I thought we were going out to lunch together." She tucks a strand of her long, brown hair behind her ear and flutters her eyelashes as she peers up at him.

"I told you I couldn't today," Grey says, sounding tired.

She juts out her bottom lip. "But you've been saying that every day. I'm getting bored of staying at school for lunch."

"Then leave campus with your friends." Grey slips his arm from her hold. "You'd be happier if you went with them, anyway."

"Why are you being such a dick?" She glares at me like it's somehow my fault.

Not wanting to get involved in their drama, I tell Grey, "I'm going to go wait over there."

Grey nods, seeming relieved. "Yeah, okay."

I take shelter in the shade and mess around with my phone while casting glances in their direction. At first, they seem like they're having a heated argument, but then Grey gives her a kiss and walks away with a smile on his face.

I find myself wondering what it would be like to have a boyfriend. I've never had the opportunity to date anyone I've liked. I've never even kissed a guy—well, unless you count the time Ari, Wynter, Willow, Beck, and I played spin the bottle and I had to kiss Beck. It was painfully awkward to say the least, and the two of us couldn't even look each other in the eye for a month. After that, I put a ban on playing any more kissing games with the four of them.

"Sorry about that," Grey apologizes as he approaches me.

"No worries." I put my phone away and follow him as he rounds the side of the school and back to where no one hangs out. It's also where Piper and the rest of Grey's friends can't see us.

He doesn't say anything right away, only stares at the parking lot where the teachers usually park. I spot Ms. Belingfutor, my Biology teacher, taking a smoke break out by one of the cars, and for some reason, that makes me giggle.

"What's so funny?" Grey asks with a somewhat intrigued, somewhat confused smile.

"It's nothing." I point over at Ms. Belingfutor puffing away. "I just think it's funny seeing teachers do stuff like that. It makes them seem normal, which just seems weird."

Grey glances from Ms. Belingfutor to me. "I get what you're saying. There was one time I caught Coach feeling up his wife in his office. But that was a little less funny and a lot more disturbing than watching Ms. B smoke."

I force back a giggle. "You really walked in on them?"

He nods with his eyes wide, as if he's reliving the horror. "It was horrible and so embarrassing, but what's even worse was Coach wanted to talk about it and make sure I wasn't traumatized. And I was, but I'd never tell him that." He folds his arms across his chest and shifts his weight as his forehead creases. "I've never told anyone that story. If the guys on the team ever found out, they'd never let me live it down."

I pick at my fingernails. "Then why did you tell me?"

"I don't know . . . maybe because you're not on the team, and you're not a guy, so I know you won't ask stupid questions, like if Coach's wife is hot."

I get his point, but still, it's not like we're even close to being friends, which brings up the huge question: why are we here?

"You said you wanted to talk to me about something, and I'm guessing it's not about how hot your coach's wife is."

"Yeah." He massages the back of his neck tensely. "I wanted to talk to you about this whole tutoring thing. I just didn't want to do it in front of your friends. They're kind of intimidating."

"My friends are intimidating?" I almost laugh. "Your friends are always making fun of people."

"That's not what I meant," he says in a panic. "I just meant they really care about you. And I knew that if I had this conversation in front of them, it'd be analyzed later and that can be . . ."

"Intimidating," I finish.

He bobs his head up and down, stepping closer to me, and I have to tip my chin up to look at him.

"Any outsider who approaches you guys probably feels a little freaked out." A lopsided smile tugs at his lips, and I stare at his mouth a few seconds too long.

"People think that about you, too. You can be intimidating to approach, especially when you're with your friends. Trust me, I know." I want to smack myself in the head for subtly mentioning the tenth grade dance. "Sorry, I didn't mean to bring that up."

"You don't need to be sorry." He cracks his knuckles, averting his gaze to the ground as he mutters, "I get where you're coming from. Back then . . . I was an asshole."

A beat of awkward silence goes by.

I clear my throat. "You said you wanted to talk about the tutoring thing."

A relieved breath puffs from his lips. "I just wanted to see where you want to meet up and what time."

"The only place I'm allowed to go other than my house is the library, and I don't want to meet up at my house." When his forehead creases, I add, "Trust me; you don't want to go there, either."

"Okay." He waits for me to embellish, but I'm not

about to give him the details about my insane home life. "So I guess it's the library."

"Sounds good. You want to meet around four?"

He scratches the back of his neck. "I have practice after school. Maybe around six?"

"Sure. That works." As long as my mom isn't on one of her lock-me-in-my-room-after-dinner kicks.

"Okay, it's a date." One side of his mouth pulls into that sexy half-grin I've seen him use on a ton of girls over the years.

I smile back, but I'm totally confused. *Date? Why did he call this a date?*

He didn't mean it literally. He has a girlfriend, for God's sake. Jesus, Luna, get a grip.

"Thanks for doing this," he adds. "It's really awesome of you. Most people aren't that nice."

I'm not that nice!

I force a tight smile. "It's not a big deal. Besides, Beck would freak if I didn't help you, and then you didn't get to play in Friday's game. He hates losing."

"I think everyone does . . . except maybe you. You seem too sweet to get upset about something like that."

"Tell that to Wynter. She won't play board games with me anymore."

"So, you're a sore loser?" He pokes me in the side teasingly, and I flinch from the sudden unexpectedness of the touch.

"Um, yeah." I struggle to remember what we are talking about as I grow flustered. *Board games. Sore losers.* "Once, I threw all the cards out her bedroom window when we were playing Texas Hold'em, and I lost, like, ten hands in a row. Then there was the whole Candyland fiasco."

"What happened with that?" he asks, seeming strangely intrigued by my board game dark side.

"I broke the heads off all the pieces." I try not to smile, even though it's kind of funny now. "But keep in mind that I was only eight, and I don't have any brothers or sisters. Whenever I played games at home, I played by myself and always won."

He struggles not to laugh. "Wow . . . that's . . ."

"Ridiculous?" I offer. "Insane? Neurotic?"

His grin slips through. "I was actually going to say funny."

"I'm glad you think so, but Wynter didn't. That's pretty much when she stopped playing board games with me. She gave me a chance a few years later, but that ended quickly. I haven't played games since."

He chuckles. "She sounds like a wimp if you ask me. So what if you broke a few game pieces and threw some cards out the window?" He pokes me in the side again, and this time, instead of flinching, my stomach does a kick flip. "I'd play with you."

"Yeah, right." My voice comes out surprisingly even, despite the fact that my nerves are jostled. "You say that now, but you'd change your mind once you witnessed the nastiness in all its temper-tantrum glory."

He drums his fingers against the side of his legs with his forehead creased. "I'll tell you what. At the end of every tutoring session, how about we play a game of cards?"

"You want to play cards with me after I help you study?" I question with doubt.

"You say that like it's weird."

"It is weird . . . You don't seem like the game playing type."

"I love playing cards. I used to play them with my dad." His face pales at the mention of his dad.

I feel horrible that we got on the topic of parents, especially his dad. From what I've heard around school, his dad passed away a few months ago at the beginning of the summer. I'm not sure how, though.

"But, yeah, anyway." Grey clears his throat and glances down at his watch. "I have to meet up with someone. Can you give me your number, just in case something happens and I can't make it tonight?"

I nod and rattle off my number, and he writes it down on his hand with a pen.

When he notes me staring confusedly at the ink on his palm, he explains, "Some friends of mine thought it'd be funny to play catch with my phone, and then one of them accidentally threw it against the wall." He shoves the pen into his back pocket. "See you later tonight." He steps by me to leave, but then stops. "You're okay with getting to the library, right? Because I can come pick you up. I know how super pricey gas is."

I catch the faintest hint of pity in his tone. I should confess right then and there that I'm not poor, that I have my parents' nearly brand new car to drive to the library. Instead, I only mumble, "I'm fine, but thanks for the offer."

"Okay, but if you change your mind, let Beck know. He knows how to get ahold of me." He stands there for a moment longer before hurrying off toward the front of the school.

Why would Beck know how to get ahold of him? The two of them have never been close or anything, and now Beck's suddenly the one who knows how to get ahold of him and is giving him envelopes before class?

By the time I make it back to my friends, Willow and Wynter have taken off, and Ari is collecting his things to head inside the school. Beck, however, is still sprawled across the grass, looking like he has every intention of staying there forever.

"Beck, can I talk to you for a sec?" I ask as I pick up my

bag and the half-eaten bag of crackers off the grass.

He sits up, stretching out his arms. "Sure. What's up?"

"See you guys later," Ari says as he gathers the last of his books. "And, Lu, give me a shout later. I think I might have a solution to your tracking problem."

"Already?" I ask, and he nods. "Thanks, Ari. I don't know what I'd do without you."

"Probably be stalked by your mom a lot more." He glances at the school as the bell echoes through the air. "I should get to class, but text me around seven or eight."

I wave good-bye to him before he turns on his heels and gets swept up in the crowd rushing for the entrance doors.

"Man, your mom's doing that crazy tracking thing again?" Beck gripes as he reaches for his backpack propped against a nearby tree. "What was it about this time?"

"My choice in clothes," I say with a sigh.

"She has control issues."

I swallow down the lump in my throat. *So do I, Beck. So do I.*

"Yeah, she does."

He yawns. "So, what did you want to talk to me about?" He holds up his hands in front of him, his eyes sparkling mischievously. "No, wait, let me guess. You want to start dating me so you can bring a bad boy home and drive your mother crazy."

"I thought Willow said you were a good boy," I tease. "Or is that just when you're around her?"

"I'm whoever I need be at the given moment," he quips, flashing me his pearly whites. "And right now, I think you need a bad boy."

"Speaking of bad boys, what was up with that envelope you gave Grey this morning? There weren't"—I look around at all the people nearby then scoot closer to him and lower my voice—"drugs in there, were there?"

"Luna, you've known me forever. Do really think I'd deal drugs in school?"

"I don't want to think you'd deal drugs, but I've seen you give people stuff."

"I never charge for the stuff, though, so it's technically not dealing. I just share with those who want to partake," he says with a devious grin. "And to answer your question about Grey, no, there weren't drugs in that envelope, but that's all I can tell you."

"How come?"

"Because it's not my place to tell." Beck squints against the sunlight as he studies me. "What I really want to know is why you two are suddenly spending time together. I thought you hated him."

"Hate's a strong word. I don't think I've ever hated him." And, if I'm honest with myself, I still have a crush on him after all these years, even after what he did to me. "I've just never talked to him because of that dance thing."

He reaches up to pat my arm. "It's okay not to like everyone."

"I know. But I don't think I should not like Grey unless you know of a reason I shouldn't." It's a lame attempt to get him to confess what was in the envelope. I don't even know why I care so much. Maybe it's because Grey knows stuff about me. Or maybe it's because I'm turning into a nosey person.

"Sorry, but I'm not telling you what was in that envelope." He stands up, picking up his backpack from the ground. "But you should probably be careful around Grey. He's an okay guy and everything, but you're too good for him."

"I'm just tutoring him," I remind him as we start toward the school. "And you're the one who got me into that mess."

"Yeah, I really shouldn't talk to people when I'm high. I become this weird, all about the love kind of guy," he says with an innocent shrug. "But I think you'll be okay. Just don't date him, especially when he never apologized for what he did to you."

"This isn't a date. We're meeting at the library, and he has a girlfriend."

"Oh, you can have a date at the library. I dated this girl once whose mom would only let her go to the library with me because she thought we couldn't do anything there but study. We did a lot of naughty things in the aisle with encyclopedias. There was this one time—"

I throw my hands over my ears. "I never, ever want to hear about your sex life, Beck. *Ever.*"

Beck laughs but drops the subject.

We walk to school, chatting about the party he's having this weekend and how I need to find a way to get there no matter what because he needs me to DJ for him.

"Beck, I'm not a DJ," I say. "I don't know why you keep insisting I am."

"I know you're not technically a DJ, but you're really good at putting mixes together and running the stereo." He winks at me. "No one else can rock it like you."

"I'll try to make it, but I can't make any promises." I'm already on thin ice as it is.

Still, I find myself feeling depressed that I probably won't be able to go. Again, I'll be the one missing out on all the fun. Even with the tracking app off my phone, my parents will never allow me out of the house that late at night, which leaves sneaking out as the only option.

Then again, maybe I deserve things to be this way for all the lies I've told lately and for all the stealing I've done. Maybe I deserve worse.

As we reach the entrance of the school, Beck holds the

door open.

"Why thank you, sir." I laugh as I step into the hallway.

My phone suddenly vibrates from inside my pocket, and I fish it out.

Mom: You are to come straight home after school.

Sighing, I type a reply.

Me: I was already planning on it.

Mom: I know, but sometimes you dilly-dally around with those friends of yours. You better walk through the front door within 15 minutes after school gets out and not a minute later. I know how long it takes to make the drive home. I even clocked it myself today just to make sure.

I shake my head. She really is insane.

Me: Okay, I get it. I'll be there at 3:45.

Mom: I'm serious about this, Luna. You, me, and your father have a lot of talking to do about what I found in your floorboard this morning.

I almost drop the phone. They found my secret hiding place. Oh. My. God. I feel sick. All the things I've hidden in there, things I can't explain how I got, things I'm not supposed to have, like makeup and nail polish and a pair of lacy panties that I've never worn, but she's going to think I did.

"No, God. No, no, no."

"What's wrong?" Beckett asks from right behind me.

"I . . . um . . ." I'm too speechless to form words.

Another text buzzes through.

Mom: You're lucky I didn't come and pick you up from school already, but I don't want you to get behind on your schoolwork. Just know that there will be severe punishments, young lady. I'm not going to let you fall into the darkness. You won't become that girl.

"Tell me what's wrong." Beck lowers his head to level our gazes. "You look like you're about to throw up."

"I think I am." I fold my arm around my stomach. "I-I have to get to class." I run down the hallway before he presses me for answers, wishing I could keep running forever without looking back.

I wish I never had to go home.

Confession FIVE

> I don't like who I am sometimes.
>
> Grey

"IT SUCKS COACH isn't letting you practice with us," Logan says as I collect my books from the locker. "By the time you get your grades up, you're going to be useless."

"Gee, thanks." I slam my locker shut then rest my shoulder against it. "You don't have to act like an asshole all the time."

He grins arrogantly. "I run this damn school. I can do whatever I want."

"Wow, what a fucking accomplishment. You know there's, like, maybe a hundred people who go to our school, right?"

Logan doesn't bother to move out of the way as a girl tries to squeeze around him to get to her locker.

"God, you've been such a fucking downer lately. What the hell is wrong with you? Is Piper not putting out or something?"

I push him out of the way to help out the girl, and he stumbles back, his shoes scuffing against the linoleum floor.

The girl offers me a tense but grateful smile then quickly spins the combo to her locker.

Logan gives me a dirty look as he regains his footing. "Screw you, Grey. You think you're better than everyone, but you're not." He backs down the hallway, sneering. "Oh, yeah, and have fun with your little tutoring thing while the rest of us who aren't stupid work our asses off to hold up the team. I'm sure you'll have a blast *trying* to learn shit from *Luna Harvey*." He says her name like there's something funny about it, probably because in tenth grade, he told everyone how she asked me out, and I rudely turned her down because I was a dick back then.

She was shier than she is now, and she wore clothes that covered up every inch of her body. The outfits were always weird, too. Like this one time, she wore a baggy sweater with bright yellow bears on it and a pair of baggy, tan pants that looked big enough to fit a guy. I want to say it didn't matter to me, but I was a jerk. I cared way too much about what people like Logan thought of me. I didn't understand that not everyone had enough money to buy whatever they wanted, including nice clothes. Now I understand more than I want to.

I understand a lot of things now, like when I saw Luna stealing stuff at Benny's store. All those horrible outfits she used to wear were probably because she couldn't afford anything nicer. She does dress better now, but I've seen her friends giving her clothes during school. It's why I took her jacket. I didn't want her getting into trouble like I did.

I stuff my books in the bag then back down the hallway in the opposite direction as Logan, calling out, "Well, at least I won't be wasting my time by hanging around at the meet up tonight for the millionth time, getting trashed and waiting around for something exciting to happen that never does."

He flips me the middle finger. "Yeah, I'll make sure to tell Piper and Jane that. Guess I'll just have to entertain them both since your dumbass isn't going to be there." He thrusts his hips a few times before spinning around and heading off toward the gym. As he walks under the banner advertising the fall formal in a few weeks, he jumps up, slaps his hand against it, and knocks it down.

He's such an asshole. I don't even know why I'm friends with him anymore other than I've been friends with him forever, and he's just around all the time. I wish I had the balls to end our friendship. I honestly want to with most of my friends, but I'm not sure I could handle being alone. Although, I feel alone even when I'm surround by people.

Bottling down my irritation, I shove out the doors that lead to the side of the school, ready to get the hell away from this place and everyone in it. But Piper cuts me off.

"Hey, baby," she says, walking across the grass toward me. "I'm glad I caught you before you left."

I'm not. "What do you want?"

"God, what's with the attitude?" she snaps. "You've been acting like this for months. It's getting ridiculous."

I take a deep breath and try again, reminding myself that I'm trying to be a better person, and this is not the way to do that. "What's up?"

She arches her back, pressing her chest against mine. "See? There's the old Grey I know and love." Her fingers thread through my hair as she pulls me in for a quick kiss.

My jaw ticks. While I want to appear like I still have my life in control, I don't want to be who I used to be anymore. I want to be someone different, someone nicer. I want to be someone who doesn't lie to their father while he's on his deathbed.

Piper starts yammering about the dance coming up next month, and I zone out, thinking about what my dad said to me right before he died.

"Make sure to live your life to the fullest. Do what makes you happy, Grey." His eyes begged me to understand his full meaning as he clutched my hand. "Surround yourself with people who make you happy. I want you to always be able to look back on your life and smile at all the great things you did."

"And my dress looks so hot." Piper hooks her arms around the back of my neck. "You're going to seriously lose your mind when you see me in it."

I feel like I'm banging my head against a wall. I haven't asked her to the dance yet, and I don't plan on it. Dances are expensive and overrated. Besides, I'm not sure we will still be together in a month. The only reason our relationship has lasted this long is because I went MIA for the entire summer after my father passed away and barely spoke to her or any of my other friends, for that matter. She didn't care that much—no one did—and when we did speak, she complained that I was, as she put it, too depressing to be around.

School has been going for a few weeks now, and she keeps making comments about how different I am. I hate that she doesn't understand. I tried to open up to her about it once, but again, she told me I was being too depressing and quickly shut down the conversation.

She doesn't make me happy.
Why am I still with her?

"Sound good?" Piper asks, batting her eyelashes.

"Um... I guess so," I say, unsure what I'm agreeing to.

She stands on her tiptoes and presses her lips to mine, giving me a deep kiss. "Yummy." She moves back. "Oh, and Grey? No more taking girls around to the back of the school. You're going to upset me. And you know, when I get upset, someone has to pay for it," she says sweetly, but her eyes carry a threat.

I frown as she waggles her fingers at me then ambles back across the grass, swaying her hips.

God, I really need to break up with her, stop dragging out the inevitable. I just don't know how to do it without pissing her off. Piper is all about the drama. I've seen her make it her mission to break down people she doesn't like. She finds out their secrets and tells every person she knows. I don't want to deal with that shit. I just want a quiet, normal life, a fresh start. A second chance to do things better, I guess.

I leave the school, feeling frustrated. As I'm rounding the corner of the building, I hear the sound of fabric ripping. The next thing I know, my books are scattered all over the ground.

Cursing, I slip off the backpack and look at the damage. It tore right along the seam, so I think it's fixable. Still, getting home today is going to be a pain in the ass.

I bend over, pick up my books, and finish the walk around to the back of the school. I move past the cars and the shed woodshop takes place in, hiking all the way to the hill about a half a mile away from school. Then I duck into the trees and retrieve my rusty, piece of shit bike I hid this morning where no one could stumble across it or see me riding it to school.

I hate the bike more than I hate Logan. It represents how much my life has changed over the last few months—falling apart and barely able to hold up my weight. I wouldn't even ride the damn thing except it takes about twenty extra minutes on foot to get home, and that would make me late to therapy/support/whatever you want to call it group. The only other option is to ride the bus, which is never going to happen. I could catch a ride with one of my friends, but they all have soccer practice right now. Besides, that might lead to questions they wouldn't want to hear the answers to.

I push the bike out of the trees and onto the dirt path, feeling lonelier than I ever have in my entire life.

Confession

SIX

I begged for a job the other day.

Grey

I MAKE IT home with time to spare, dripping in sweat.

"Grey, come play basketball with me!" my eleven-year-old sister Mia shouts as I pedal up the driveway.

"I wish I could, but I have to go somewhere," I say as I jump off the bike and wheel it up to the garage.

She frowns as she dribbles the ball. "You're always too busy."

"I know. I'm sorry." I prop the bike against the garage, feeling bad that I've been such a terrible brother lately. I've just been too busy trying to keep what's left of the family together. "How about I set a couple of hours aside this Saturday? We can do anything you want."

Her eyes glint with hope. "Even if it's going out for ice cream?"

"If that's what you want to do." I just hope I can scrounge up enough change for it.

She frowns again. "But we can't afford stuff like that anymore."

"You shouldn't worry about money, Mia. You're just a kid."

"Everyone else is always worried," she mutters. "I even heard Mom talking to Aunt May about how we're going to end up on the streets. Is that true? Are we going to be homeless?"

Seeing her worry like this breaks my heart.

"No, we're not going to end up homeless," I say, though sometimes I worry about that myself. "Mom just says things sometimes when she gets stressed."

"But we're poor. And don't people who are poor end up homeless?"

"Just because we don't have as much money as we used to, it doesn't mean we're going to be homeless." I take the ball from her and shoot a one-handed basket. "Now start making a list of all the things you want to do on Saturday, and we'll make sure to do as much as we can." That gets her to smile.

"Okay, but it's going to be super long with lots of crazy stuff," she warns as I jog up the stairs. "So be prepared."

"I'll make sure to be ready for all sorts of crazy stuff," I promise her then open the door and step into the kitchen.

On the outside, the house still resembles the same home I grew up in: two stories with trees in the yard and a lawn I'm forced to mow. On the inside, it's empty.

After my dad passed away four months ago from cancer, my mom has been selling off furniture, appliances we don't need—pretty much anything she can until the house sells.

"We can't afford it anymore," she said to me the day a realtor showed up with a for sale sign.

"But this is Dad's house," I snapped, angry that she was getting rid of the place that carried so many memories of him.

Tears welled in her eyes, and I instantly felt like the worst son in existence. "I know it is," she whispered, "but, Grey, there's not much else I can do. Your father and I . . . We didn't plan for him to get sick and . . ." Tears streamed from her eyes as she stared at a framed picture of him on the wall. "I don't know what else to do," she said more to herself.

I dropped the subject after that, even though it kills me every time the realtor shows someone our house.

"You look tired," my mom notes as she glances up from the stack of overdue bills on the kitchen table in front of her.

She's the one who looks worn out with her bloodshot eyes, and she's still wearing her pajamas. She used to be one of those moms who was always up and running before everyone else. Now she's usually late for everything and doesn't have time to clean up. But with everything she's taken on, it's not her fault, and she's still a good mom.

"I stayed up late, trying to catch up on assignments." I set my torn backpack on the table covered with overdue bills. "Can you fix this?"

She picks it up and turns it over, examining the hole in the bottom. "I think I can. What happened? Did you snag it on something?"

"No, it's just old. I knew it was going to happen sooner or later." I open the fridge and hold back a sigh at the lack of food inside.

"Honey, I'm so sorry," she says. "I can buy you a new one if you want me to. I just got some extra shifts at the diner and—"

"Mom, stop worrying. It's not that big of a deal. It's just a backpack." I open the cupboard and grab three packs of fruit snacks. My mom has been bad about stocking the cupboards with food, partly because she's distracted and partly because we're low on cash. "I have to go to that thing again, but when I get back, can you drive me to Benny's? He said to stop by today and fill out an application." I begged him to let me apply because no one else in town would even consider hiring me after the shoplifting ordeal.

She presses her lips together, on the verge of crying. "I hate that they're making you go to these sessions. It's not fair after what you've been through."

"We've all been through stuff," I tell her. "I made the choice to do what I did. I'm just lucky the store owner didn't press charges. And I only have to go for another week. I can make it through one more week."

She nods, dazing off, thinking about God knows what. It could be the bills, her nightshift at the diner she started working at after my dad died, her day job at the pharmacy, or her son who decided to steal a soda, a bag of chips, and a frozen package of steaks and got caught.

The owner agreed not to press charges, just as long as I attended this support group/therapy session. Since I live in such a small town, there aren't any individual sessions, so I have to sit and listen to people who have gotten into trouble with drugs, stealing, vandalism—pretty much everything. I really do regret what I did. I was just really hungry and tired of eating fruit snacks and Top Ramen.

My mom removes her reading glasses and sets them down on the table. "Grey, I really don't like the idea of you getting a job, especially when you're struggling in school."

I glance down at Luna's phone number on my hand. I felt like a dumbass when I had to write it down. I knew Luna was wondering why I didn't just enter it into my phone. I didn't lie to her about my friends breaking it. But the incident happened a couple of weeks ago, and right now, there's no money to replace it, so I'm stuck using the house phone.

"We need the money." I tear open a fruit snack bag, tip my head back, and empty the whole pouch into my mouth.

"And I found someone to tutor me. We're starting today, so I either need to borrow the car or need someone to give me a ride to the library later tonight."

"Tutoring sounds expensive. Maybe I can help you."

"I love you, Mom. I really do. But you've tried to help me with my homework before, and you always end up getting pissed off. And the person who's tutoring isn't really a tutor. She's just a . . . ." I'm not sure what to call Luna. Up until the other day when I saw her steal from Benny's store, we barely spoke to each other, even if we have gone to the same school since kindergarten. We're definitely not close, but at the same time, I feel like she might understand my situation. "She's just a friend, not an actual hired tutor."

"Oh, okay." She relaxes a bit. "That was really nice of her."

"Yeah, it is." I'm not surprised Luna agreed to help me, even with what happened our sophomore year. She's just that way—really nice and sweet, something I'm not used to.

Stuffing the rest of the fruit snacks into my pocket, I wander back to my room to put my books on my bed. Then I pull out the envelope Beckett gave me. I'm still unsure what I'm going to do with the money inside—whether I'm going to spend it or not. I want back what I gave up for it, but my family needs the help. And once I spend it, what I gave to Beck will be gone forever.

I hide the envelope under my mattress where my mom won't find it then leave my room. I yell bye to my mom then head out the front door before she can say anything to me. She's been so stressed out over the last few months, and I hate that she now has to worry over her son's life falling apart.

I'm trying to get my shit together—get my grades up, get a job, and start paying for my own stuff. If I wasn't such a spoiled brat to begin with, the change might not have been so hard. But up until my father got sick, and even a little bit after, I was a cocky asshole who always got his way. I'm trying not to be that person anymore, because I get it now—what it feels like to have the whole world against you sometimes. And what it feels like to be truly ashamed of the person you are.

"You're a good son, Grey," were my dad's final words to me. He looked up at me from his bed, pale and thin, just bones and skin, as he clasped my hand. "I'm so proud of the man you've become."

He was so wrong. I wasn't a good person. I was someone who stood around and watched people get bullied and who did it himself sometimes. I was an asshole. I never did anything good. And I let my dad die, thinking I was the opposite. I didn't even have the balls to tell him the truth.

My eyes burn with tears as I wind around the corner of the block to the main street that runs through town. I wipe my eyes before I pick up my pace for the entrance door, noting the time on the town clock and realizing I'm early.

I slam to a stop when I spot Luna walking up the sidewalk in my direction with an older woman and man at her side. Either they're her parents or her grandparents. I can't tell because they look older, at least sixty or so.

Luna looks different than she does at school, more tense and depressed. She isn't wearing the shorts and tank top she had on earlier, the ones that show off her long, lean legs and smooth skin. I remember the first day she came to school dressed differently. It was toward the beginning of junior year, and everyone was talking about it. Some people were making fun of how she got the clothes.

"She must have robbed a store or something," I remember Piper saying. "Seriously, there's no way she can go from thrift store shit to designer."

I didn't say anything, only nodded. I hardly ever said

much, which didn't make me any better than the rest of them.

Not everyone was rude about it, though. I remember a couple of my friends talking about her "hot ass." She does have a hot ass, and those legs of hers go on for miles. But the outfit she has on now covers all of that up.

"I still can't believe what you've done," the woman seethes at her as she jerks open the door to the building I'm supposed to go into. "You know better than to have those kinds of things. After everything I've taught you, you should know better. You shouldn't want that kind of stuff."

Luna enters the building, biting her nails, and the woman and man go inside with her.

I briefly contemplate the idea of ditching the therapy session and just going home. The last thing I want is for people at school to find out what I did or why I did it. I don't think Luna is the kind of person to tell anyone, though, so I crack my knuckles, square my shoulders, and pull the door open.

The woman is still chewing out Luna as I enter. Thankfully, no one else has arrived, because she's making a scene, and Luna looks horrified enough without an audience.

"It's ridiculous that we're even here," she snaps, standing on her tiptoes to get in Luna's face.

The man remains close to Luna, backing her into a corner, as if they're trying to make "intimidate Luna" a team effort.

"I can't believe my daughter has to come to a place like this, but you need to learn your lesson because my punishments clearly aren't working. Hopefully, this place will give you some insight to how you're going to end up if you keep heading in this direction. You know what kinds of people come to these meeting, Luna? Drug addicts, thieves, whores.

They're just like your aunt Ashlynn. Is that how you want to end up, Luna? Do you want to be whore? Because those clothes and makeup I found make you look like one."

Whoa. This woman is intense.

I contemplate backing out of the room and waiting outside or maybe even stepping in and stopping them, but the man glances in my direction and gives me a judgmental look that pisses me off. I carry his gaze, daring him to say something to me. He glares back before looking away.

Yeah, douchebag, look away.

The woman—Luna's mom—fiddles with Luna's hair and tugs on the bottom of her sweatshirt that already reaches her knees. Then she does the same to her own hair and button down shirt.

"You have exactly ten minutes to get home after the meeting ends. If you're late, you'll get punished, do you understand?"

"Yes," Luna mutters with her eyes fixed on the carpet.

"I'd pick you up myself, but your father and I have a church meeting," she continues. "Your phone better show you at home at five ten."

"I said I understand." Luna squeezes her eyes shut.

"This is your own fault," the man, who I assume is her dad, says in an icy tone. "You did this to yourself by making the wrong choices that have embarrassed this family. Think about that while you're here. You've been such a terrible person. If you keep going down this road, do you know where that's going to get you in life? Nowhere, that's where. Losers stay losers, Luna, so stop being one."

With that, the two of them turn to leave. As they pass me, the man gives me another nasty look, and the woman's eyes narrow on me.

"See? That's the kind of people who belong here," she whispers loudly enough for me to hear. "He looks like a troublemaker."

"I think that's Gary Sawyer's son," the man replies as he shoves open the door. "So that's no surprise."

Hearing him talk about my dad that way makes me want to beat his ass. My dad was a good person, who yeah, let me get away with more shit than he should've, but he never yelled at me and tried to intimidate me by telling me I'm a bad person.

Getting into a fight with an old dude is the last thing I should be doing, though, so I curl my hands into fists and focus on breathing until the two of them leave the building.

"Goddammit," Luna curses as she yanks off the sweatshirt and tosses it on the floor. "Why do they have to be my parents? Why? Why? Why?" She stomps on the shirt several times before she notices me. Then her cheeks turn red. "What are you doing here?" She sounds choked up.

"Probably for the same reason you're here." I point at the circle of fold up chairs in the middle of the room. "For the session."

"Oh." She scoops up the sweatshirt from the floor. "How long have you been standing there?"

I pretend to be casual, even though I just witnessed her parents rip into her. "Not too long."

She assesses me as she ties the shirt around her waist. "You saw them yelling at me, didn't you?"

I offer her an apologetic shrug. "How'd you know?"

She readjusts the bottom of her tank top that was hidden under the sweatshirt. "Because I know that look on your face. You feel sorry for me. Wynter gets the same look on her face every time she sees my parents get mad at me." She pauses. "Thanks, though, for trying to lie about it to spare me the embarrassment."

"You shouldn't be embarrassed. They should."

She eyes me over warily. "Even after the temper

tantrum I just threw?"

"I would've lost my shit, too." I step toward her. "I would've yelled at them, though."

"I wish I did." She frowns, unconvinced, and then forces a laugh that sounds all kinds of wrong. "I guess you just got a glimpse of what I can be like when I lose games, right?"

I don't say anything. I'm not sure what to say. She's embarrassed, but I don't want her to be. I want her to feel comfortable around me, especially since we're going to be spending time together while she tutors me.

Her cheeks flush. "I'm sorry you had to see that. My parents are just really intense, especially when I mess up."

"I get it," I say, though I don't. Yeah, my mom and dad have gotten pissed off at me when I have gotten into trouble, but they usually just ground me.

"Do you?" she mumbles, staring off into empty space. "Because I don't."

"Everyone's parents get pissed at them sometimes," I tell her in an attempt to make her feel better.

"But does everyone's parents haul them to a group therapy session because they found makeup and nail polish and worry they're going to turn into a prostitute?" she challenges then shakes her head. "I'm so sorry. I shouldn't be talking to you about this. You don't need to hear about my problems."

"You're fine. You can say whatever you want. I swear I won't tell anyone." I mean it, too. I owe her for what I did to her in tenth grade, and now might be my chance to make up for how horribly I treated her.

Apparently, she doesn't believe I'm being that genuine, because uncomfortable silence stretches between us.

"They really brought you here because they think you're a prostitute?" I ask, breaking the silence.

"They think makeup leads to prostitution. And nail

polish. And stupid, lacy, black panties," she mumbles with an exhausted sigh.

Black, lacy panties? Is that what she has on under there? My gaze deliberately sweeps over her long legs hidden by those loose jeans, her narrow waist, her chest, her lips . . .

I tear myself from my lustful thoughts as she peers up at me through her eyelashes, looking as innocent as can be.

Okay, how the hell can her parents think she's going to turn into a prostitute? She's, like, the sweetest girl ever.

"You thought I was here because I shoplifted, didn't you?" she asks, fiddling with the hem of her shirt.

"No," I lie. That's exactly what I thought.

She continues to nervously wring the bottom of her shirt, pulling it high enough that I catch a glimpse of the bottom of her flat stomach. "It should be." She swiftly shakes her head. "I'm sorry. I usually don't ramble this much, especially to people I don't know. I think I'm just stressed out."

"You do know me." I offer her a lopsided smile that seems to fluster her. "We've been in the same school together for practically forever."

"Yeah, but up until the thing at . . . Benny's"—she stares down at her feet again, seeming ashamed—"we've only said, like, maybe ten words to each other, ever since . . . well, you know."

I want to apologize to her for the dance, tell her the whole story of what happened, tell her I didn't spread that rumor about her, but I'm not sure if that'd be enough. I acted like a dick when I turned her down. I could've just given her an excuse, told her I was busy, but no, I had say no fucking way, because I was a cocky shit who wasn't much better than Logan.

What would my father have done if he knew exactly how bad a person I was? That I wasn't the good man he knew? That, when I was at school, I was the opposite?

"So what if we didn't used to talk? We're talking now." I duck my head to catch her eye. "You can talk to me about whatever you want. Isn't that why we're at this place? To talk about our problems?"

"I guess so." She stares at me for a heartbeat or two then sits down in one of the chairs and pulls out her phone from the pocket of her sweatshirt.

I watch her mess around with her phone for a bit. Her head is down; her long, brown hair concealing her face; and her shoulders are hunched over. While she's usually shy, she isn't this timid and offish.

When I finally sit down beside her, she doesn't glance up at me, but I feel her tense as my shoulder brushes hers.

"Everything okay?" I ask, trying to get her to look up at me.

"Yeah." She clears her throat as she scoots over an inch.

It throws me off a little. Usually, girls move closer to me, not away. I guess I deserve it from her.

Her eyes remain on her phone, her fingers scrolling through texts messages. I try not to read what's on the screen, but it's hard not to glance down every once in a while.

> *Ari: So, if you bring your phone to school tomorrow and give it to me for a couple of hours, I can swap out phones. U can have a backup to take with you and one to leave wherever. That way, your parents can still get ahold of u whenever, but they won't know where u r. Or they'll think you're at wherever your phone is, anyway.*

Jesus, her parents are way beyond intense. It makes me feel even shittier for the stuff my friends put her through. Not only did she have to suffer through them teasing her, but she had to go home and deal with her parents.

She types a response, thanking Ari at least ten times

before she switches to another thread.

> Wynter: A new band I found that I think you'll love. It's not mix music or anything, but it's got a good beat to it. Cheer up, girly. We've all got your back. Always and forever.

I feel the slightest bit jealous of Luna and her friends and how much they seem to care about each other. Mine give me nothing but shit for getting put on academic probation. I can't even imagine telling them about my other problems.

Luna clicks on an audio file titled "There's No 'I' In Team" by Taking Back Sunday, and a song blasts through the speaker of her phone. She casts a panicked glance around the empty room then at me.

"Is it okay if I listen to this?" she asks. "Because I can turn it off if it's bothering you."

"You're fine. In fact, turn it up."

She relaxes as she cranks up the music and sings along. Apparently, she already knows the song. I lean back in the chair, stretching out my legs, and tap my fingers to the beat. She smiles at me when she notices my fingers drumming against my knees, and I return her smile. It's probably the most content I've felt in weeks, and part of me wishes the song would keep playing forever so the moment would never have to end.

Like everything else, it does, and the room eventually grows quiet again.

"Does Wynter always send you songs to cheer you up?" I ask.

"How'd you know this was from Wynter?" she questions, setting her phone down on her lap. "Did you read my messages?" She doesn't seem angry, only curious.

"Sorry. I didn't mean to read them. They were just kind of there, you know. And I'm kind of fascinated by you and your friends."

"You mean my *intimidating* friends?" she says with a trace of a smile.

Getting her to smile makes me feel proud, like maybe I'm taking a step in the right direction of getting her to forgive me.

"I've decided they're just intimidating to outsiders. They seem like good friends."

"They are. They've always been there for me."

"It's good you have them. I'm kind of jealous."

"Of *me?*"

I nod and twist in the chair, facing her. "I just think it'd be nice to have friends I can tell anything to without worrying they'll make fun of me."

"I don't tell my friends everything," she utters softly. "Not because I think they'd make fun of me or anything—I know they'd never do that. There's just some things I'm embarrassed of . . . like the thing you saw me do the other day."

"You shouldn't be embarrassed. I really do understand." More than I want to tell you.

"Why I stole . . . It's not as simple as you think." Her head angles to the side as a contemplative look crosses her face. "Can I . . . ? Do you care if I . . . ?" She looks away from me. "Never mind."

"No, go ahead. Say what you're going to say. The guy who runs this thing is going to be here soon, anyway, and he's going to ask everyone a shitload of questions."

She immediately frowns. "Really?"

"But you don't have to answer them if you don't want to."

"I wish I didn't have to talk at all."

"I think a lot of people here are the same way. It's hard talking about your problems, isn't it?"

She nods, chewing on her bottom lip, bringing all of

my focus to her mouth. Her lips look soft and natural, and I think I prefer the look over Piper's heavily done lips. Every time we kiss, I end up getting lipstick all over, and it's a pain in the ass to get off.

"How long have you been coming to these meetings?" she asks.

"A few weeks." Should I say anything about why I'm here? Fuck it. She's going to find out sooner or later. "I was caught stealing from Mountain Ridge Grocery, and the owner, Larry, said he wouldn't press charges just as long as I came to a month's worth of meetings."

Her eyes widen in astonishment. "You were caught stealing?"

"It was really stupid. I don't know why I thought I could get away with it. My shirt looked so bulky."

"What'd you take?" she asks, mildly curious.

I pick at a tiny hole in the knee of my jeans. "Soda, chips, and a steak."

She seems unfazed by my confession, which makes me wonder just how many times she has stolen.

"Is it . . . ? Was it the first time you ever stole?"

I nod. "What about you? Was that day at Benny's your first time?"

She shakes her head with her lips fused.

"I'm sure you have a good reason for doing it, though," I add.

She looks sad and regretful. "You think too highly of me. Everyone does. I'm not as good of a person as everyone thinks I am."

"Or maybe you just don't see yourself clearly because of other stuff."

"What kind of other stuff?"

"I don't know, like, because of the things your parents say to you." *That my friends and I used to say to you. Why can't*

I say it aloud? Just say, I'm sorry.

She opens and flexes her fingers as she stares down at the scars on her hands.

I open my mouth to apologize, but I can't figure out the right words or if there are any right words. A simple sorry doesn't feel right, not after all the stuff we did to her, the things we said. Logan even spread a rumor that her body was covered with the same scars she has on her hands. He never explained how he could possibly know that, but no one cared. They only believed it.

"What happened?" I ask, grazing my fingers along her palm.

She shivers, her hand trembling.

"Sorry," I apologize, pulling away. "Do they hurt?"

"No, they're just a little sensitive." She stretches out her fingers. "Our house caught on fire when I was four, and I was stuck in my room for a while. I got the scars when I was crawling across the floor, trying to get out. There are a couple on my knees, too, but they're really hard to see."

"Holy shit! That had to be scary."

"I can't really remember what happened. Sometimes, when I'm asleep, I dream I'm crawling across the floor in the middle of flames, and then someone scoops me up, but that's about all I can remember."

I reach out and trace my fingers along the scars again. "Did it hurt? I mean, when your hands were burned?"

"Yeah, it did. That part, I do remember." She shudders from my touch again, but this time, I don't pull away.

It's not like I've never touched a girl like this before. I used to flirt a lot and was known as a touchy, feely kind of guy. Usually, girls flirted back. But Luna remains still, staring at my hands with a combination of fascination and tension.

I stroke her palm, wondering how long she'll let me touch her before she pulls away. Hopefully, she'll let me for a while, because I find the movement comforting, like we're connecting somehow. Or maybe it's because I'm having an actual, real conversation.

I ask, "How'd the fire start?"

She rips her gaze off my fingers on her palm. "From what my parents say, someone started a fire in the fireplace that spread throughout the house."

My jaw drops to my knees. "So it was started intentionally?"

"That's the story. The police never did find out who did it."

"You say that like you don't buy the whole story."

"Sometimes, I don't."

"Why not?"

"I don't know . . ." Her forehead furrows. "When I dream about what happened, I can remember being carried out of the house. The thing is, my parents say a fireman rescued me, but I swear it feels like I knew the person . . . I felt so safe in their arms . . ." She shakes her head. "But, anyway, I'm probably remembering things wrong since I was so little."

I trace the tip of my finger down one of the longer, angular scars. "Have you ever told your parents about the dreams?"

She nods. "They're the ones who told me I'm probably remembering wrong. They said there was no way I could remember something that happened when I was four years old and that I should just be glad the fireman got me out of the house. They do that a lot—try to tell me how to think."

"I'm not surprised," I say. "Have they always been that way? So . . . intense?"

"Pretty much." She rotates in her seat so we're both facing inward and our knees are only inches apart. "One of my first memories is of them collecting all my toys, bagging them up, and throwing them in the trash. Then I got this big lecture on how I was too old to play with toys, and it was time to grow up and start learning to behave properly. I was five when she did that."

"You were *five*? That's fucking crazy. My younger sister's eleven, and she still has a toy box and everything."

"That's just one of the many stories when I felt like I had to grow up too fast." Her expression unexpectedly fills with worry. "I'm sorry for talking so much. I don't even know why I'm telling you all of this. I don't usually talk about this with anyone except my friends, and that's only because they've seen my parents do"—she flicks her wrist, motioning behind us where her parents reamed into her moments ago—"what you saw them do."

"I told you that you could talk to me. And I like listening to you talk." I like having an actual conversation that carries depth.

"Really? Why? My stories are so . . ."

"Real? Honest?"

"I was going to go with messed up."

"Still, they're real. I haven't had a real conversation in a long time." *Since my father died.* "Whenever I'm with my friends, they always want to talk about sports or who they screwed around with at last weekend's party. And Piper . . . All she wants to talk about is the dance and what party we're going to hit up." I stop myself as Luna's demeanor shifts. "Are you okay?"

"Yeah, I'm fine." She tries to shrug it off, but I can tell that she's lying and that something is bothering her. My bet is Piper did something to Luna. I wouldn't be surprised since I've seen Piper do a lot of messed up shit to people over the last year while I was dating her, and I just stood by and watched.

"So, you have a little sister, huh?" she asks. "That's got

to be nice, not being the only child."

"It's nice sometimes, but she can be a pain in the ass when she doesn't get her way." Although, she has been quieter lately, which is why I've been trying to spend more time with her.

"Still, it's better than being the only child and being the sole focus for your parents." Her phone hums from her lap, but she doesn't pick it up.

"I've never looked at it that way, but I get what you're saying," I reply. "There's been a ton of times I've gotten away with stuff because Mia had my parents distracted with something she did."

"Do you guys do a lot of stuff together?"

"We didn't used to, but ever since . . . my father died, I feel like I need to spend more time with her."

"That has to be hard, losing your dad."

"It was—is hard." I pretend to have an itch on the corner of my eye to cover up the tears trying to escape. "He was really involved in my life. He's actually the reason I'm so into sports. When I was about four, he started taking me to soccer games, baseball games, football—pretty much every single sport you can think of. When I started playing sports myself, he never missed any of my games, and he was the same way with Mia. She was really into dance for a while, and he always went to her recitals."

Her eyes get misty. "He sounds like a good dad."

"He was the best." My voice cracks. "He had a hard time when he got sick, because he couldn't do as much stuff with Mia and me anymore. I think he did more stuff than the doctor's thought he should."

"What was he sick with?" she asks then hurriedly adds, "Never mind. You don't need to tell me if you don't feel like talking about it."

"No, it's okay. He died of cancer." I remember the day

my mom and dad sat Mia and me down to tell us. It becomes harder to fight back the tears. "It was crazy. It was like, one minute, he was perfectly healthy, and the next, he was telling us that he was sick. He didn't look sick at first, but then he started chemo, and he got weaker and frailer until he didn't even look like my dad anymore . . ." I trail off as my hands start to shake.

"Grey, I'm so sorry." She places a hand over mine, steadying it. "We don't have to talk about this if you don't want to."

"No, I want to," I tell her, surprised by how much I really do. "I haven't actually talked to anyone about it. Even with my mom, I don't feel comfortable because I'm afraid she's going to cry, and Mia is the same way. Every time I bring him up, she gets upset. And my friends . . . None of them are good listeners like you are, and they make me feel bad whenever I bring it up because they think I'm being too depressing."

"Well, I'm here if you ever want to talk."

I open my mouth to tell her that I'd really like to talk more, but the door swings open, and five people wander in, putting an end to probably the most honest conversation I've ever had.

Confession

SEVEN

> *I usually don't have a purpose for the stuff I steal.*
>
> *Luna*

WHEN I WAS fourteen, I stole a jacket when my mom was taking me school clothes shopping. It wasn't even a jacket I liked. It was too big and bulky and a horrible shade of puke green.

Right before I jacked it, I was following my mom around the store, watching her put clothes in the cart that I was supposed to wear while listening to her ridicule every person around us.

"Oh, look at that girl, Luna." She pointed at a girl around my age who was wearing a tight black dress, matching boots, and had a stud through her nose. "Imagine how she'll end up in a few years. Probably on the corner of a street." She didn't even say it quietly, and the girl gave us a nasty look.

I was beyond embarrassed and wanted to say something, but like always, I kept my mouth shut. But I felt something silently snap inside me, break, and I stole for the very first time in my life. For the briefest second, I felt in control, like I was somehow yelling fuck you to my mom without actually saying the words aloud.

After I made it out of the store with the jacket, I gave it to a homeless woman standing near the store, like somehow that made me a better person. It didn't.

I've known what kind of person I am ever since I was seven years old, and my parents tried to explain to me how I was supposed to act, what I was supposed to wear, and who I was supposed to be. I remember thinking it didn't sound like someone I wanted to be, which had to make me a bad person.

I spend most of the session listening to the rest of the group talk about their problems while silently drowning in my own. I desperately want to steal something. My hands twitch to snatch something up and hide it in my pocket. I long for control, long to breathe for two goddamn seconds. But I can't go anywhere.

Or can I?

I glance at the exit door several times, debating whether to get up and make a quick trip to the store. I could be in and out in five minutes. What if my parents found out I left, though? All it would take is for one of their church friends to spot me, and word would get back to them.

What do I do?

What kind of person am I to be sitting here, contemplating this?

I'm so fucked up.

My head is crammed with thoughts that are in no way related to the session, and I can barely think straight. Thankfully, Howard, the guy in charge, doesn't push me to talk. Grey talks, though, during what Howard calls sharing-our-feelings time.

"I felt bad about what I did." His hands are balled into fists as he stares down at the floor. "No matter why I stole the stuff, it wasn't fair to just take it from someone else, you know? But it felt like this other person took over and let me justify putting that stuff in my pocket." He lifts his head, and our gazes collide. "But I don't think that makes me a bad person."

It feels like he's trying to send me a message, like he gets me. I wish he did. Maybe then I could finally open up to someone and release the pressure building in my chest instead of having to steal in order to do so. He doesn't understand me, though, even if he thinks he does.

Grey has stolen a total of one time, and I'm guessing it was just a rebellious act to get a rush. He doesn't understand what it's like to go to the store with the sole purpose of stealing, what it's like to feel like you have to do it; otherwise, your entire world will spin out of control. He isn't sitting here, contemplating running out the door just so he can put something in his pocket to get some messed up form of temporary peace.

But he does know more about me than he did twenty minutes ago. I don't know why I told him all those things about my family and the fire. It just sort of poured out of me. And it seemed like I had the same effect on him when he told me all those things about his family and his dad.

I've always been told I'm a good listener, but I never thought the day would come when I'd be one for Grey Sawyer. Watching him talk about his dad, I saw a sweeter side of him, one I didn't think existed.

"I totally get what you're saying," a woman in her mid-twenties with short, black hair says, drawing me out of my thoughts. "It's like when I used to get high. I'd always justify what I was doing, but after I crashed, I always felt so fucking bad about what I did. I don't think what I did made me a bad person; I just made bad fucking choices. I wish my sister could see how hard I'm trying and forgive me. I know

I did a lot of terrible shit to her, but I've been trying to get my shit together, you know?"

"Give her some time," Howard says. "I know it's hard, but like with how you're still healing over your addiction, your sister needs time to heal, too."

The woman nods, anxiously thrumming her fingers on her knees. "I hope so. I really do . . . I miss her."

I think about my own parents at home and wonder if they'll ever forgive me for the stuff they discovered about me today. I doubt it. They were already upset from finding the stuff. And when they asked me how I got the money to pay for everything, I couldn't come up with an answer, and they somehow put two and two together.

"You stole it, didn't you?" my mom asked, but it wasn't a question. Somehow, she just knew her daughter was a thief. "I should've seen this coming."

"This is partly your fault." My dad put some of the blame on my mom, which surprised me. Usually, they blamed me for everything. "Clearly, you haven't been controlling her enough."

"I've been trying"—she slammed her fist against the table—"but she's uncontrollable. She doesn't do what she's told. I don't think I can help her anymore."

Shock ricocheted through me. Never in my life had I seen her so . . . out of control.

"Well, she definitely doesn't get that from my side of the family," he said, shoving his chair back from the table to stand up. "Find a way to fix her."

I expected her to make me burn all the stuff she found, but I should've known it wouldn't be that easy.

Going to the sessions for a week is only the start. I'm also not allowed out of the house except to go to school, to the sessions, and to the library for an hour a day. The last part was only a stipulation because I told my mom I had a school project to work on that required after school time with a group and that we're supposed to meet up at the library. Part of me lied just so I could get a break from the house, but I also didn't want to back out of tutoring Grey when I promised him I would.

But that's not my biggest problem. I'm basically on my parents' version of house arrest, which means I'll be around them more, which means I'm going to want to steal more but won't have a chance to.

Crap. What am I going to do? How am I going to deal with this?

"Luna, the session is over."

My palms are damp with sweat as I blink out of my trance. To my surprise, almost everyone has cleared out of the room.

Grey is standing in front of me with concern in his eyes. "You kind of zoned out. Are you okay?"

I glance at the time and realize I have five minutes to get home. The only way I'll make it is if I run.

"Crap, I'm going to be late." I spring from the chair as panic sets in.

Grey has zero time to move out of my way, and my chest collides with his as my forehead knocks into his chin.

"Shit," he curses as he trips back, clutching his chin.

I slap my hand over my mouth. "Oh, my God, I'm so sorry."

"It's fine." His face is contorted in pain as he rubs his chin.

I glance from the door to him. "Are you sure?"

"Yeah, I'm positive." He lowers his hand, and his lips tug into a joking smile. "You have a really hard head, though."

I let out an edgy laugh, my gaze darting to the door again. "I know I'm going to sound like a jerk, but I have to get home, like, right now or my mom's going to freak out."

"You don't sound like a jerk, and I swear I'm okay." He waves at me to go.

I shoot him a grateful look then rush for the door. "Sorry I bumped you in the head," I call out.

He strides with me, flattening his palm against the door to open it for me. "Are you still going to be able to make it to the library tonight? It's okay if you can't."

The instant I step outside, I pause. My instinct is to run into a store, but shit! I don't have time.

It feels like a weight is crushing my chest as I turn away from the stores and speed walk toward the corner of the street. "No, I can make it. I told my parents I have a group project I have to work on." I pause at the end of the sidewalk, deciding which route is the quickest. "Which way's faster?" I mutter, dragging my fingers through my hair.

"Where do you live?" Grey appears by my side. I tell him my address, and he ponders something for a second before he veers to the right. "Come on. I know a shortcut."

I run after him, my sneakers thudding against the concrete. "One that will get me home in three minutes?"

"That all depends."

"On what?"

He shoots me a challenging grin. "On how fast you run."

He takes off, and I race after him. People walking through the neighborhood openly gawk at us as we sprint past them, laughing. When the sidewalk reaches a dead end, Grey doesn't slow down, running straight for a six-foot, wooden fence that separates the neighborhood from a small tree area. He stops when he reaches the fence and crouches down with his hands linked.

"Hop on, and I'll boost you up," he says, barely out of breath.

I trip to a stop, gasping for air. *I really need to start*

exercising more.

"Are you sure? I don't want to hurt you."

He gives me an are-you-kidding-me look. "I think I can handle it."

I prop my foot into his hands and grasp the top of the fence. He grunts as he stands up and hoists me up. I get my balance then jump down onto the other side, landing in the dirt on my hands and knees. Then I trip to my feet and stumble for the trees.

I hear a soft thump behind me as I barrel into the trees. I glance over my shoulder and see Grey jogging after me.

"What? Did you think I was just going to let you wander into the forest by yourself when it's almost sundown?" he teases as he gets ahead of me and runs backward down a dirt path that cuts straight through the trees. "What kind of a guy do you think I am?"

"I have no idea." I might have thought I had an idea, but I'm not so sure anymore.

He smiles, like he's reading my thoughts, then reels around and quickens his pace. I struggle to keep up with him and his ridiculous athletic skills.

"How do you know about this shortcut?"

"I take it home sometimes," he answers with his eyes on the path ahead.

"I thought you drove your truck to school?" I ask, but instantly realize my mistake.

He glances out of the corner of his eye at me. "How do you know I drive a truck?"

I give him what I hope is an indifferent shrug. "Doesn't everyone in this town know what everyone drives?"

"Yeah, I guess." His head tilts back as he gazes up at the pale pink sky.

I study his profile: his lips I once dreamed of kissing, his scruffy jawline I've always wanted to run my fingers across, his skin that looks so soft and is somehow not drenched in sweat like mine is right now. I'm not sure how I got to this moment, running home with a guy I've secretly liked since forever who saw me steal and saw my parents chew me out. Saw that I'm not the nice girl everyone thinks I am. Why isn't he running in the opposite direction?

"I don't have my truck anymore." Pain is in his eyes. "I sold it when my dad died. It was hard, because he was the one who gave me the truck."

"I'm so sorry. That had to be hard."

"It was, but we needed the money." His gaze fastens on mine. "No one's noticed I don't have my truck anymore, not even my friends."

"Not even Logan?" I ask breathlessly as I swat branches out of my way.

He shakes his head. "Logan's a self-centered dick. The only way he'd notice is if he suddenly needed a ride somewhere."

"What about Piper?" I cringe at the hint of jealousy in my tone.

Since when do I sound jealous? That's not like me. Or is it? Maybe I've never gotten the chance to be jealous before, and it's really a huge part of who I am.

A hollow laugh leaves his lips. "Yeah, Piper and Logan are kind of the same way. It's okay, though. I'd rather them not notice. Then I don't have to tell them why I had to sell it."

"I get what you're saying," I pant out, wiping the sweat from my brow. "I don't talk to my friends about everything. I love them to death, but sometimes, I worry about stuff."

He hops over a log blocking the path. "Worry about what exactly?"

"That they won't love some of the things that I do . . . won't understand why I do the things I do." I dodge around a pothole in the path then turn to my side right as a revelation smacks me across the face. Grey is going to see the home I live in and know I'm not stealing because my family lives in poverty.

I search for an excuse that will get him to turn around and go home before we make it to my house. Before I can think of a good lie, though, the trees thin and my two-story home with a lavish front yard and three car garage comes into view.

I guess it's time to tell the truth. It was going to happen eventually, anyway. Besides, after he opened up to me about his dad, I feel terrible for lying to him and letting him believe I'm a better person than I really am.

I suck in a breath and blurt out, "I know you think I stole because I'm poor, but I'm not. I'm just a bad person who steals stuff."

He carries my gaze even when the path curves sharply to the right, and I have to look away to regain my equilibrium. Silence sets in, the awkward kind that makes me squirm. I dare a glance in his direction then cringe at the disgust in his eyes, the same disgust he had the day he turned me down for the dance.

"Thanks for telling me about the shortcut." I pick up the pace, even though my legs are furious with me.

He doesn't come after me, which is good since I'm pretty sure I won't be able to look him in the eye ever again.

I make it home with seconds to spare, getting the door shut right before my mom calls.

I know I should feel grateful that I made it home in time and avoided further punishments, but all I feel is trapped and in desperate need to get control again. I can't breathe. I swear the walls are about to close in and crush me to death.

A small part of me wishes they would.

Confession
EIGHT

> Sometimes, when I'm in my room alone, I let myself cry.
>
> Grey

LUNA DOESN'T SHOW up at the library. With how horrified she looked when she ran away from me, I'm not surprised. I could see in her eyes that she thought I was judging her, and why wouldn't she think that? It's not like I have a great track record of being a nice, nonjudgmental guy.

But I wasn't judging her. While I don't fully understand why she stole, I don't think she's a bad person. After I saw how her parents treat her, I think I understand why she thinks she's, though.

I call her when I get home, but she doesn't answer, so I end up asking my mom for help with my English paper, which turns into a disaster. She freaks out when she discovers that the assignment is about Shakespeare's work.

"But I haven't read anything by him."

"Me, either," I tell her, trying to make her feel better.

She scowls at me from across the kitchen table. "You're telling me you haven't been doing the reading assignments?"

"I tried, but I could barely make it through the first

scene." I lower my head into my hands. "I feel like an idiot. I shouldn't have waited until my senior year to try to get my grades up."

"Honey, you're not an idiot, and I don't want you to ever say that again." She reaches across the table and tugs on my arm until I look at her. "We'll get your grades up."

I force a smile, hoping she's right, that somehow she can help me make good on the promise to be a better person. Getting my grades up is part of accomplishing that.

I wish I hadn't screwed around so much for the last few years. Then maybe reading Shakespeare wouldn't be like trying to understand Latin.

"What happened with the girl who was supposed to tutor you?" Mom asks as she reads over the assignment sheet again.

"She had something come up and couldn't make it," I lie as my stomach grumbles.

My mom glances at me then at the clock. "Wow, I didn't even realize it was that late. I should make dinner." She pushes back from the table, wanders over to the cupboard, and takes out three cans of Ravioli. "Why don't you call her and see if maybe she can meet you another day?"

My hunger pains increase at the sight of the cans. "That might work." But I'm not sure Luna would be too happy to help me after what happened unless I somehow convince her that I'm not the douchebag I used to be.

"Mom, can I ask you a question?"

"Of course, honey," she says as she presses the can opener into the top of the can.

I pick at the cracks in the table. "Say there was this person who was an asshole to someone for a really long time. Then one day something happened, and he decided he needed to change, but the girl he wanted to be friends with was someone he did some messed up stuff to. How would he go about convincing this girl that he's not a jerk anymore?"

She narrows her eyes at me as she rotates the handle on the opener. "Grey Sawyer, have you been mean to girls?"

"Not lately . . . But, yeah, I have . . . in the past," I confess, ashamed.

She pries the lid off the can. "I thought I raised you better than that."

"You did. I just didn't listen to all the amazing stuff you taught me." I try to dazzle her with my most charming smile.

She wags a finger at me. "Don't try to charm me, young man."

"Sorry. I'm trying to change, though . . . be better . . . be the person Dad thought I was."

She grows quiet, and when she speaks again, her voice is overflowing with emotion. "Your dad didn't *think* you were a good person. He *knew* you were."

I shake my head. "He might've thought I was, but . . . I've done some messed up stuff, and everyone at school knows it."

She chucks the lid of the can into the trash below the sink then wipes her hands clean on a dishtowel. "Well, I guess it's time to start showing everyone the good side of you." She pulls out the trash bag from the bin and ties it up. "And you can start with taking the trash out for your mom."

I get up and take the bag from her.

As I'm heading for the back door, she says, "And, Grey, if you want to show this girl you're a nice guy, you can start by telling her you're sorry."

"You think it's that easy?"

"No, but I think it's a start."

Could it be that easy?

I hope so.

I spend the rest of the evening eating dinner with Mia

and my mom while trying to think of what I'm going to say to Luna tomorrow and how to apologize to her. After I eat as much as I can, scraping the plate clean, I get ready for bed then head into the office to say good night to my mom. But I stop just outside the door when I hear her talking on the phone.

"I know we're behind on the mortgage, but things have been rough lately." She pauses, and when she speaks again, her voice is wobbly like she's fighting back tears. "Fine, I understand. I'll come up with the money." She hangs up and bursts into sobs.

I give her a moment to cry before I knock on the door.

"Just a second," she says quickly. I hear her rustling around with something, and then she calls out, "Okay, you can come in."

I open the door and step in. Papers and folders are scattered all over the floor and stacked so high on the desk I can't even see the computer. She's kneeling in the center of the mess, her eyes red from crying.

"Hey, honey." She starts sorting through the papers. "Did you need something?"

"I just wanted to say good night." It's hard to see her like this—so broken down.

"Good night, sweetie." She smiles, but it looks forced.

"I start work in a few days," I remind her. "So I need to either borrow the car or get a ride there."

"Are you sure you're going to be able to handle a job?" she asks distractedly as she sifts through a small stack of papers that look like medical bills.

I lean against the doorframe. "Yes, I'm sure."

We've had this conversation at least ten times already, and I've given her the same answer. If I didn't think I could handle a job, then I wouldn't have begged Benny again today to take a risk on me. Thankfully, he took pity on me, mostly because of my father.

"Your father was a good man," he said as he struggled to turn on the computer mouse. "You know he helped me out when he was your age. It was when I first opened the store." He pounded the mouse against the counter. "Damn technology. I told Margret I didn't want an upgrade, that my system was fine, but she said it was getting too complicated without having electronic records of everything."

"Here, let me help you." I took the mouse from him, flipped it over, and turned on the power button. "It should work now," I said, handing it back to him.

He looked at the mouse dubiously then set it down on the pad and clicked it. His eyes lit up as he stared at the screen. Then he smiled at me. "Grey, you have yourself a job."

He hired me for weekends since I have school and practice on weekdays. That is, if I ever make it back on the team. Truthfully, I think I would have asked for weekdays if my college career wasn't riding on a sports scholarship.

"There it is!" my mom exclaims as she waves the paper in the air.

"What is that?" I inch into the cluttered room.

"It's the title to your father's first car." She hops over a plastic bin that's in the middle of the room and hands me the paper. "Your uncle Nate's been storing it for your dad since forever. He was going to give it to you as a graduation present, but . . ." She forces a lump down in her throat. "But, yeah, I thought it might be better to give it to you now."

I look down at the title. A 1966 Chevy Impala.

"We should probably just sell it," I say quietly.

"That's really up to you." When I open my mouth to protest, she adds, "Your father wanted you to have that car. If you sell it, I won't take the money. You can put it away for college. Besides, the car isn't really worth anything in the condition it's in right now."

"Does it run?"

"Kind of."

"How can something kind of run?"

"I'm not sure." She twists a strand of her hair around her finger, thinking. "How about we go and talk to Nate before school tomorrow? I can drive you there before I have to go to work, and if the car runs, you can drive it to school."

"Are you sure you'll have time to do that?"

"Of course."

"Okay. I guess that sounds good." I glance down at the title again.

My dad even signed it over to me. I don't know why, but I find myself tearing up. He must have done it when he found out he was sick.

"Honey, what's wrong?" Mom asks. "I didn't mean to upset you."

"I'm not upset." I wipe my eyes with the sleeve of my shirt as I back out of the room. "I need to get to bed." I turn to leave yet pause in the doorway. "Mom, thanks for giving me this. It . . . It means a lot." I leave the room before I start bawling.

When I get to my room, I take out the envelope I hid under the mattress earlier today. I thought I'd have more time to decide if I wanted to use the money, more time to decide if I was ready to give up the signed baseball my dad gave to me at the first Yankee's game we ever went to.

"My dad gave it to me at the first game we ever went to," he said with pride as he handed me the signed ball.

"Thanks, Dad." I looked down at it in awe, knowing I was never going to forget the moment.

I suck back the tears and write my mom's name on the front of the envelope along with the message: *Someone once helped me out when I needed it, and I want to pay it forward.*

Hope this helps. Then I sneak out the front door and put it in the mailbox.

I hate being sneaky about it, but I know my mom will never take the money if she knew where I got it. I also know it's not enough money to solve all our problems, but it'll hopefully help keep my family afloat until the house sells.

After I return to my room, I close the door and take a good look at the emptiness—another painful reminder of how much everything has changed, how my dad's gone and is never coming back. He'll never come to another one of my games again. There won't be any more Sundays spent watching our favorite teams play. There won't be any more celebration dinners.

All I have left now are memories of him and a beat up old car.

With the title still clutched in my hand, I crawl into bed and cry myself to sleep.

Confession

NINE

> I like junker cars more than I liked my truck.
> Grey

FIRST THING THE next morning, my mom walks out to the mailbox to stick a bill inside. By the time she returns to the kitchen, she looks as if she has seen a ghost.

"Everything okay?" I ask her as I butter a slice of toast.

She shakes her head, her gaze descending to the envelope in her hand. "It's nothing." She turns the envelope over several times before shoving it into her purse. Then she plasters on a fake smile. "You about ready to head to Uncle Nate's?"

I put the butter back in the fridge. "Yeah, let's go."

We drop Mia off at school before we drive to my uncle Nate's house. My mom prepares to leave the second he gets the engine started, muttering that she needs to make a quick stop at the bank before she heads to work. I'm glad to hear her say that, because I was a little worried she might not use the money.

She gives me thirty dollars before she heads for her car. "It's for gas," she says when I open my mouth in protest.

"And I don't want to hear you argue. You're taking the money."

I stuff the bills into my wallet. "Thanks, Mom."

"Just make it last as long as you can." She gets into her car and drives away with the tires kicking up a cloud of dust.

Once she's gone, I concentrate on the car in front of me. It's in worse condition than I imagined. The passenger door is dented, the entire outside is practically bondo, and it's in serious need of a paint job. On a positive note, the tires are in good condition, the interior is pretty decent, and there's hardly any rust.

"She could be a real beaut with some body work and a new paint job," my uncle Nate insists as I lap the car, eyeballing all the scratches and dings.

"Would it be worth anything if I fixed it up?" I feel guilty for bringing it up, but I need to know.

The money I gave my mom last night isn't going to last very long, and I'm worried my family is going to be kicked out in the streets. I know my dad would rather me sell the car and pawn off his baseball to keep that from happening, contrary to what my mom believes.

Uncle Nate runs his hand over his head. "You want to sell it?"

I crouch down to inspect a large dent in the bumper. "Maybe."

"Yeah, you could get a lot if it was fixed properly," he says, giving the tire a soft kick with his boot.

"Really?" I run my fingers along a small spot of remaining cherry red paint.

"I could help you fix it up," he offers, sliding his hands into the pockets. "Your dad and I were supposed to start at the beginning of this year, but we . . . We never got around to it."

I shove down the pain rising in my throat as I stand

back up. "Yeah, I'd like that. Thanks, Uncle Nate."

"No problem. I'm happy to help. Just promise me you'll really think about it before you sell it."

"I promise." I wave good-bye then slide into the driver's seat.

I try to focus on the positive side of having a car again as I pull into the busy school parking lot. I wish I was running late, because I know it's going to draw attention.

"What the hell happened to your truck?" Logan appears by the door the moment I climb out of the car.

"I traded it in for this," I lie as I grab my bag from the back seat.

He cringes at the nails-on-chalkboard noise the door makes as I push it closed.

"That's seriously your car?"

"It's a classic," I say like I know what I'm talking about. Really, I'm just repeating Uncle Nate's words.

"Classic means old, and old stuff is usually a piece of shit," he sneers, picking at a small section of paint that's left.

I push him away from the car. "Don't touch the car if you're going to be a jerk about it."

"Oh, come on, Grey." He shoves me back. "You're acting like you actually like this piece of shit."

"You know what? I kind of do," I tell him truthfully. I knew it the moment I saw it, dings and all. Turns out, I'm a classic car kind of guy, just like my dad was when he was my age. At least, according to my uncle Nate.

Logan gapes at me like I've lost my damn mind. "What the hell is going on with you? You spend all summer blowing everyone off, and then you come back to school and barely talk to anyone. It's like you think you're better than everybody."

"I don't think that."

"Then what the fuck's going on with you?"

I picture telling him about my promise to become a better person and see him laughing in my face in response.

"I have to get to class." I sidestep around him and head toward the sidewalk.

"Piper thinks you're acting stupid, too." He follows me. "She spent an hour last night talking to me about you."

"I'm glad you two are getting along." I scan the grass area, the benches, and the trees for a certain brown-haired girl with really big eyes. I desperately want to talk to Luna so I can tell her I'm okay with what she confessed yesterday.

"So that doesn't bother you?" Logan questions as we reach the sidewalk.

"Does what bother me?" I ask when I spot Luna and her friend Ari crossing the parking lot. She's wearing an oversized, bright orange hoodie that looks big enough to fit me, along with a pair of loose khakis. Her hair is down and wavy, and she doesn't have a drop of makeup on.

As I'm openly staring at her, she laughs at something Ari says, and it makes me smile.

"Dude, are you checking out Luna Harvey?" Logan asks, sounding appalled.

I realize that I've stopped walking and that he's watching me. My first instinct is to say no, but I find myself shrugging.

"So what if I am?"

"You've got to be shitting me." He shakes his head. "So, is it the baggy clothes that turn you on? Is that part of your new"—he waves his hand at my car—"whatever's going on with you?"

"She doesn't dress like that all the time," I growl. "And who cares if she does? She's a nice person, which is more than I can say about you."

"You think I give a shit about being nice?" He laughs in my face. "Girls don't want nice guys, man."

I clench my hands into fists to stop myself from punching him in the face. "Just drop this, okay? It's none of your damn business."

"You know she'll never put out for you, right? Girls like that don't." He glances in Luna's direction and shakes his head before looking back at me. "Do yourself a favor; go and find Piper, say you're sorry, and let her fuck some sense back into you."

"Why would I apologize to Piper?"

"For blowing her off yesterday."

"I have no idea what the hell you're talking about," I say. "I didn't blow her off."

"She thinks you did, so just say you're sorry before she dumps your sorry ass and looks for something better." He grins as he points at himself. "Someone like me."

I open my mouth to fire off a comeback, but Luna and Ari pass by us, and my attention travels from Logan to Luna. Her eyes pop wide the second she sees me. Then she grasps Ari's sleeve and hurries toward the school.

I swing around from Logan and chase after her.

"What the hell are you doing?" Logan yells. "You've freakin' lost your mind!"

I blow him off and continue jogging after Luna.

"Luna! I need to talk to you."

Ari glances over his shoulder at me with his brows dipped before he looks back at Luna and whispers something to her. The two of them keep power-walking toward the school as she says something back to him. He responds with a stern look.

Huffing with frustration, she slows to a stop and waits for me to catch up.

"Hey," I say as I reach her.

"Hey," she replies, still clutching Ari's arm.

"Hey," I tell Ari as I slide the strap of my backpack that

my mom fixed last night higher on my shoulder.

Ari looks from her to me then shifts his weight. "Um, hey."

Silence stretches between us until Luna finally cracks a tiny smile.

"That was a lot of awkward *heys* in ten seconds' time," she says.

I smile. "It kind of was, wasn't it?"

Ari snorts a laugh. "I think we broke a record."

"Well, we've always been good at being super awkward." She playfully nudges her shoulder against Ari's.

"We're definitely gifted with awkward," he replies, grinning at her.

Again, I find myself both intimidated and jealous of Luna and her friends and how comfortable they are with each other.

I felt a momentary comfortableness yesterday when we talked, and I wish I could experience it again. And again. And again.

"May I talk to you for a second?" I ask Luna, sounding more nervous than I normally do.

"About what?" She seems equally as nervous.

"About what happened yesterday . . ." *And I want to apologize to you, but not in front of Ari. I want to be alone so I can make sure to do it right, to say everything I need to say.*

Luna plays with a bracelet on her wrist. "I don't know if there's anything to talk about."

"I think there is." I inch toward her and lower my voice. "We need to talk about a lot of stuff."

Ari clears his throat. "I have to stop by Mr. Belsteron's classroom this morning," he tells Luna. "I'll catch up with you later, okay?"

Luna tenses as he backs away from her. "Can't you wait, like, five minutes?"

"You'll be okay." He casts a glance in my direction, and I detect the faintest bit of a warning in his eyes. "You better be, anyway."

Ari is a timid guy who's never been in any fights, not even verbal ones, so I'm shocked he has the balls to threaten me. I think I might respect him for it.

Luna watches him go until he vanishes into the school. Her shoulders rise and fall as she inhales and exhales then turns to face me. "Before you say anything, I just want to say I'm sorry."

Wasn't that my line?

"Sorry for what?"

"For running off, for not thanking you for helping me get home in time, for blowing the tutoring thing off . . ." She slips her hands into the front pocket of her hoodie. "For lying to you and letting you think I was poor and that I needed all that stuff I took from Benny's."

"You don't need to apologize. I'm sure you have your reasons. And I'm the one who should be saying sorry, anyway."

Confusion swirls in her eyes. "For what?"

"For reacting the way I did in the forest," I explain. "I think you misunderstood me. I want to talk to you about what happened and about other stuff, too. About—"

"Hey, shit face." Logan appears by my side. "Piper's looking for you. She needs to talk to you."

"That's fucking fantastic," I say through gritted teeth, "but I'm talking to Luna right now."

A malicious look flashes across his face before he turns all of his attention toward Luna. "Oh, hey, Luna, I didn't see you there," he says, scrutinizing her clothes. "I don't know how I missed you, though, in that god-awful outfit you're wearing. Tell me, is it like a split personality thing?"

"Is what a split personality thing?" Luna asks with a

guarded expression.

"The whole dressing like a freak one second then dressing like a cock tease the next." When Luna blinks at him in shock, his grin broadens. "I saw you at that party, the one the cops broke up. You were wearing that slutty, black dress that barely covered your ass." He reaches toward her like he's going to grab her ass.

I smack his hand away and slam my hands against him, jostling him back. "Don't fucking touch her."

"Or what?" Logan crosses his arms with a stupid smirk on his face. "You'll yell at me? Hurt me? Get jealous?"

"I'll beat your ass," I warn. "Which we both know I can do."

His smile falters, more than likely remembering the drunken fight we got into at the beginning of the summer when I gave him a black eye and almost broke his nose.

"Dude, why are you being such a dick? Luna knows I'm just messing with her." He turns to Luna. "Right?"

She rolls her eyes. "Sure."

"She's only saying that because she's nice," I say to Logan in an icy tone. "She knows you're being a jerk."

"It's fine," Luna says to me as she backs away. "I have to get to class. I'll see you later, maybe."

Before I can work up a protest, she whirls around and runs for the school, putting her headphones in. Logan laughs at her, muttering something about going to change into her alter ego. I start to chew him out, but Piper saunters up to me with three of her friends.

"You look hot today," she says, hauling me in for a kiss.

I hate when she does this—puts on a show for everyone.

When she steps back, she runs her finger along her lips, fixing her lipstick. "I have to go paint some banners for the pep rally on Friday, but I need to talk to you later. Maybe we can hang out after school."

"I have some stuff to do after school," I tell her, and two of her friends trade a look before narrowing their eyes at me. "Can't you just tell me now?"

"Look, I know you've been stressed ever since your dad died." Piper skates her hands up my chest, loops them around my neck, and stands on her tiptoes to whisper in my ear. "But I think it might be time to move on. I've been trying to ignore how much of a jerk you've been lately, but it's starting to get old, and I'm not sure how much longer I can put up with it. You blow me off all the time. And you refuse to get a new phone, so I can never even text you, which is so goddamn annoying."

"This isn't about being stressed," I growl through clenched teeth. "I really do have shit to do after school."

"Then take me to lunch." She presses her tits against my chest and grazes her teeth along my earlobe. "I just want to talk about the dance. I promise it'll be worth it." She steps back and puts on a phony grin. "I'll meet you at your truck." She blows me a kiss then walks away with her friends.

"Guess you haven't told her you don't have your truck anymore," Logan comments with a grin.

I stare at Piper over by the benches, laughing with her friends about something. *The dance? When did I agree to go to the dance?*

It doesn't matter. I can't do this anymore. I can't pretend these shallow, meaningless conversations are enough. I can't pretend I don't want more. It's time to end things with her. Yeah, shit may hit the fan, but I'll deal with that if I have to, because I can't do this anymore.

I turn my back on Logan and leave.

"Eventually, people are going to get tired of your shit,

Grey," he yells after me. "And then what are you going to do?"

I don't know. I really don't.

I guess I'll find out soon, though.

Confession

TEN

> *I'm avoiding Grey on purpose because I'm a coward.*
>
> *Luna*

I'M FIDGETY, RESTLESS, nervous. At least, that's how I feel whenever I'm at home. All I want to do is go to the nearest store and get rid of the anxiety smothering my chest, but my parents are always watching me.

When I'm at school, I'm not as anxious, even though Logan has made it his mission to torment me. It's like sophomore year all over again. Only, this time Grey isn't joining in with him. He's actually trying to get him to stop, but Logan's having no part of it.

"Nice sweater," he says the moment I step foot into the busy hallway. "Did you used to be fat or something? Is that why all your clothes are too big for you?"

I ignore him, shove in my headphones, and hurry to Wynter's locker to get some clothes from her. But the same thing happens every morning for the next three days. Only, Logan becomes crueler.

"You're a closet slut. That's why you dress like this, isn't it?" he accuses one day when I'm wearing a dress.

Piper busts up laughing from beside her locker, and her group of friends join in. "Logan, don't tell me you're thinking about touching that."

Logan's eyes darken as his gaze drinks me in from head to toe. "I don't know. It might be interesting to see what she's got hiding under there." He reaches for the bottom of my dress.

I slap his hand away. "Don't ever touch me." I sidestep around him and dash down the hallway with the sound of their laughter hitting my back.

I don't get it at all. My dress isn't even short, but it's like he wants me to feel ashamed of myself. Sometimes, I do. Sometimes, I think maybe my mom and dad are right, that I shouldn't be dressing like this. Then I look in the mirror, and for the briefest moment, I recognize myself.

Grey has tried to talk to me a couple of times, but I've been standoffish. I feel bad, but I'm worried he'll ask me more about my confession in the forest. And I'll have no choice except to lie to him or tell him about the messed up inner workings of my mind. I stew in that guilt every time I see him, every time I walk into class and he attempts to catch my eye. I sit down as far away from him as I can, though mostly to avoid Logan.

And during the therapy sessions we attend, my parents make sure to drop me off right on time and pick me up the second the meeting is over, so I only have time for hellos and good-byes. I don't see Grey at lunch throughout the week, either.

On Thursday, my avoiding-the-truth routine takes an unexpected turn when I show up to class before Grey does.

When he runs in right as the bell rings, he drops in the desk beside mine. "Hey," he says, a little out of breath. "How are things going? I haven't talked to you much since the other day."

I dare a glance across the room at Logan and find him watching the two of us like a hawk.

"I've been really busy. Sorry."

"It's okay." He sweeps strands of his brown hair out of his eyes then leans across the aisle to whisper, "How are things at home?"

I anxiously peer around the classroom, noticing how many people are watching us.

"You know what, never mind," he says, reclining back in his chair.

The room grows quiet as the teacher begins class.

I'm jotting down notes when a folded up paper lands on my desk. I pick it up, look at Grey, and he smiles at me.

Confused, I unfold the paper.

I want to make sure everything's okay, but I can tell you're nervous to talk about it aloud, so I thought I'd just write you.

I press the tip of the pen to the paper and write:

Everything's fine. I'm still grounded, and I'm only allowed to leave the house for school and sessions, but that's okay. It's not the first time I've been in trouble like this. Quick change of the topic question, but do you still not have a phone? Or do you just like to do things old school? ;)

When I fold up the note and hand it to him, our fingers brush, and my skin tingles from the contact.

His lips quirk as he reads the letter. Then he picks up the pen, scribbles something down, and hands the paper back to me.

I haven't gotten around to buying one yet. It's a long story.

It sucks that your parents won't let you out of the house. If you ever need someone to bust you out, let me know. I make a good getaway driver.

A smile tickles at my lips as I respond:

I bet you do. I promise I'll be okay. Besides, if my mom caught me sneaking out with a guy, she'd lock me in my room and throw away the key.

I hand him back the note, and this time, he frowns as he jots down something before giving it back.

I hate that it's like that for you. I mean, I get that parents sometimes need to punish their kids, but there's a fine line between punishing and being a warden.

I take a deep breath and write:

I know. All I can do is count down the days until school ends. Then I can go off to college and finally be my own person. That is, if they let me go to college. If they have their way, I'll stick around until some guy they approve of requests my hand in marriage.

I hand him back the note. He reads what I wrote then quickly pens something down. As he reaches over to hand it to me, our fingers brush again, and he smiles at me. I have a feeling he did it deliberately, and the idea makes my heart skip a beat.

I unfold the piece of paper.

First of all, what century do your parents think we live in? And second, don't let them decide that for you. Promise me you'll do what you want to do, that you'll go to college, and that you definitely won't marry a guy they pick out for you. You deserve so much better.

I press the tip of the pen to the paper, surprised how easily I write, *Okay, I promise.*

I pass the note to him, and a smile graces his lips as he reads it.

"Grey Sawyer, would you like to share with the class whatever you and Luna seem to find so fascinating?" Mr. Gartying suddenly asks with his eyes locked on us.

"Nah," Grey replies coolly while my back goes as rigid as a board.

"That wasn't really a question." The teacher signals for him to stand up. "Bring me the note."

My heart sprints at the idea of the teacher reading the

note aloud to the class. It's been sprinting a lot lately. Maybe it's time to do something about it. Give in. Cut class and go downtown. Alleviate the stress that has been bearing down on me.

Grey looks from me to Mr. Gartying then stands up. "Sure." When he reaches the front of the classroom, he tears the note into pieces. "There you go." He hands the pieces to Mr. Gartying.

"That just earned yourself detention." Mr. Gartying discards the torn up paper into the trashcan. "Now, take a seat, and no more passing notes." He muses over something. "Huh. I never thought I'd have to say that again."

Grey calmly walks back to the desk and drops down in his seat. I want to thank him, but I'll wait until the bell rings to avoid getting us in more trouble.

"Thanks for doing that," I tell him after the bell rings. I pile my books into my arms, slide out of the chair, and cast a glance out the window, contemplating if I still want to ditch. I do feel a bit better now after what Grey did for me. "I'm sorry you got detention."

He tucks his book under his arm. "It was worth getting detention. Just as long as you do something for me."

I head for the doorway. "And what's that?"

"Stop shutting me out." He gives me that adorable half-smile I've seen him use when he's flirting. "I miss talking to you."

I nod, baffled over the smile. Is he flirting with *me*?

"I have to get to the gym," he says, glancing at the clock above the teacher's desk. "But maybe we can get lunch together tomorrow?"

Is he being serious? He wants to have lunch with me?

"Um . . . sure."

"Good." He winks before spinning on his heels and stepping out into the crowded hallway.

I linger in the classroom for a second longer, processing what just happened, before I dazedly step out of the classroom and get swept up in the crowded hallway.

Confession

ELEVEN

> I don't feel that upset about breaking up with Piper. In fact, I'm kind of relieved.
> Grey

I'M GLAD LUNA'S talking to me again and even agreed to go to lunch with me tomorrow. I would've asked her to go with me today, but there's something else I have to do, something important.

"What happened to your truck?" Piper asks with her nose crinkled at my car.

I open the door to climb in. "I sold it a while ago."

She fires her infamous bratty scowl at me from over the chipped roof of the car. "I'm not riding in this piece of crap."

I retrieve my keys from the pocket of my jeans. "Then I guess we're not going to lunch."

Invisible daggers shoot from her eyes as she jerks open the door and drops into the passenger seat with a huff.

I exhale in relief. While I'm not thrilled about going to lunch with her, I need her to come with me so I can break up with her and move on with my life. Over the last couple of days of listening to her ramble about the dance and her encouraging Logan to torment Luna, I know it's time to let go of *everything* and get a completely new start. No more hiding behind my old life. No more being afraid of being alone. No more worrying if Piper will ruin my reputation. My reputation wasn't that great, anyway.

At least, that's what I keep telling myself as I drive to the drive-thru and listen to her chatter on and on about all the people who annoy her. After we get her order, I park the car in front of the restaurant and turn off the engine.

"I was thinking that you could match your cummerbund and tie to my dress. It's pale pink," Piper says as she peels off the lid of the bowl of salad she ordered.

I unwrap the peanut butter sandwich I brought with me. "I'm never going to wear anything that's pale pink."

"You will if you want to go to the dance with me." She grins haughtily as she grabs a plastic fork out of the paper bag. She nibbles on the lettuce while frowning at my lunch. "Why did you bring a sandwich if you knew we were going to get lunch?"

"Because." I take a bite of the sandwich and chew it slowly to avoid saying anything more.

It's crazy. I've dated Piper for almost a year, and I'm not even comfortable enough to explain my situation to her. While I haven't told Luna everything, I plan on doing so when I get some alone time with her. I've already told her so much, more than I've ever told anyone.

Piper adds more dressing to her salad and stirs the lettuce around with a fork. "That's the most pathetic sandwich I've ever seen." She sets the fork down in the salad bowl, flips down the visor, and grimaces. "There's not even a mirror in this pile of crap. What the hell, Grey? How am I supposed to fix my makeup?"

As I sit there, listening to her, I try to figure out what the hell I saw in her a year ago, why I thought I needed to start dating her. I remember thinking she has a hot body, something she always shows off in tight, short dresses. She likes to go to parties and is friends with a lot of my friends. I knew she could be a bitch, but I didn't really care about that. She puts out, and that was all that mattered. Back then, that was enough, but not anymore.

I set the sandwich down on my lap. "Piper, we need to talk."

She must sense something in my tone because she flips up the visor and folds her arms across her chest. "Don't you dare try to break up with me right before the dance."

"That dance isn't for another three weeks."

"Three weeks isn't that far away."

"I'm sure you'll be able to find someone else to take you." I flick the keychain with my fingers as I think of the right thing to say that will cause the least amount of drama.

"Is this about Luna Harvey?"

I tense at her mention of Luna. The last thing I need is for Piper to go after her.

"Why would you think this is about Luna?"

"You think I'm blind? I've seen you look at her when you think no one is paying attention." She flips her hair off her shoulder. "It's pathetic. Picking her over me. Most guys would kill to be with me."

"Then I guess you won't have a problem finding someone else to take you to the dance," I say flatly.

"You're going to regret this," she huffs, reaching for the door handle. "By the time I get finished with you, no one will want to touch you."

"Calm down," I say as she kicks open the door. "I'm sorry you're upset, but I can't keep doing this. We were never . . . really right for each other."

"Oh, I'm not upset." She plants her heels on the ground, tugs on the bottom of her dress as she stands up, and then reaches back in to snatch up her purse from the seat. "I'm pissed off. No one breaks up with me. You knew that when you started dating me. I warned you that if you so much as tried to break my heart, I'd end you."

I shake my head. "I didn't break your heart. We weren't in love, Piper. You know that."

"Obviously, but that's not the point." She digs her phone out of her purse. "The point is you broke up with me after all that whining and sulking I put up with over the summer, and I'm not going to let you get away with this. By the time I get through with you, you're going to have no one left." She slams the door so hard the entire car groans in protest. Then she storms off toward the entrance of the restaurant, putting her phone up to her ear.

I grip the living daylights out of the steering wheel and take a few measured breaths. That was even worse than I thought it was going to be. Still, threats and all, I'm relieved it's over. Maybe now I can move on from that chapter of my life.

Except, in the back of my mind, I worry about what's going to happen if she does make good on her threats, mostly because I'm worried she's going to try to do something to Luna. I can handle Piper's temper tantrums, but the last thing I want is for Luna to have to.

I'll just have to make sure that doesn't happen.

By the time I make it back to school, Piper has told almost everyone she broke up with me at lunch. Thankfully, that's the only rumor that seems to be spreading around the hallway. Still, I can't help noticing that some of my so-called friends are acting differently, like Logan. He takes a moment to corner me in the hallway and express his "concern."

"I just hope you don't go all loner crazy like Jay," he says, looking way too happy over the idea.

Jay was the last guy who dated Piper. After spreading

around a rumor that he was in a cult and spent a lot of time hurting animals, most of his friends cut ties with him. I'm ashamed to admit I was one of them.

Maybe I deserve what's coming. Maybe I deserve worse.

"Why are you being such an asshole?" I ask as I open my locker. "We used to be friends."

"Yeah, we were never really friends." He leans his shoulder against the locker with his eyes on the people traveling through the hallway. "We've hung out and stuff, but we've never really liked each other. Most of the time, I hate you. You think you're the shit, but you're not." A slow smile spreads across his face as he looks at me. "Haven't you ever heard 'keep your friends close and your enemies closer'? Good luck with what's heading your way." It's a threat. Clearly, he has every intention of helping Piper destroy me.

I spend the next couple of classes trying not to notice how differently people are treating me. But they're avoiding me like I have the plague. It takes me until the last class of the day to figure out why.

"Piper said Grey Sawyer has herpes," a girl whispers to her friend as I enter Biology.

Herpes? Really, Piper? That's the best you can do?

"Yeah, which must mean she has it, too," I say to the girls.

Her eyes widen as she seizes her friend's arm and scurries to the opposite side of the room from me.

Shaking my head, I take a seat at my usual table and wait for class to start. No one sits by me, and no one seems too enthusiastic to be my partner when the teacher hands out a group project assignment.

I feel uncomfortable sitting there all alone. *You did this to yourself. If you'd been nicer, then maybe people would have your back.*

"So, you have herpes, huh?" Beck drops his books down

on the table and pulls out a chair to sit down.

"That's what I've been told." I try not to appear too relieved when he sits down, but I am. Like, a ton.

"You know, I've seen Piper come up with a lot crazy rumors, but this one might be the most disgusting one she's ever spread." Beck flips open his book as Ari joins us, sitting down in the chair across the table from me. "She must be really pissed off at you. But everything pisses her off when she doesn't get her way."

"That, it does," I agree as I crack my textbook open.

I wait for him to start asking questions about what happened between Piper and me, but instead, he nods his head at Ari.

"I'm not sure if you two have officially met, but this Ari, my partner in crime and the guy who will get us an A on the assignment."

Ari rolls his eyes as he reads through the assignment packet. "I'm not going to do all the work for you."

"That's what you say now, but we both know that's not how things are gonna go down," Beck tells him cheerfully then looks at me. "He says this every time, but then he gets frustrated and takes over when he realizes how much I suck at homework."

"It all turns out okay, though," Ari says, opening his binder. "Beck makes up for it by giving the presentation to the class, which I suck at."

"So, what does that leave me with?" I ask, twirling my pen with my fingers. "Because I'm not that great at science, and normally, I rock with giving the presentation, but I'm not sure how the class is going to react when they all think I have herpes."

Ari sighs as he removes his glasses to clean the lenses with the bottom of his shirt. "People really are stupid, aren't they? Who believes anything Piper Talperson says? That girl should've lost all her credit when she tried to convince people back in seventh grade that broccoli was a fruit and that it grew on trees. She even tried to argue about it during debate class and told a story about the broccoli tree she once saw growing in her backyard."

Beck reclines back in his seat with his hands tucked behind his head. "How did I not know about this?"

Ari slips his glasses back on, shrugging. "It's not like we ever talk about her."

"True," Beck says with a bob of his head.

God, if Piper heard what they were saying, she'd lose her mind. I find myself smiling at that.

I spend the rest of class working on the assignment with Ari and Beck and listening to them tell stories about some of the stuff they've done. They bring me into the conversation whenever they can. They're really easy to talk to, like Luna, more accepting than I'm used to. Watching them joke around with each other forces me to realize how crappy my friends have been over the years and how much time I've wasted by hanging out with people I never felt comfortable with.

When the bell rings, I collect my stuff and head out of the classroom. People continue to give me nasty looks as I make my way to the parking lot with Ari and Beck, but I do my best to ignore them.

"So . . . Have you gotten your grades up yet?" Beck asks casually as we cross the grass.

Ari is detached from the conversation, engulfed in some kind of text conversation on his phone, but he does glance at me when Beck asks the question.

I pat my pockets for my car keys. "A little bit."

"You think you're going to be able to play in the game tomorrow?" he asks, spinning a keychain around his finger.

"Maybe. It all depends on if I can pass the exam in

English." I don't think I will, though.

"Did you get another tutor?" he asks, seeming marginally interested in my answer.

"I have it handled," I say with a shrug. It's a lie. I don't have it handled at all, but I don't know anyone else besides Luna who is smart enough to tutor me.

He nods. "Cool. Maybe we have a shot at winning."

"Yeah, maybe." I feel like a jerk for lying, but what else am I supposed to say?

We part ways and get into our cars.

The drive home gives me time to clear my head. Maybe this thing with Piper won't be as bad as I thought. Perhaps it'll help me get rid of everyone who simply used me, like Logan. I want a fresh start, right? Well, that also means making new friends.

I'm feeling pretty okay by the time I pull up into my driveway. As I climb out of the car, though, the oxygen suddenly gets ripped from my chest as I notice the sold sticker slapped over the for sale sign in the front yard.

I drift into the house in a daze, trying to convince myself that it's a good thing. It means my mom won't have to worry about a mortgage she can't afford. My family needs this. But it hurts to know the house I grew up in won't be my house anymore. I want to cry. Instead, I put on a smile so my mom won't know how upset I really am. No one will.

Confession

TWELVE

> I haven't stolen anything since Benny's, and I feel like I'm losing my mind because of it.
> Luna

THURSDAY EVENING, I eat dinner with my parents, listening to them gossip about all the people in the town who don't live up to their standards. I tune them out for the most part, allowing my thoughts to drift to Grey.

I'm still not positive what I'm going to tell him if he brings up the stealing incident tomorrow. I can't lie to myself, though. All confessions aside, the idea of going to lunch with him has me excited. I just hope Piper doesn't flip out about it. That's the last thing I want.

"Luna, you're going to be working this Saturday and Sunday after church," my mom announces as she scoops a spoonful of lasagna onto her plate.

I blink from my thoughts and focus on what she's saying.

"Your father and I will be out of town for the weekend for the church camp program, but my mother will be coming to stay with you," she explains. "We've made her a list of rules that she'll make sure you follow. And don't think you can get away with stuff just because she's old. Remember, she took care of Aunt Ashlynn."

I stab my fork into the food on my plate. Eighteen years old and she still gets me a babysitter.

"Who am I working for?"

"For Benny at his store." She sets the spoon into the pan. "And you won't be getting paid for it."

"This isn't a job," my father says as he digs into the pasta. "This is part of your punishment."

I set the fork down, no longer hungry. "Did you . . . ? Did you tell Benny that I stole from him?"

My mom lets out a sharp laugh. "Like I'd ever tell such an embarrassing thing to anyone." She picks up her fork, shaking her head. "We told him we thought it would be good for you to help our community, that you were becoming too spoiled and need to experience what it's like to work. And it'll help improve our family's appearance. You've been causing a lot of our church friends to gossip about us lately."

"Okay," I say quietly.

"You're lucky Benny is giving you this opportunity," she continues. "He turned down the offer a few times, but we were persistent, so be grateful for this chance and don't argue."

I actually like the idea of helping out Benny. Perhaps it can alleviate some of my guilt. There's just one problem. Or a fear, anyway. What if I can't control myself? What if I'm in the store, and all I can think about is taking stuff off the shelves when Benny isn't looking? I haven't stolen since that day, but every time I get stressed, it's all I think about.

"Maybe I should help someone else," I subtly suggest. "Someplace that's not a store."

"You'll help the person you stole from," my mom snaps. "And you'll do a good job."

I nod without further argument. *I can do this*, I tell

myself. *I'll be out of the house, far away from them and way less stressed, which will help with the impulse.*

After I've scraped my plate clean to avoid any "waste not, want not" speeches, I clean up and head for my room.

"Luna, come here for a second," my mom calls me back to the kitchen table.

I free a quiet breath as I back up. "Yes?"

She meticulously examines me. "I've been thinking about something."

A chill rolls over me. Great. This can't be good.

She reaches up and fusses with my hair. "I think it's time for a haircut, something way shorter. Maybe something like Mary Persting's daughter."

I jerk back. No way am I cutting my hair as short as Mary Persting's daughter. Hers is shorter than Beck and Ari's hair, for crying out loud.

"I like my hair this way."

Her expression hardens at the sound of my clipped tone. "Watch how you talk to me, young lady."

I try again, forcing myself to be calmer. "I'm sorry, but I don't want to cut my hair. If I do, then I won't be able to pull it up and keep it out of my eyes."

"If we cut it short enough, it won't hang in your eyes."

My fingers curl inward, and my nails stab into my palms. "Please don't make me do this."

"Stop arguing with your mother," my dad warns from the kitchen sink. "If she says to cut your hair, then you will cut your hair. If she says jump, you will ask how high. If she tells you to clean the house, you will thank her for giving you a roof over your head."

I bite down on my tongue until I taste blood.

"I'll schedule an appointment with Donna for the end of next week. You will go, or you won't be allowed back in the house." The threat in her eyes makes me shudder. "And be grateful I'm taking you to a salon. I could do what we did last time and cut it myself."

I swallow hard as the painful memory strangles me. I was twelve and had worked so hard to grow my hair all the way down my back. Then, one day, my mom decided she hated the long hair after someone commented on how trashy I looked.

"Nice girls don't keep their hair that long," she said. "Right now, you don't look like a nice girl."

I didn't want my hair short, and I tried to run. She had my father pin me down in a chair while she hacked off my hair. Her movements were so rough she even nicked my brow, and I still have a faint scar from it.

"I'm tired of the arguing, of you breaking the rules," my mom continues. "This is the final straw. If you don't stop disobeying, your father and I will have no choice but to take more drastic measures." My mom shoves the chair back from the table and snatches up the empty pan as she rises to her feet. "Now go and work on your homework."

Fighting back the tears, I run out of the kitchen and upstairs to my bedroom, locking the door behind me. I pace the floor several times, telling myself I'll live, that it's just hair. There's no need to get overdramatic. But as I catch a glimpse of myself in the mirror, I can't keep the tears from overflowing.

I'm wearing a long-sleeved, yellow and pink shirt, and I don't even like yellow or pink. I have no makeup on, and while I'm not a huge fan of it, I do like lip-gloss and eyeliner sometimes. My hair is the only thing I've ever had control over. I've always kept it long so I can braid it, put it up, leave it straight—do whatever I want with it. What happens when it's gone? Will I even know who I am when I look into the mirror?

I glance out the window, debating whether to climb out

and run to the store. Take back control. Alleviate the pressure in my chest. Be the bad person my parents always tell me I am.

You're such a terrible daughter, a disappointment. I don't know what's wrong with you.

I curl my fingers inward and fight down the compulsion as I grab my phone to text Wynter.

Me: SOS

She responds within two seconds.

Wynter: On my way.

THIRTY MINUTES LATER, Wynter is crawling through my bedroom window and into my room.

"Man, I haven't climbed up that tree since freshman year," she says as she plucks a leaf out of her hair. She inspects the mud caked on the bottom of her four-inch, platform shoes. "I forgot what a pain in the ass it is."

"I'm sorry for making you do it." I sink down on the edge of my bed. "But I knew they wouldn't let you come up. They're too pissed off at me."

Her eyes skim my bare walls, my organized computer desk, and my perfectly made bed. "It's okay. I'm cool with climbing up a tree for you." She takes a seat beside me. "I have to prove my love for you somehow, right?"

I crack a small smile. "I guess so."

She wiggles around then leans against the headboard and stretches out her legs, getting comfortable. "All right, spill the beans. What happened this time? Or is it still that thing about the clothes?"

I comb my fingers through my hair. "She wants me to cut off all my hair."

"What the fuck?" she says a little too loudly.

I cover her mouth with my hand. "Shh . . . Or they'll hear you."

"Sorry." Her lips move against my palm.

I pull my hand away. "It's okay. I'm the one who should be saying sorry. I mean, who makes their friend climb up a tree?"

"The most awesome friend ever." She puts a hand over mine. "Look, I know how tough it's been for you. I've known you for, like, forever, and I've seen the shit your parents put you through. And your dad is really, really scary, especially that time when you accidentally microwaved a fork."

"We didn't do that on accident, remember? Beck told us that, if we did, it would melt into silver."

"God, we were really naive back then" She gets a faraway look in her eyes. "Sometimes, I miss it, though." She looks almost pained, and I wonder if she's thinking about something other than the memory of trying to melt the fork.

"We're still kind of naive sometimes," I say. "Think about some of the dumb stuff we've done, like sneaking out to parties."

"That's not naive." She smiles again, shaking off whatever's troubling her. "It's called having fun, which most people do . . . But, anyway, you're missing my point. My point is, for the last ten years, I've watched your parents try to control you, and while I love you and how nice you are to everyone, I think you sometimes let people walk all over you. You always try so hard not to upset anyone, even people like Logan who freakin' deserve to be told to fuck off."

I frown. "I don't like making people upset."

"I think that's because your parents branded that into your head. They are trying to get you to act that way toward them, but it ended up becoming a big part of who you are." She squeezes my hand. "I'm not saying it's bad to be nice, but you're eighteen, and it's time to start living your life for *you*. You can say what you feel sometimes, and it'll be okay, even if someone's feelings do get hurt."

"They'd kick me out," I whisper. "If I pushed them too much, they wouldn't let me live here anymore. They've been saying that a lot . . . more than they normally do. I can feel it coming."

"You don't know that for sure." She pulls a pillow onto her lap and picks at a loose thread. "My mom and dad never go through with half the threats they make."

"Mine do. You know my mom has a sister, right?" I ask, and she nods. "Well, did you know that my grandma kicked her out of the house when she was seventeen because she was dating a guy they didn't like? They didn't even give her a chance to break up with him. They just told her to get out and didn't let her take any of her things with her."

"If my parents were that way, I'd be screwed." She pulls her legs to her chest and rests her chin on her knees. "What happened to her?"

"I have no idea. No one's seen her since she left. At least, that's what my mom says."

"Was your mom upset when it happened? I know what she's like now, but back then, she had to be different, right?"

"My mom already had me by the time this all happened. There was a huge age gap between her and her sister, but that's not really my point. My point is that my mom has always been as strict as my grandma, and I know she'll kick me out. I think she's already considering doing it, and the messed up part is I kind of wish she would. But I don't know what I'd do. I don't have any money, and none of my family would take me in. I don't have anyone." I don't realize I'm crying until she scoots forward and wraps her arms around me.

"That's not true at all. You have me. You have Ari, Willow, and even Beck. We'll all be there for you, no matter what."

I sniffle. "Even if I'm homeless?"

"You'll never be homeless. You can always come live with me. I've been thinking about getting my own place, anyway. Hell, maybe I'll move into the pool house this weekend. I doubt anyone would notice."

"Your parents notice you. They just get distracted sometimes."

"Yeah, tell that to my empty house. Neither of them have been home in, like, two weeks, and I don't even know where they are."

I pull back. "Really?"

She nods then heaves a sigh. "It doesn't matter. I'm almost eighteen; it's not like I need an adult around."

"Yeah, but they shouldn't just take off and leave you alone for that long," I say. "And, if they do, they should at least tell you where they're going."

"I'm used to it by now." She gives a what-are-you-going-to-do shrug then sits up straight and lowers her feet to the floor. "But enough about our lame-ass parents. Let's talk about something fun."

I scoot to the edge of the bed. "Like what?"

She waggles her brows at me. "Like why Grey Sawyer keeps giving you sexy-boy eyes."

"He's not giving me sexy-boy eyes. He looks at me like he does everyone else."

She rolls her eyes. "See? There you go, being naive."

"I'm not being naive," I argue. "I'm just being realistic."

"How is that being realistic?"

"Because Grey Sawyer would never, ever give me sexy-boy eyes. He just wants my help with something."

"Help with what?" she asks, watching my reaction closely.

I give a half-shrug. "Getting his grades up and stuff." Not a total lie.

"I thought you already helped him with that?"

I pick at my fingernails as guilt swells in my chest. "I kind of blew him off."

"Wow, I didn't know you could be so mean." She prods me in the side with her finger. "I'm kidding. He probably deserves it for treating you like shit."

"He's not a bad person," I tell her. "And just because he was mean to me once, it doesn't mean I need to stand him up when he needs help."

"Do you still like him?"

"What? No way." I pretend to be appalled.

She grins like the Cheshire Cat. "You so do. Oh, my God, how did I not see this?"

"Because there's nothing to see," I say indignantly. "I don't have a crush on Grey Sawyer."

"Okay." Sarcasm drips her in voice. "If you did, I'd be okay with it."

"I thought you hated him?"

"I do, but if he's nice to you and you like him, then as your best friend, I kind of have to like him, too. Besides, I sorta feel bad for him after what Piper did."

"Yeah, I heard that rumor. I doubt it's true."

She *pfts*. "Of course it's not true. Piper's just a bitch."

I trace circles on the bedspread. "Do you really think she broke up with him? Or do you think she's making that up, too?"

"Who knows? But I wouldn't put it past her." She scrapes at the purple polish on her nails. "You could always just ask him if it matters to you."

"I don't think it matters." At least, I don't want it to, but it kind of does.

"I can see why it would. I mean, you like him, and if he broke up with her, then that makes him more of a good guy."

"Why would that make him a good guy?"

"Because Piper's an evil bitch, and staying with an evil bitch and pretending their bitchiness is okay makes you a bitch, too. So, for his sake of ever getting a chance to date you, I hope he's the one who dumped the Wicked Bitch of Ridgefield High."

"Grey doesn't want to date me," I stress. She continues to give me that know-it-all look, and I sigh exhaustedly. "Can we drop this and figure out what we're going to do with my hair?"

"Hm . . ." She thrums her finger against her lips then gathers my hair into a loose bun on the back of my head. "You wouldn't look that bad with short hair."

I take another look at my reflection in the mirror again and shudder. "I'd look awful. And my hair is the only thing I have left that's mine."

"Yeah, you're right." She releases my hair then sits back with a look of determination on her face. "We'll figure something out, but only if you promise me one thing."

"Okay . . . ?" My tone conveys my reluctance. Sometimes, making promises to Wynter means making promises to get into trouble.

"That tomorrow night after the game, you'll sneak out and come to Beck's party," she says with a glimmer of hope in her eyes.

My mood nosedives even more. "I can't. I'm already on thin ice with my parents."

"You have to. Ari even fixed that tracking app thing

and got you a new phone, so that won't be a problem." She clasps her hands in front of her. "Please, Luna. Beck's older brother is going to be there, and I need you to be my wing-woman."

"You know Beck's going to flip out if he sees you flirting with his brother. And then you two will end up fighting."

"I can handle Beck and his temper tantrums. You know I've had a crush on Theo for years. He's not like my other crushes. This one's stuck."

"You've had a lot of crushes. Why don't you just focus on other ones who aren't one of our best friends' brothers?" I suggest with naive hopefulness. Deep down, I know she won't do it. When Wynter sets her eyes on a guy, she never backs down until she gets him.

"I made a promise to myself a long time ago that, the moment Theo came home from college, I'd do my thing." She shimmies her hips. "And I fully intend on going through with that promise tomorrow night."

I sigh. "Fine. Get your thing on, but when you and Beck get in a fight, don't say I didn't warn you."

"So, that means you'll come to the party?" She taps her feet against the floor, bursting with eagerness. "Pretty please, say yes."

I should tell her no. Not take the risk. But then I look at my hair, my beautiful hair that might be gone next week.

"They have this overnight, camp church thing they're doing this weekend, so my grandma is babysitting me." I roll my eyes at the absurdity of being babysat. "She's a pretty heavy sleeper, so I might be able to sneak out if she falls asleep early."

She squeals way too loudly, and my eyes widen as I hear the sound of footsteps heading down the hallway.

"Crap. Someone's coming." I leap for my bed and push open the window.

"See you tomorrow." She kisses me on the cheek then hops out onto the tree branch. "And we'll fix this problem with your hair. I promise."

Someone bangs on the door right as I slide the window shut.

"Luna, open the door this instant," my dad demands with another hard knock.

I rush across the room, take a few calculated breaths to calm down, and then unlock the door and open it. "What's wrong?"

His gaze darts over my shoulder. "Is someone in here with you?"

I shake my head and step back as he pushes into my room. He checks in the closet, looks out the window, and then bends down to look under the bed. As he stands up, he catches sight of something sticking out from under my mattress and grabs it.

"Why do you have a photo of Aunt Ashlynn under your mattress?" he yells, causing me to cower back.

"Um . . . I don't know." What am I supposed to say? I have it because she's my idol. Yeah, that would go over well.

His face reddens as he strides toward me and grabs my wrist. "Do you have any idea how much this would hurt your mother!"

I back up against the wall. "I'm s-sorry."

"Oh, you're sorry." He leans into my face, his fingers digging into my skin. "News flash, Luna, sorry doesn't mean anything. Apologies are worthless. What you do, the choices you make, can't be erased."

An exhale trembles from my lips. "I know, but people can forgive people . . . And sometimes people can change."

"You'll never change. You're just like her. I can see it in your eyes." He lets go of me and rips the photo into pieces. "I'm not going to tell your mother about this, but only because I want to spare her the pain and embarrassment."

I rub my wrist where he grabbed me. "Okay. Thank you." What I don't get, though, is why having the photo would cause my mother pain. Or why he's so upset.

"I'm not doing this for you. I'm doing it for your mother because I care about her, which you clearly don't. You're so selfish. Your mother can't always see it, but I can. I've told her time and time again that we just need to accept that you'll never change and to let you go, but she won't." He storms out of the room. "Get to bed." He slams the door behind him.

My legs quiver as I climb under the covers. I try to go to sleep, but I'm too wired after what just happened. I toss and turn, trying to relax, but I can feel the fear under my skin. I've been getting on my parents' nerves more with each passing day, and soon, they're going to do to me what my grandma did to Aunt Ashlynn.

Part of me is terrified, while a small part of me feels . . . relieved.

Confession
THIRTEEN

> I'm afraid of being alone with guys.
>
> Luna

FLAMES IGNITE, BURNING everything in their path.

"Hang on. I've got you, Luna."

Arms pull me against them as heat blisters my skin.

Who are you?

I know you.

I can feel it.

"Hang on, okay?" they say as we reach the caving stairway. "And no matter what, no matter how bad things get, I want you to hang on. Promise me you'll hang on, Luna."

"I promise," I gasp, struggling to get air.

I'm afraid, so afraid. I can't breathe, and my hands and knees hurt. Everything hurts, but I know I have to be strong.

"I'm going to get you out of here," they promise before running straight through the fire, out the front door, and into the fresh air where I can breathe again.

FRIDAY MORNING, I mess up. Instead of heading straight to school, I drive to the gas station, pretending the car needs gas. But I'm not really here for fuel. I'm here to try to deal with what happened last night with my dad.

My wrist aches as I wander up and down the aisle, eyeing the snacks while occasionally glancing at the cashier, who seems more interested with texting on their phone than with what I'm doing.

Since she isn't paying attention, this should be easy, yet I'm hesitating. I keep thinking of the last time I stole and how Grey caught me. How ashamed I felt when I saw him watching me. How nervous I was when I followed Benny up to the front of the store to empty out my pockets.

I almost leave the gas station with empty pockets, but then I receive a text from my mom, reminding me that my grandma will take me to my session today and that I'm to obey her no matter what. Something snaps inside me, and I reach for the nearest candy bar and start to tuck it into my jacket pocket.

"Don't even think about it," the cashier says.

My attention whips to the front of the store. She has her phone in her hand, but her eyes are locked on me.

"I'm tired of you little teenage brats ripping me off." She glares at me. "So unless you plan on paying for that, I suggest you get the hell out of my store before I call the cops."

My cheeks flood with heat as I toss the candy bar back on the shelf and rush down the aisle with my head tucked down. "I'm sorry," I mutter as I pass her.

"Don't come back here again," is all she says.

I quicken my pace and run out the door. Only when I make it to my car do I breathe again.

Oh, my God. That was close. Too close. Just like Benny's.

Things are getting out of hand. I need to stop. I need to break this addiction. I just wish I knew how.

"PLEASE PUT ME out of my misery if I ever look that stupid while I'm dancing," Wynter mutters under her breath as we watch the cheerleading team try to get everyone amped up for tonight's game. "I can't believe we have to miss second period just for this."

We're sitting on the highest row of the bleachers in the school gym, munching on licorice and gummy worms. Willow and Ari are with us, arguing about something they read in the news this morning. Beck is stuck sitting in the front row with his team, looking bored out of his mind.

Now that I'm at school with my friends, I feel a little better than I did this morning. But getting caught trying to steal weighs heavily on my mind. Still, I do my best to focus on my friends and keep my worries hidden.

"Since when do you care about missing class?" I ask Wynter as I prop my boots onto the bench in front of me.

"I'd rather go to class than watch this shit," Wynter complains as she slumps against the wall and folds her arms. "It's such a stupid tradition."

I pick at a hole in the knee of the frayed, black skinny jeans I'm wearing. "Yeah, it is, but we have to be here."

"We could always cut," she suggests with a hopeful look.

"If I'm going to the party tonight, I'm not going to risk cutting class." I offer her a stick of gum, and she snatches it from my hand. "Now chill out. It'll be over in, like, forty-five minutes."

"Fine. I'll be good, but only because you're going to the party with me." She stuffs the stick of gum into her mouth. "What time are you coming to my house tonight?"

I drop the pack of gum into my open backpack then lean back against the wall. "That all depends on when my grandma falls asleep."

"The party starts at eight, and I want you to come over early enough that I can pick out an outfit for you." She pops a bubble. "I have this really, really cute, black, flower dress that would rock with a pair of knee highs and those boots you're wearing."

"I might be later than eight." I slide the strap of my navy blue, silky top higher as it starts to slip off my shoulder.

"Beck hates when we're late to his parties." She avoids my gaze, messing around with a zipper on her skirt.

"Since when do you care so much about Beck?" I question. "Or is this about Theo?"

She gives me an innocent look. "I just really want to be there for Beck. That's all."

I'm not buying it, but I let it drop. "You can go early, but there's no way I'm getting out before eight."

"I'm going to be late, too," Willow says, pulling her hair into a messy bun and fastening it with an elastic band. "I have to work until nine."

"I can't make it until nine, either," Ari tells us as he digs through his bag for a pen. "I have to do this thing with my dad."

"See? It works out," I tell Wynter. "We can all be late together. And Theo can wait."

Willow starts to laugh, but her amusement fades as her gaze swings to the side of me. "Oh, hi, Grey."

I glance up just as Grey sits down beside me. Air gets trapped inside my lungs when he barely leaves any room between us, sitting so close our shoulders touch.

Why is he sitting so close to me? And why do I like it so much?

Grey's gaze drags up and down my body, lingering on my lips for a split second before he focuses on Willow. "What's up?" he says then gives Ari one of those chin-nod things guys do.

Ari waves back, tucking a pen behind his ear. "Hey, how's that stuff coming along with the Biology project?"

"Good. I printed up some info," Grey replies, putting his feet up on the bench in front of him. "I'm not sure if I totally understand everything I read, though."

"That's okay. We can go over it in class." Ari pulls out a grey, knit cap from his bag and tugs it on his head. "You don't need to stress too much about it. Beck was right when he said I'd get us an A yesterday. I have a habit of taking over, and I can't . . ." Ari's expression floods with panic for an instant. "I have to get good grades no matter what."

"I'll try my best not to mess that up for you," Grey says, resting his arm on his knee.

"I'm not worried about that." Ari's focus drops to his phone as the screen lights up.

I stare at Grey perplexedly. Since when do he and Ari chat like that? The last time I saw them together, they could hardly get out hey.

Grey turns to Wynter, struggling not to smile. "Wynter, I see you found your way to the gym."

"Only because I was forced to," she replies with amusement.

Grey shifts his weight, scooting closer to me. I struggle not to note how amazing he smells, like soap and cologne, but I notice. A lot.

"Why aren't you up with the team?" Willow asks Grey as she slips on a black and red hoodie.

"Yeah, that's an excellent question." Wynter crosses her arms. "Why aren't you up there with the rest of your douchebag friends?"

"I'm still on academic probation," he answers, glancing down at where the team is sitting. "It's okay, though. It's been pretty interesting watching all of this"—he gestures down at the gym floor where our mascot, a blue and gold fox, is doing a cartwheel—"from a different perspective."

"You don't get to play in tonight's game?" Willow frowns when Grey shakes his head. "That's so sad. With how much time you've spent practicing in gym class, you should get to play."

"It's okay." He shrugs it off. "I still might get to if I can pass the English exam."

"The one we took today?" I ask.

He nods, glancing at me from the corner of his eye. "I got a C on the one I took this morning, but Mr. Gartying offered to let me do a retake after school. If I get a B, then I get to play in tonight's game, but I doubt I will. It's not like I can learn an entire course within a few hours." His lips tug into a small, defeated smile that makes the guilt in my stomach knot.

I'm confused. I had Beck check with Grey to make sure he found himself another tutor, and Beck reported back to me that Grey said he had it handled. Clearly, he was lying.

Wynter jabs me in the side with her elbow.

"Ow." I grip my ribs. "What was that for?"

"He needs help studying," she hisses as she nods her head in Grey's direction. "Hint. Hint."

"It's okay." Grey offers me a smile. "I really don't think studying for a few hours will do any good."

"You clearly haven't studied with Luna and Willow, have you?" Wynter tells Grey as she laces up her shoe. "If the two of them help you, you'll get an A. Trust me. They've helped me a ton of times, and I'm a pain in the ass to teach."

Grey looks skeptical. "And you care because . . . ?"

"I don't care, but I know someone who . . ." Wynter's eyes drift to me, and I shake my head.

Please, please, don't say anything about me liking him, my eyes silently beg with her.

"I don't want Beck to be pissy, and he will if we lose the game," she feeds him as an excuse, and I relax.

"Thank you," I mouth to her.

She shrugs and focuses back on Grey. "And from what Beck says, you"—she makes air quotes—" 'kick ass.' And the team really needs your help to win."

"Winning's a team effort," Grey says. "Even if I do play, we still might not win."

"But it'd help if you played, right?" Wynter continues on with the charade.

Grey lifts his shoulders, shrugging. "I guess so."

"Then count me in for tutoring," Willow declares as she slips on her backpack. "I need to practice my teaching skills, anyway. I'm supposed to start tutoring my neighbor's kids next week."

"Are you sure?" Grey asks, but he already appears less stressed than he was a minute ago. "I don't want you to feel like you have to. I'm cool with just sitting out this game."

"I want to help, but we should head to the library, like, right now." Willow hops to her feet. "And meet there at lunch and during any of your free periods." She jumps up onto the bench in front of her, and then her gaze drops to me. "Are you coming, Lu?"

Wynter raises her brows at me. "Yeah, Lu, are you going to help out a *friend* or what?"

I shake my head at her sneaky little emphasis on the word *friend*. But I get up, anyway. It's probably my fault he has to take the test over since I was too scared to face him and tell him the truth.

I smile at Grey. "Yeah, I'm in. I should've helped you to

begin with."

"It's not your fault," he says, leaning in and keeping his voice low. "You've had your own problems to worry about. How is everything with your parents and . . . stuff?"

"It's fine. Things are fine." *Lies. Lies. All lies.* I have the marks on my wrist to prove it.

He nods but appears unconvinced. "I don't want you to feel like you have to help me, but if you want to, I'd really, *really* appreciate it."

"I want to help you," I promise. "I should've helped you before. I thought you had help, though. Beck said you were handling it or something."

"I had my mom try to help me," he explains with a shrug. "But that didn't work out very well."

I shoot him a grin. "Stick with me and Will, and you'll be fine."

His smile reaches his eyes, and butterflies flutter in my stomach at the sight of it. Hopefully, Wynter can't tell I'm secretly giddy. It'll only convince her more that I like Grey.

Willow and I say good-bye to Ari and Wynter, and then the three of us jog down the stairs.

"You really think you can help me get a B?" he asks us as we reach the sidelines at the bottom of the bleachers.

Willow and I grin at each other.

"You're going to ace this," I assure him with a light shoulder nudge. "Trust me."

He doesn't look very confident, which only makes me hope I can back up my promise. If there's one thing I'm good at, though, it's school, so I should be able to help.

As we hurry down the side of the gym, I notice an abundance of heads turn in our direction, just like when Grey and I went behind the school. Beck even gives a what-the-hell look. Piper also notices, pausing mid-cheer to blast me with a death glare.

Grey swings around to the other side of me and blocks me from her view, placing his hand on the small of my back. "People seriously need to get over themselves," he mutters as we push out of the gymnasium doors. "It's like they can't get over stuff. First, it's the car, and now it's this stupid thing with . . ." He trails off, tensing.

But I know what he was going to say. *This thing with Piper.*

"So they finally noticed you got rid of your truck, huh?" I ask as we start up the hallway, heading for the library.

"Logan noticed the moment I pulled up in my new car," he answers then wavers. "Or new old car, anyway."

"I saw you had a new one." My boots squeak against the floor as we slow to a stop in front of the doors that lead to the library.

He finally moves his hand away to open the door and lets Willow and me walk in first. "Yeah, I got it a few days ago. It was my dad's . . . It's old, but at least it runs. And it's all my family can really afford right now." He looks away, seeming embarrassed by the admission.

I'm a little surprised by it. Grey's family was always so well off. He had a nice truck—which, yeah, I guess he sold—nice clothes, and they live on the wealthier side of town.

Suddenly, some of the stuff he has said to me makes more sense, like the fact that he hasn't had a phone for weeks.

"I think old cars are cool," I tell him, not wanting him to feel embarrassed. "They have so much history, and I bet so many amazing things happened in that car. People learned how to drive in it. Someone probably had their first kiss in there. A baby could've even been born in the backseat."

Grey's face twists in disgust. "Okay, I really hope the last one didn't happen."

"It probably didn't, but still, it's cool to think about the history of your car." I drop my books onto an unoccupied table in the back corner by the computer stations. "If it could talk, it could tell you all sorts of stories."

"Most of my stories would be about my dad." A small, sad smile rises on his lips. "My dad owned the car for, like, two decades or something. From what my uncle says, he used to race it."

I find it almost fascinating to watch Grey talk about his dad. While he gets emotional, there's also so much happiness in his eyes. I wonder what it would be like to have happy memories of my parents.

"It sounds like he was pretty cool," I say.

"He is—was." He softly laughs, shaking his head. "There was this one time when I was ten, and he tried to outdrive a cop to avoid getting a ticket, which probably would've worked better if he wasn't driving a minivan. He ended up getting a ticket and told me he'd take me to a baseball game if I didn't tell my mom."

"Did you ever tell her?"

"No way. I would've kept my mouth shut even without the bribe. It's guy code not to rat out your best friend."

"Your dad was your best friend?" The idea seems crazy to me, but with how highly Grey speaks about his dad, I'm not too surprised.

He nods. "He really was."

"I can't imagine being best friends with either of my parents." I absentmindedly fold my fingers around my wrist.

"I don't blame you. Your parents are . . . intense." He rubs his hand across his forehead. "I saw you at the store the other day with your mom."

My mood goes *kerplunk*. "You did?"

He nods, seeming remorseful. "I wanted to come up to you, but I was afraid your mom would rip my head off."

I duck my head and let my hair curtain my face as my

cheeks heat. I'm mortified he probably saw my mom pat me down when I came out of the store. She didn't even let me get into the car. She made me stand in front of the car and spread my legs and arms out like a criminal while she searched my pockets.

"You don't need to be embarrassed." He brushes my hair out of my face and lowers his head, leveling his gaze with mine. "Your parents should be, not you. They're the ones who made the scene, and they should be grateful you're nice enough to put up with their shit instead of freaking out on them."

"Maybe, but it's still hard to be the one standing there while they're doing the embarrassing stuff."

"I know. I wish it wasn't that way for you. I wish I could make it better."

"I wish I could make it better for myself and finally stand up to them. I wish I could be a better person." I bite my lip at my unexpected confession.

"It doesn't make you a bad person because you haven't stood up to them yet. You're not weak, Luna, at all. Some of the stuff I've seen you put up with . . ." His Adam's apple bobs up and down as he swallows hard. "And you forgive so easily."

"It's not that big of a deal," I say quietly.

He shakes his head. "Yes, it is." Another swallow. "There's so much I want to say to you."

We stare at each other until a group of people walk in, making a lot of noise and crushing the moment into smithereens.

I realize his fingers are still in my hair a split second before he does. He looks at his hand, and then our gazes collide as his fingers tangle through the locks, pulling me closer instead of pushing me away.

Willow coughs as she sets her bag and books down on

the table. The noise startles me, and I jump back, leaving Grey blinking in shock.

I hurry and plant my butt in a seat. "What's up?" I ask Willow.

"Nothing's up with me." Her tone carries an underlying meaning, but she doesn't overload me with questions like Wynter would. She sits down in the chair across from mine and looks up at Grey. "You wouldn't happen to have your test from this morning, would you?"

"I have it in my locker," he says, gripping the back of the chair.

"Would you mind getting it?" she asks. "If I can see which questions you missed, I'll be able to get a better feel for where we should start."

"Sure." Grey flashes me a smile before he saunters off for the doors with a spring in his walk.

I watch him walk away until he vanishes out the doors, and then I turn back to Willow. "What was with the strange look you gave me when I sat down?" I take out a pen from the spine of my notebook.

She thumbs through the pages of a textbook. "I've just never heard you talk that much before to someone outside of our group."

I check the time on the clock above the front desk. "We didn't talk for that long, did we?"

"You two stood there for over five minutes, talking to each other like no one else was around," she says. "I was starting to feel like a third wheel."

"I'm sorry." I fold my arms on top of the table. "I didn't mean to. We just sort of started talking, and I . . . got lost in the conversation, I guess."

She clicks a pen and jots something down in a notebook. "Don't be sorry, but I do want to know what's going on, especially with how Wynter acted. She's never been nice to Grey or anyone in his group before."

I grimace. "She thinks I have a thing for Grey."

"*Thinks?*" Her brows rise. "Or *knows?*"

"I don't know." It takes all my strength not to smile as I picture Grey and how he had his fingers in my hair. "Maybe knows."

She doesn't seem all that enthusiastic. "Has he ever said sorry to you for what he did?"

"No, but he's a lot nicer to me, and he's done . . . stuff that's really helped me out."

"Like what?"

"Just stuff."

"Luna, you do know I can tell when you're lying, right?" she says. "It's okay if you don't want to tell me, but just say so. It makes me question how good of friends we are when you lie."

She's right. I'm not being a very good friend by lying to her. And I've lied a lot to her—to all my friends—especially over the last few days.

"I'm sorry for lying." I pull the lid off my pen with my teeth. "There's just some stuff that's been going on that I'm not ready to tell anyone yet."

"But you told Grey?" It's not an accusation, just a simple statement.

"He kind of found out by accident," I explain to her.

"What was an accident?" Grey asks, sitting down in the chair beside me.

Willow sneaks an I-have-this look in my direction then smiles at Grey. "Luna and I got invited to Pete Ashfon's summer/fall bash," she lies without missing a beat. "But it wasn't on purpose."

"I hate going to that stupid party." Grey slides his test across the table toward Willow. "It takes forever to get to his house, and by the time my friends and I get there, they're wasted and ready to pass out."

"We're not going." Willow sneaks a glance at me. "Luna and I kind of made this pact."

He leans forward with interest. "What kind of pact?"

Willow looks at me, and I sigh but explain, "When we were sixteen, we decided that we'd never go to any parties thrown by"—I choose my next words carefully—"the popular crowd."

"But you go to Beck's parties." He rotates to face me, propping his elbow on the table.

"Beck's not really popular. Yeah, he talks to you guys at school and while you're practicing, but at the end of the day, he's ours." Willow winks at him so he knows she means that lightheartedly.

Grey chuckles, his eyes crinkling at the corners. "So what makes someone popular? Because, this whole time, I thought I knew, but now I'm not so sure."

"You know, I'm still trying to figure that out myself," Willow muses as she looks down at Grey's test. "I'll let you know when I figure it out." She scans over each question he got wrong while muttering under her breath.

He turns to me. "You're seriously never going to go to a party if it's thrown by someone who's popular, even if someone asked—no, begged you to go?"

I shrug. "I made a pact with Willow, and you can't break a pact with your best friend." I stretch out my legs underneath the table. "Besides, the last time I went to a party, the police broke it up, and my parents had to come get me."

"Are you going to Beck's party tonight?" he asks, pushing up the sleeves of his dark blue shirt.

I nod. "I actually am, but only because Wynter begged me to go."

"What about the game?"

I shake my head. "Sorry, but I can't make it to that. I

have to go home straight after school. I really wish I could go, though."

A pucker forms at his brow. He glances over at Willow before he turns inward and leans closer to me. "Your parents are letting you go to a party, but not a soccer game?"

I snort a laugh. "God, no. Even if I wasn't grounded, they wouldn't let me go anywhere."

His face contorts in confusion. "Then how are you going to the party?"

"My parents are out of town and my grandma's babysitting me," I clarify. "She sleeps like a rock, so it should be easy to sneak out."

He doesn't even so much as flinch from the mention that I have a babysitter. "That's good . . . that you're going to it."

"Are you going to be there?" I ask, massaging my wrist as it starts to ache again.

He nods. "And I was thinking we could talk for a while when we're there. I know we were supposed to hang out at lunch, but I think I might have to ask you for a rain check so I can study." His gaze descends to my arm, and then his brows dip. "What happened to your wrist?"

My chest tightens as I glance at the bluish purple dots on my wrist. "It's nothing." I cover the marks with my hand. "I just did something stupid on the trampoline and ended up getting my arm caught in the springs."

"Since when do you have a trampoline?" Willow gives me a suspicious look.

"It was on Wynter's," I lie in an uneven voice as I tuck my arms under the table.

Willow presses me with a look, and I shoot her a pleading look back, begging her to let it go.

Shaking her head, she pulls out a highlighter and drags it across the page.

I know, the moment we're alone, she's going to bring it up, and I have no idea what I'm going to tell her. The truth? God, my dad would freak if I did, but that doesn't mean I want to lie to Willow. She's one of my best friends, and I've already been lying too much lately.

"I want to talk to you because I have some stuff I really need to tell you that I should've told you a long time ago," Grey whispers, tucking a strand of my hair behind my ear. "But now I think maybe there's some stuff you need to tell me, too, like where those bruises came from, because they sure as hell aren't from trampoline springs." He reaches under the table, and his fingers graze my injured wrist. "I don't want you to be afraid. You can trust me."

My heart thrashes in my chest every time his skin comes into contact with mine. "Okay."

He smiles, trying to make me feel more at ease, but I don't know if I'll ever be able to relax.

When my dad saw the marks this morning, he warned me that I was supposed to tell people it was an accident.

"If anyone asks, say you hurt yourself on a trampoline," he said as he glared at me.

"But we don't have a trampoline," I muttered as I stirred my cereal, feeling too sick to my stomach to eat.

"Lie, then. You're good at that, aren't you?" He slammed the cupboard and turned to me. "People don't need to know what a terrible person you turned me into," he warned. "This is your fault. If you'd just behave, then I could control my temper."

I silently got up and walked out the door to go to school, but when I made it inside the car, I screamed until my lungs ached. That was when I made the decision to drive to the gas station.

"Let's get started with this," Willow announces as she highlights a sentence on the page of a textbook.

Grey keeps his hand on my wrist, eliciting shiver after shiver from me.

"I'm all ears, teacher," he tells Willow.

She smiles then jumps right in, explaining to him why he missed certain questions.

I help whenever I can, but I'm distracted by what's going to happen at the party tonight when Grey and I talk. And what if we're alone? I've never been alone with a guy other than Ari and Beck before, and there's so much unsaid between Grey and me.

What happens if I break down and tell him everything, and he discovers the nice Luna he thinks he likes doesn't really exist?

Confession

FOURTEEN

> The kiss was kind of preplanned, even though I pretended it was sporadic.
>
> Grey

I'M NERVOUS AS hell taking the test, but after spending lunch and every free second I could get throughout the day studying with Luna and Willow, the questions make more sense than they did the first time around, which has to be a good sign.

I wait at my desk for Mr. Gartying to finish checking my exam, growing more anxious every time he strikes the marker across the sheet of paper. Finally, he drops the marker, picks up the paper, and scoots his chair back from his desk.

"So, did I pass?" I ask nervously.

"Why don't you take a look for yourself?" He strolls up to my desk and places the test down in front of me.

I pick it up and smile at the red B+ on the top. "Fuck yeah!" I can't wait to tell Luna and Willow. God, that's a new feeling—wanting to tell someone.

It was crazy enough when I told her I couldn't afford a new car. I let it slip out on accident, but she didn't miss a beat and even told me she thought old cars were cool. My developing obsession with her deepened in that moment.

"Watch your language, Grey," Mr. Gartying warns robotically then grins. "Now go and win us the game."

I nod and head out of the classroom, making a quick pit stop by my locker to grab my bag and books before jogging to the parking lot. The game is in a couple of hours, and I still have to attend my very last group therapy session before I suit up.

As I'm hurrying toward my car, I pass by Beck, who's sitting on the trunk of his car, looking bored as hell.

He glances up from his phone at me. "So, did you pass?"

"Yep, got a B plus thanks to Willow and Luna." I swing my bag around in front of me to unzip it and tuck the test inside.

"Good. Maybe we won't get our asses kicked, then." He lowers his feet to the ground and hops off the trunk.

"Hopefully not, but you do know, just because I get to play, it doesn't guarantee us a win, right?"

"Obviously, but it gives us a better chance."

I used to love the pressure people put on me to win. I'd get amped up on it. With all the stressful stuff going on in my life, though, I feel almost too pressured.

"What are you doing out here, anyway? School got out half an hour ago." And Beck's definitely not one to spend any extra time at school.

He glances around the mostly empty parking lot then shrugs. "I had some business to take care of, but I'm starting to wonder if the customer is going to be a no show."

I drape the handle of my backpack over my shoulder and rummage around in my pocket until I find my car keys. "I've actually been meaning to talk to you about the baseball." I shift my weight, hating that I have to talk to him about this. I hated approaching him to begin with, but Beck is known as the go-to guy around our town. Thankfully, he's a good enough guy that he hasn't told anyone and doesn't act all weird about it. "I had to use the money, so you can go ahead and sell the baseball."

"That sucks, man," he says with sincerity.

"Yeah, it does." Uncomfortable, I glance at my watch. "Look, I've got to go. I have to be somewhere in, like, ten minutes."

"That's cool. I need to get going, anyway." He pulls out his key fob and presses the unlock button, causing his car to beep. "I won't be doing any sales for a few weeks, so if you happen to come up with enough money by then, let me know."

"Okay. I will." But I know there's no way I'll ever be able to come up with the money.

He starts to get into the car then pauses and turns back to me, seeming undecided about something. "Grey, I don't want to go all big brother on you, but since Luna doesn't have a big brother, that's always kind of been my role." He spins the keychain around on his finger, considering something. "You don't have the greatest track record with her. I get that people can change, and you seem like you're trying to, but if anything happens to her, if you hurt her at all, I'll fucking kick your ass, okay?"

"I'm not planning on hurting her," I assure him. "Trust me. That's the last thing I want to do."

"Yeah, but sometimes, people don't intend to hurt others, but it just sort of happens." He opens the car door. "She's a really sweet girl, and in my opinion, she forgives way too easily. Just make sure you don't fuck her over. Don't take advantage of how nice she is. Too many people do that to her already . . . And just, treat her right, okay?"

I nod, and he goes from super intense to the relaxed Beckett I've always known.

"See you at the game," he says then gets into his car.

I watch him drive away, feeling unsettled. I've been working on changing and being a better guy, but suddenly, that doesn't seem like enough. I need to do better. I need to make up for what I did to Luna. Somehow.

Blowing out a breath, I head toward my car parked at the back, but I mutter a curse when I spot Piper's car next to mine and her leaning against it. She's alone, a rare occurrence for her, and she seems preoccupied with her phone.

I stare in the opposite direction, hoping to escape without her noticing me. She hasn't said much to me since we broke up, though I did catch her glaring at Luna when we left the gym earlier. Not a good sign. If she wants to rip me apart, that's fine. But I won't let her do anything to Luna.

"What? Are you too good to even say hello to me?" Piper calls out right as I reach the rear end of my car.

So fucking close.

I toss a quick glance at her as I unlock my car. "Nope. Just in a hurry."

"You seem in a hurry a lot lately," she remarks, propping her hip against her car door. "Like this morning when you ran out of the gym with *Luna* and *Willow*." Her heels click against the asphalt as she walks toward me. "You know, I've seen guys lose their minds when I break up with them, but I've never seen them lose their minds this badly."

The lock clicks, and the door creaks as I yank it open. "*You* broke up with *me*? Isn't that what you're telling everyone?"

"What else would I tell them when that's what happened? She feigns innocence. "I mean, I can't keep going out with a guy who has herpes."

"Nope. I guess not." Deciding not to play her game, I duck into the car and start to close the door.

She snatches ahold of it, and my fingers slip from the

handle. "I know you care, even though you're pretending you don't. You're just like me, Grey. You've always cared about what people think. That's what made us such a great couple."

"I *used* to care what people think, which is why we broke up." I slant to the side and extend my hand for the door handle.

"Screw you," she snaps, shuffling back. "You act like you don't care, but you do, and if you don't yet, you will once I'm finished with you." She puts her hands on her hips and grins at me, but it's all for show. Deep down, I have rattled her.

Lifting her chin, she reels around and makes her way back to her car, and I slam the door then drive to the center of town for my very last therapy session. The closer I get, the more my worries of Piper fade as my excitement to tell Luna about the test grows.

It's crazy how I'm so excited just to share something like this with someone. A couple of weeks ago, I wouldn't even have told anyone about my struggles with school. Six months ago, I wouldn't have cared enough to get my grades up.

After I park my car in the parking lot adjacent to the building, I jog to the entrance and step inside. I immediately seek out Luna and spot her sitting in one of the fold-up chairs, frowning at something on her phone. She's still wearing that pair of tight, black jeans and the blue top she had on earlier that shows off the freckles on her shoulders. Now, though, she has a jacket tied around her waist and a braid in her hair.

Since I'm running a bit late, almost everyone else has made it here except for Howard, the therapist, so the session hasn't started yet.

I start to step toward the circle of chairs when Luna's

gaze elevates to mine.

I freeze as our gazes weld, and a revelation slaps me across the face. I'm going to kiss her. Really soon. It's not a big deal. It really shouldn't be, anyway. I've kissed enough girls, ones I've spent way less time with. In fact, I once kissed a girl one minute after meeting her. Logan dared me to do it, and he cheered me on when I pressed my lips to the very shocked but very enthusiastic-to-kiss-me-back girl. This thing with Luna feels like an epic, life changing moment, though.

She rushes over to me. "So?"

"So what?" I play dumb.

She jokingly swats my arm. "You know what. Did you pass?"

I chuckle. "Yeah, I passed."

"You did!" She claps her hands and jumps up and down. "I'm so happy for you."

"I couldn't have done it without you and Willow."

"It was mostly Willow. I didn't do that much."

"Give yourself more credit, Luna. You helped me out a lot." *More than I think you realize.* I fold my arms around her and pull her in for a hug. "I want to say thank you for helping me out. Not just with the test thing, but for listening to me and letting me talk about my dad. I didn't realize how much I needed to talk about him."

"I'm glad I could help." She stiffens in my arms as she places a hand on my back.

I trace my finger back and forth across the bottom of her back until the tension leaves her body, and she fully hugs me back, tucking her head under my chin. God, her hair smells so good, like strawberries and vanilla. I breathe in the scent before slightly tipping my head to the side to look at her.

"You did more than just help me. You listened, and not

many people do that, especially for someone who's treated you so shitty and who still needs to say he's sorry, which he's fully planning on doing, but the right way." Before I can back out, I brush my lips across hers so softly she probably won't be able to tell if the move is accidental or not.

She gasps against my mouth, and my fingers tighten as the desire to kiss her deeper pulsates through me. I graze my lips against hers again, and this time, she moans.

Holy. Fucking. Shit. I almost lose it.

"No kissing inside the building," Howard mutters as he brushes by us.

Luna's cheeks are bright pink as she scrambles away from me with her fingers pressed to her lips. I carry her gaze, even though I'm kind of nervous myself. I can't tell what she's thinking, whether she liked the kiss as much as I did.

"Everyone have a seat," Howard says from the circle.

"We should probably sit down." The corners of her mouth pull into a coy smile as she turns around and sits.

I take a seat next to her and drape my arm along the back of her chair. She glances at her phone, seeming bothered by something on the screen. I want to ask her what's bothering her, but Howard starts the session, so I don't get a chance.

People start talking, but I barely hear anything, too fixated on every time Luna shifts her weight, when her shoulder grazes mine, when she crosses her legs and her knee brushes against my jeans. My body and mind are hyperaware of everything she does to the point where it's driving me insane, but in the best way. I'm not sure I've experienced this kind of a connection with someone before.

Halfway through the session, she starts rubbing her bruised wrist, and I'm reminded we still have so much to talk about. I know she didn't get those bruises from a trampoline. No, those marks look like they came from fingers, and after seeing how Luna's parents treat her, my bet is that one of them did it.

I only hope she'll trust me enough to open up and tell me the truth.

Confession

FIFTEEN

> I'm terrified of my parents.
>
> Luna

"IS EVERYTHING OKAY?" Grey asks the second the session is released.

"Yeah, why?" I stand up from the chair and put on the jacket to cover up my outfit.

"You seemed a little distracted with something on your phone." He runs his fingers through his hair, making the strands go askew. "Like someone sent you a message that was bothering you."

I open my mouth to lie to him—to be the liar I am—but the truth just sort of tumbles out. "It was an email."

"Okay." He chews on his lip, deliberating something.

God, I can't believe I kissed those lips. Holy shit!

"Can I ask what it was about?" he asks. "Or is it too personal?"

"I have this aunt, my aunt Ashlynn," I start, shocked I'm telling him this. Then again, he already knows so much about me. Maybe that's why it feels so easy to tell him stuff. "She's kind of the bad seed of our family. My grandma kicked her out of the house when she was around my age because she was doing a lot of bad stuff."

"What kind of stuff?"

"I'm not really sure. I mean, I've heard a couple of stories about her hanging out with the wrong friends, getting caught drinking, and coming home late, but no one's ever specified what got her kicked out."

"That seems like mild stuff to get kicked out of the house over."

"Yeah, but I'm not surprised." I zip up my jacket. "I'm actually surprised my parents haven't kicked me out yet after everything I've done."

"You really think they'd kick you out?" he asks, baffled.

I shrug, pretending it's not as big a deal as it is. "They've threatened me before."

"Luna . . . I'm so sorry. That sucks that you have to worry about stuff like that."

"It is what it is." I wander toward the door, knowing my grandma is going to have a meltdown if I don't come out soon, and Grey walks with me. "I've always kind of known there's a chance I'd get kicked out of my house before I graduated. My parents made sure of it. Every time they're mad at me, they bring up my aunt Ashlynn's situation, but no one ever brings up what happened to her after she was forced to leave, and I used to make up all these stories in my head of what happened to her. Sometimes, my thoughts would go to a dark, twisted side, and I'd picture her lying in some rundown building, dead. But sometimes, I wonder if she had, like, this really awesome life where she could be herself."

"Is there any way you could find out where she is?" Grey asks as we stop in front of the door.

"I used to think there wasn't. I mean, every time I ask my mom if she's heard from her, she gets really upset and says she hasn't spoken to Ashlynn since she left." I splay my hand against the door to push it open, but then draw back when I spot my grandma's car parked out front. I'm not ready to go out just yet. I need just a few more moments to talk with Grey, a few more moments of peace. "But I got an email today from someone claiming to be her."

"*Really?*" His eyes widen. "How long has it been since you've seen or heard from her?"

"I was four when she got kicked out, so about fourteen years ago."

"What did she say in the email?"

"That she wanted to meet up with me to see how I'm doing. She didn't say how she got my email address or anything . . . I'm not even sure why she'd try to contact me instead of someone else in the family."

"Maybe she knows you're more understanding than your family," he says. "Or maybe she's reaching out to you because she knows you might reply to her."

"But how could she know that?" That's what doesn't make sense. How could she possibly know what kind of person I am? Was it evident back when I was four that I was going to turn into an utter disappointment for my parents? "And how did she get my email address?"

Grey suddenly grows uneasy. "Are you sure it's her? Maybe someone is pretending to be her."

My brows draw together. "Why would anyone do that?"

He scuffs the tip of his sneaker against the carpet. "To hurt you." He sighs heavily. "Luna, I need to tell you something, and I'm not sure how you're going to react."

I move away from the door as someone walks by us. "Okay . . . ? You're making me a little worried."

"I don't want you to worry, but you need to know." He takes a deep breath. "Piper might try to come after you."

"*What?*" That is so not what I was expecting him to say.

"I promise I won't let anything happen," he adds in panic. "I just want to make sure that you're careful whenever you're around her."

"But I didn't do anything to her. I barely even know her," I say in a high-pitched voice.

"You might not have purposefully done something to her, but she mentioned you when I was breaking up with her, and it made me nervous." He blows out a deafening breath. "I know how she is when she gets pissed off at someone . . . like with me and that stupid rumor she's been spreading."

I smash my lips together as anger simmers under my skin. How can she be so hurtful to someone?

"I don't get why she brought me up when you broke up with her. I'm just a girl you talk to sometimes."

"You think you're just a girl I talk to sometimes?" He searches my eyes for something. Then, looking unsure of himself, he reaches forward and laces his fingers through mine. "Luna, you're probably the first girl—no, the first *person* other than my dad that I've ever *really* talked to."

I stare down our intertwined fingers. "And you think that's enough of a reason for Piper to come after me?"

"I've seen her try to ruin people over less." He squeezes my hand, drawing my attention up to him. "But I won't let her do anything to you. She can come after me—I'm okay with dealing with her drama—but she better not even so much as spread a rumor about you."

Something occurs to me then. "Wait. You don't think she's the one who emailed me, do you? Because there's no way Piper could know about my aunt Ashlynn. Not even all my friends know about her."

"I doubt it's her, but you never know." He yanks his fingers through his hair with his free hand, tugging roughly at the roots. "If she overheard you talking about her even one time—if anyone did—then I wouldn't put it past her to look into it and do something messed up like email you and pretend to be your aunt. It is kind of weird that your aunt suddenly contacted you after fourteen years at the same time all this shit is going on with Piper."

"I don't talk to many people about it, though, so I still don't think it could be her." Or maybe that's just false hope.

"But you talk to me about it?" He holds my gaze, and I don't look away, even when my skin warms.

"I know." My uneven tone makes my face flush hotter.

"Just be careful until I can find a way to get Piper to chill the fuck out, okay?" He lightly grazes his finger along the inside of my wrist.

"How are you going to do that?" I question. "She doesn't seem like the kind of person who just chills out over stuff."

"There are ways to break her down. She may pretend she's perfect, but she's not." His jaw sets tightly as his eyes drift to our linked hands. "If you want to walk away from this, I'll understand."

Walk away from what? Whatever this thing is that's going on between Grey and me? I could do that. It might be easier. Then again, I've never walked away from any of my friends, no matter what was going on in their lives, and I care about Grey enough that I'm not about to walk away from him, either.

"I don't want to walk away," I say, giving our hands a swing.

Relief washes over his expression. "Good. I'm really fucking glad to hear you say that, even if that makes me a selfish asshole."

"You're not a selfish asshole." My gaze flits to the door as someone honks a horn. "I better go. That's probably my grandma. But I'll see you at the party."

He nods, and with great hesitancy, I slip my fingers from his and turn for the front door.

"This thing with your aunt," Grey says as we step outside into the fading sunlight. "I think, if it is her, it might be good for you to meet her and see how she's doing. Maybe it'll help you realize you're not as bad a person as your parents try to make you believe. But promise me that you'll make sure it's her before you agree to meet her."

"I promise I will. I was planning on it, anyway."

"Good." The tension in his body alleviates, and his gaze fleetingly drops to my lips. "See you tonight at the party?" he asks, and I nod.

Looking super happy, he turns and heads for the corner of the street.

I call out, "Good luck with your game."

He smiles from over his shoulder. "Thanks. I have a feeling you just gave me good luck."

My heart beats wildly in my chest as I float toward the car in a haze, wondering what's going to happen at the party tonight. I don't want to set my expectations too high, but at the same time, I feel giddy.

I realize as I slide into the passenger seat that I don't think I've ever been giddy over a guy before. My mom was wrong. Dating can be fun, if that's even what Grey and I are doing.

"Who was that guy you were talking to?" my grandma asks as I shut the door.

I draw the seatbelt over my shoulder. "Just some guy who goes to my school."

"And a guy who has to go to this place." She glares at the single-story brick building where the sessions take place.

"He's not a bad guy." No, Grey isn't a bad guy at all, something I'm learning more and more each day. He's sweet and caring and has such soft lips.

I never thought in a million years Grey would ever kiss me or be my first kiss outside of my circle of friends. Then again, never in a million years did I think Grey would be the first one to find out about my kleptomania. Life is kind of crazy that way, so full of twists and turns and unexpectedness, like my aunt contacting me from out of nowhere. I just really hope it turns out to be her.

My grandma adjusts her thick glasses higher on her nose then shoves the shifter into drive. "Why do you look flushed?"

"It's hot in here," I lie, cranking up the air conditioning.

"It's not hot." She violently twists the knob, flipping the air right back off. "And those pants you're wearing are too tight." That is all she says to me before steering out onto the road.

She doesn't say anything for the rest of the drive and hardly speaks to me during dinnertime. Unlike my mom, my grandma is a woman of few words. She has the same views on clothes and how a person should act, but she isn't as verbal about it. She likes to make statements and sort of leave them hanging in the air for people to figure out the underlying meaning.

"Your hair looks tangled," means, "Go comb your hair." "Your shoes look worn out." Translation: "Buy some new shoes." Or, my personal favorite: "You're too tall." Yeah, I'm not sure what the heck she really meant by that one. It's not like I can just stop being tall.

But the silence gives me a lot of time to think about how I'm going to handle this thing with Aunt Ashlynn, and eventually, I come up with a plan. I just cross my fingers it doesn't backfire on me.

At around eight o'clock, my grandma pokes her head into my room. "I'm going to bed. Lights out."

I scoot toward the edge of the bed. "Wait. May I ask you something?"

She impatiently taps her finger against her watch. "If you must."

"I'm doing a project at school about my family, and I need some information about all of my family members. I was wondering if you could tell me Aunt Ashlynn's birth date."

"Can't you ask your mother?" she snaps.

"The project's due on Monday," I lie way too breezily. God, I'm becoming a real pro. "And I need to work on it this weekend."

"What a ridiculous project." She huffs an exasperated breath. "It's July twenty-fifth." Then she flips off the lights, backs out of my room, and slams the door.

July twenty-fifth. Okay, that's a start.

I sit on my bed in the dark for a half an hour to make sure she's asleep before I sneak out my window, scale down the tree, and jog to the corner of the street where Wynter is waiting for me in her car.

"Holy shit!" she exclaims when I yank open the door and dive inside. "What the hell, Lu? I didn't even see you coming."

"That's because I have ninja skills," I tease, hunkering down in the seat. "Hurry and drive away so I can stop worrying my grandma's going to spot me."

"She's, like, eighty years old. She probably can't even see in the dark." Still, she presses on the gas and peels away from the curb.

I only straighten in the seat when we're miles away from my home. Then I kick off my sneakers, crank up some music, and prop my feet up on the dash, tapping my toes to the rhythm.

"How many people do you think are going to be at this

party?" I ask as I roll down the window, and a cool breeze blows inside.

"I don't know." She turns on her blinker as she taps the brakes at the intersection. "Probably a lot since they won the game."

"They did? That's good. I wish I could have been there to watch them win." I tilt my head toward the window, unable to stop smiling.

"You do, huh? That's interesting since you've never cared about sports before."

"I have, too," I respond. "I've even watched Beck play a few times."

"And you were bored the entire time." She cranes the wheel into a turn down the side road that leads to her and Beck's neighborhood.

"Stop implying stuff."

"Just say it, then, and I'll let it drop."

"Say what?"

"*Luna*," she warns.

"Oh, fine. I wish I could've been at the game so I could see Grey play, okay?" My feet fall to the floor as I sit up and put my shoes back on. "There. Are you happy?"

"Very." She grins at me as she parks the car in her driveway. "But I don't get why you're making a big deal out of this. So, you like Grey. Who cares? Just own it. You've liked guys before and never cared when I teased you about it."

I know, but still . . ."Sometimes, I feel like I'm being ridiculous going after a guy who shot me down once. Like I'm being naive and getting too caught up in him before I even get to know him."

"I don't think you're being naive." She silences the engine, turns off the headlights, and extends her hand for the door handle to get out. "I mean, it's not like you've done anything other than talk to him and help him with his grades."

I bite down on my lip. "That's not entirely accurate."

"*What?*" She gapes at me through the darkness. "Oh, my God, you kissed him, didn't you?"

"No," I say, unbuckling my seatbelt. "He kissed me."

The interior light clicks on as she pushes open the door. "Did you like it?"

"Like what?" I ask, even though I know what she meant.

She rolls her eyes. "Duh. The kiss."

I shrug then nod. "Yeah, it was . . . nice." Way, way, nice. "Much better than that gross kiss with Beck."

"Okay, first of all, that kiss with Beck doesn't count because it was . . . well, with Beck. And second of all"—she lets out a squeal as she claps her hands—"I'm so happy for you!"

"I'm kind of happy for me, too," I admit as I get out of the car, but under the happiness lies fear: fear of getting hurt, fear of Grey learning too much about me and not liking what he sees, fear of Piper ripping me apart, fear of Logan tormenting me to death. There seems like so much going against Grey and me, but I've been through high school hell before. "But will you promise me one thing?"

She bumps the door shut with her hip. "That all depends on what it is."

"That you won't say anything to anyone about this, not until I talk to Grey some more."

"Sure," she says, "if that's what you want."

"It's what I want." At least until I figure out what exactly is going on with Grey and me. Sure, we kissed, but it's not like we've been out on a date or anything. Maybe he just wants to be friends who kiss, something Beck and Wynter tried once for a couple of weeks when we were in middle school. Needless to say, that turned into a disaster.

"We so have to pick you out a smokin' hot outfit,"

Wynter declares as we enter her foyer.

"I don't want to dress smokin' hot, just nice." I slip off my shoes by the front door and pad across the marble floor, heading for the split stairway.

"Okay," she says easily, but I can tell it's going to be a pain in the ass for us to agree on an outfit.

After sifting through her closet for an hour, I end up putting on a red dress that's fitted at the top and flows out at the bottom. I top it with a three quarter sleeve leather jacket and ankle boots. I leave my hair down in waves and add a drop of lip-gloss, eyeliner, and mascara. Wynter goes with a longer, backless dress and gladiator sandals. She pins up her hair and stains her lips dark red.

I check my phone every so often to make sure no one calls. If my grandma does find out I snuck out, my mom will call me. I'm not sure what I'll do if that happens, especially since I left my other phone with the tracking app at home. So, not only will I have to explain why I'm not at the house, but she'll discover what I did with my phone. All I can do is pray to God that my grandma doesn't wake up and look in my room. But, no matter how worried I am, there's no going back now. I made the choice of what kind of person I am—one who picks parties and friends over doing what their parents want.

Willow and Ari show up as we're getting ready to leave. Willow's sporting the tank top, plaid shirt, and jeans she went to work in, and Wynter insists she has to change.

"Beck said the party is fancy casual," Wynter explains when Willow puts up an argument.

Shaking her head, Willow snatches the short, black dress from Wynter's hand and steps into the closet to put it on. "Fine. But don't get used to this. I like my grungy look."

"What the hell is fancy casual?" Ari asks as he sits down on the edge of Wynter's bed.

Wynter shrugs as she piles makeup into a glittery handbag. "I don't know, but it got her to change out of her work clothes, didn't it?"

"Why does it matter how she's dressed?" Ari asks, self-consciously glancing down at his blue jeans and plaid shirt.

"It doesn't," she says, adding another pin to her braided up-do. "I really don't care if she dresses up or not. I was just trying to get her out of her work clothes."

"Should I change, too?" Ari asks. "Or do I pass the Wynter outfit inspection?"

"Hm . . ." She folds her arms as she critiques his attire. "I don't know. I think there might be something missing." She steps toward him and playfully ruffles his hair with her fingers. "There you go. Much better."

Ari rubs his hand over his hair, flattening it back into place. "Was that really necessary?"

"Maybe not, but it was fun," she replies. "Besides, I think you might be able to rock the whole sexy, bed-head look. You know, mix it up a little. You've had the same look since I met you."

"Thanks for the suggestion," he responds dryly, "but I think I'll keep my look."

Wynter gives a nonchalant shrug. "Didn't hurt to try, did it?"

He sighs tiredly as he leans back on his elbows. "So, how long do we have to stay at this little shindig? Because I have to get up early."

"You always have to get up early," Wynter points out as she slips on a pair of hoop earrings.

"I have to make sure I'm home at a decent time, too," I say, sitting down in the chair in front of the vanity. "It's too risky to stay out for too long."

"Don't worry, princess; we'll get you home by

midnight," Wynter teases as she slides a silver cuff bracelet on.

"Thanks, Prince Charming," I quip.

Her eyes sparkle with hilarity. "Prince Charming? I thought that was—"

"Shush," I warn, wagging a finger at her. "Don't even think about bringing him into this."

Ari's gaze dances back and forth between the two of us. "Bring who into what?"

"Luna likes Grey," Wynter shamelessly spills the beans. "And he kissed her today."

"Way to keep a promise, you traitor." I lean forward, snatch a pillow from the bed, and chuck it at her.

It smacks her in the face, but she only laughs. "I didn't think that included Ari or any of our other friends."

"And Beck already knew about it, anyway!" Willow shouts from the closet. "Well, not the kissing part, but that Grey likes you."

"How the heck does Beck know that?" I ask.

She sticks her head out of the closet. "I'm not sure. He said he could just tell." She ducks back inside. "But he told me he gave Grey a lecture on how to treat you."

I drop my head into my hands. "Jesus, that's so embarrassing."

"Why? If Grey likes you, he should be glad you have friends looking out for you," Ari says.

I peek at him through the cracks in my fingers. "Were you there when he did it?"

"No, but I'm glad he did." He shoves up the sleeves of his shirt. "Grey seems like he's going through some kind of personality change, but that doesn't mean that we all don't worry he's going to end up hurting you."

"I'm not as breakable as everyone thinks," I say, circling my fingers around my bruised wrist.

"We know that," Wynter chimes in, "but that doesn't mean we like seeing you get hurt. We all saw what Grey and his friends put you through sophomore year, and we never want to see that happen again." She places her hands on my shoulders and looks me dead in the eyes. "Just promise me that you'll be careful, take things slowly, and let us have your back."

"Fine," I say. "But please try to lay off the lectures for a while."

"I'll try, but I'm not making any promises." She jumps back as the closet door swings open, almost hitting her.

Willow curses as she trips out, tying the plaid jacket around her waist. "Oh, my God, there are too many shoes in there."

"There's no such thing as too many shoes." Wynter evaluates Willow's outfit with wariness. "You're really wearing the jacket like that?"

Willow nods, giving her the death glare. "And no more arguing about my outfit. This is what I'm wearing. Deal with it."

Wynter's lips twitch as she notes Willow's unlaced boots. "All right." She collects her house keys and purse from the dresser, and then the four of us head out the front door.

Beck only lives a few blocks down, so we decide to walk there.

As we stroll up the sidewalk underneath the glow of the streetlights and moon, Ari and Wynter fall into a conversation about why her neighbors have Christmas decorations still up.

Willow seizes the opportunity to pull me back into a private conversation. "You never told me what happened," she whispers, nodding at my black and blue wrist.

"It's not a big deal." My fingers stiffen as I cover my

wrist.

What do I tell her? The truth? It seems so easy, just a few words I have to utter, but confessing something about my family that would make them look like bad people scares the shit out of me. What if my dad finds out? What if he kicks me out like he has been threatening? What if? What if? What if?

What if I stop being so scared all the time and took control for once without stealing? What if I just went to parties that I wanted to go to without sneaking down trees? What if I kissed guys I wanted to without planning on marrying them? What if? What if?

What if I was me all the time and did what I wanted without worrying about what my parents or anyone else thought?

"My dad and I had this argument, and he . . . He kind of grabbed me." My pulse soars as soon as the words leave my lips.

"Your *dad* did that to you?" She sounds absolutely horrified.

"I-It was an accident," I stammer. "He didn't mean to, and I did make him really mad."

"I don't give a shit if he meant to or not," she hisses with her hands on her hips. "Luna, it's never okay for someone to hurt you, even if they're mad at you."

"I know." Uttering the truth aloud is like reality slapping me across the face.

I knew since the moment the bruises formed that what my dad did wasn't okay. That he grabbed me too hard. That, no matter what I did, he never should have put his hands on me like that.

"You need to tell someone." She hooks arms with me. "Promise me you won't just let this go like you let everything else go."

I nod, making a promise I'm unsure I'm ready to make.

Could I really do it? Could I really tell someone what goes on inside my house? If I did, then I know I'd be making a choice. I'd be choosing to move out, because there's no way my parents would ever let me back in the house if I betrayed them like that. And even if they didn't kick me out, I don't think I'd be able to go back into that house, because . . .

The truth is, I'm terrified of my parents.

Confession

SIXTEEN

I'm a closet DJ and dancer.

Luna

BY THE TIME we arrive at Beck's two-story, brick home at the end of a cul-de-sac, the party is in full force. Music can be heard from all the way outside, cars line the driveway and the street, and a large group of people crowd the side balcony.

Wynter squares her shoulders as we stand at the edge of the lawn. "All right, let's do this." She loops arms with Ari and me then leads us toward the front door. Willow's arm is still linked with mine as she jogs across the grass to keep up with us.

"Man, why does Beck always have to invite so many people?" Willow gripes as we reach the front door. "He probably doesn't even know half the people here, and the ones he does know, he hates."

"Yeah, but all the noise is a great distraction." Wynter releases her grip on Ari and me and pushes open the door.

"From what—" I start to say, but the music drowns me out.

Inside, people are crammed into his spacious living room, dancing and grinding all over each other. A huge line has formed in front of the downstairs bathroom, and couples are wandering upstairs toward the bedrooms.

I scan the faces, searching for Grey, but with how many people are here, it's impossible to tell if he's here or not.

"Jesus, Beck went overboard this time!" Willow shouts over the music, shaking her head in disgust as she watches some guy jump up and down in the foyer. "I don't even recognize half of these people!"

"Me, neither! But the game today was supposed to be for the championship or something," I explain. "Maybe that's why."

"Or maybe he's just having a really shitty day," Wynter yells as she heads toward the dance floor with her eyes targeted on a tall, older guy with similar features to Grey. "I'll catch up with you guys later! I'm going to get a drink!" Before I can stop her from what she's about to do, she dives into the mob.

"She's trying to hook up with Theo, isn't she?" Willow asks me, frowning.

I shrug. "She might be."

Willow purses her lips. "Beck's going to get super pissed if he finds out."

"I'm going to get super pissed about what?" Beck asks, appearing out of nowhere. He's dressed up in a pair of nice jeans and a plaid, button down shirt, but the backward baseball cap he's sporting gives him a chill vibe. Hm . . . Maybe that's what Wynter meant by fancy casual. He also has a drink in his hand and looks a little buzzed.

"That we're not going to dance," Willow responds with an indifferent shrug.

"*Pft*, yeah, right. Everyone dances at my parties." His gaze drags up and down Willow. "Since when do you wear dresses?"

Willow self-consciously messes around with the jacket around her waist. "Since Wynter forced me to. Don't get used to it. This is a onetime thing."

"You look"—he muses over something—"hot." Then he smacks Willow on the ass, a move Beck does a lot, but only on girls he's flirting with. "I didn't know you had it in you, Willow."

Willow goes from all bug-eyed to utterly livid. Instead of chewing him out, she reaches around and slaps him on the ass. The four of us trade a look then erupt in laughter.

"Sorry about that," Beck apologizes to Willow then glances down at the cup in his hand. "I think I might've had one too many."

"I'll let you off the hook just as long as you promise never to smack my ass again," Willow warns.

After a second of dithering, Beck looks up from the cup and grins. "Okay, I promise, but if you ask me to smack your ass, then all bets are off."

"I'll never ask you to smack my ass," Willow promises, seeming a little squirmy.

"We'll see." Beck raises the brim of the cup to his lips, throws his head back, and chugs the drink down before his bloodshot eyes land on me. "I need to talk to you."

"Okay?" I'm so confused. "About what?"

A grin breaks out on his face as he crunches up his cup and tosses it aside. "About how much you kick ass." He wraps me in a big bear hug and whispers in my ear, "Grey made the winning shot tonight."

"That's awesome." I circle my arms around him. "But I'm not sure what that has to do with me kicking ass."

"Because he wouldn't have even been in the game if it wasn't for you."

"Willow helped, too," I remind him. "Way more than

me."

"Yeah, but I don't think it was just the getting a good grade that made him play better than he ever has," he says. "I was a little worried he might be out of it with all this shit going on with Piper, but he seemed really focused and relaxed, even when we were losing. I think that might be about you. You have that effect on people."

I'm not sure what to say or how I feel about Beck's theory.

"Is he here?"

"I haven't seen him"—he pulls back, keeping his hands on my upper arms—"but I made the whole team promise they'd show up, so I'm sure he'll be here." He gives me a pat on the arm before spinning around. "Let's go and get you lovely people some drinks then hit the dance floor so I can get Willow to relax."

Willow gives an exaggerated sigh, but I catch a sparkle of amusement in her eye as she follows Beck.

When we get to the kitchen, Beck mixes everyone a drink. None of us are that big on drinking, so we take a few sips while Beck downs half of his. After he sets his cup down on the counter, he grabs my arm and tells Willow and Ari, "We'll be right back." Then he drags me across the kitchen and pushes his way to the corner of the living room.

"Work your magic," he says as he gestures to the stereo hooked up to his laptop. "You should be able to get into your account from my computer, right?"

"Yeah, but nothing I turn on is going to be any better than what you've already been listening to." I frown when I spot Piper and Logan watching me from the foyer, chatting about God knows what.

Beck tracks my gaze. "Do you want me to ask them to leave? I don't even know why they're here. I didn't invite them."

"It's fine. They'll just cause a scene if you do." I rip my attention away from them and focus on the stereo. "You really want me to do this?"

He rotates his cap forward. "Absolutely. I love your taste in music. It's so unique and different."

I almost laugh as I wind around the table. Unique and different. God, no wonder my parents hate me. They love ordinary and blending in.

Shoving thoughts of my parents aside, I click open my music account. It takes me five tries to get the password right since I haven't been allowed to go on the internet in ages. Once I figure it out, I open one of the mixes I put together during the rare occasions my parents let me go to a friend's house. Then I adjust the bass and tweak the sound before stepping back.

A hypnotic beat booms from the speakers, and a satisfied grin spreads across Beck's face as he rubs his hands together. "Dancing time."

We squeeze toward the middle of the dance floor as the song slowly builds up, growing louder and louder.

"What about Ari and Willow?" I ask when we find a space on the floor.

With a drunken grin, Beck cups his hands around his mouth and shouts, "Ari! Willow! Front and center!"

Although people gawk at us like we've lost our minds, Beck just shrugs it off. He has never been one for caring what other people think.

We start to move to the beat.

"You're not going to do the robot this time, are you?" I ask him.

"I wasn't planning on it, but now that you brought it up . . ." He charms me with a grin before he backs up with his arms out to the side, clearing some room. Then he proceeds to do the robot right there in front of everyone, and there's nothing left for me to do but roll with it.

He laughs as I rock out, doing a head bang, and I giggle as he strikes a pose.

"You guys are so dorky," Willow comments as she joins us, "but I love you for it."

"Of course you do." Beck dances around her, grabs her arm, and spins her around.

She throws her head back, laughing when he does it again. As the song lulls to a sexy beat, he hauls her against him, and they sway back and forth, rubbing against each other, getting down and dirty.

I look away from the two of them, feeling as if I'm imposing on some sort of sexual moment.

"Ari, dance with me?" I ask with my hand extended toward him.

"You know I suck at dancing," he says but still takes my hand.

We dance for what feels like hours, laughing and messing around.

As I'm standing there in the middle of the packed living room, dancing with three people I love more than anything, I become hyperaware of how much fun I'm having, maybe the most fun I've ever had. Whether that makes me a bad person or not, that's the kind of person I am. The kind who likes to dance, who likes to laugh with their friends, who loves picking out music, who loves being . . . well, free, like the walls are wide and there's so much space, so much air.

"I need some water!" Ari shouts, fanning his face.

"I'll come with you!" I start to tell Beck and Willow we'll be back, but Beck's hands are wandering all over Willow's body, and she seems perfectly okay with being fondled.

I quickly look away, startled. Ari appears as uncomfortable as I do, and we both silently agree to just let them be and head out to the back deck without them. Unlike the side porch, the back deck is an extension from Beck's parents' room, and not many people are out there.

"Well, that was . . . interesting," Ari says, digging a bottle of water out of a large cooler.

"I know. Maybe they're a little drunk or something." I rub my hand across my forehead. "I don't think Willow drank that much, though."

He unscrews the lid off, hands the bottle to me, and gets another one out for himself. "You don't think we should stop them, do you?"

I take a swig of water then shake my head.

Ari unenthusiastically nods. "But isn't it going to make things weird if they hook up?"

Huh. I hadn't really thought about that.

Before I can say anything, though, his phone rings, and he fishes it out of his pocket. "Shit. It's my mom. She probably forgot I was going to the party and thinks I'm still in the house." He presses talk, wandering down the stairs and into the shadows of the backyard.

I plant my backside down on a patio chair and sip on my water, staring up at the night sky dusted with stars, waiting for Ari to return. From the tidbits he has told me about his family, his mom has some sort of mental illness, and the meds she's on make her forget stuff, like picking him up from school, buying food, and paying the bills. Ari's dad seems like a nice guy and tries to take care of the household, but he works crazy hours, and Ari and his older brother do a lot of things, like run errands and make sure the bills get paid. His brother even skipped going away to a college and, instead, takes classes online so he can be around to help out.

By the time Ari climbs back up the stairs, his shoulders are slumped, as if the weight of the world is bearing down on him. "I have to go home. My dad's working the nightshift tonight, and my mom needs help with something at the house."

I start to get up. "Do you want me to go with you?"

He motions for me to stay put. "It's okay. Stay and have fun for the both of us, okay?"

"If you need anything, call me," I say, sinking back down into the chair.

He nods then disappears into the house.

The people who were out on the porch when we first came out have migrated to the back lawn to play Frisbee, so I relax back in the chair.

While I've always been okay with being by myself, I find myself wishing I wasn't out here alone. I think about going back inside to find Beck and Willow, but what if they're up in one of the rooms? I could always go and find Grey, but I'm not sure I feel that daring just yet. And wandering around alone . . . What if I run into Piper and Logan? I don't want to put up with drama tonight. I just want to relax.

I take out my phone to read the email that is supposedly from Aunt Ashlynn as I work up the courage to track down the guy I like. As I'm typing a quick response, asking her when her birthday is, I hear the back door open.

"I was beginning to worry you didn't come," Grey's voice sails over my shoulder.

A goofy smile rises on my face. I quickly hit send then look up at him. "I was starting to wonder the same thing about you."

He steps onto the deck beneath the porch light, and I discreetly check him out. He always looks good, but he looks extremely sexy tonight in a pair of loose-fitted jeans and a black, thermal shirt with the sleeves pushed up. Like Beck, he has a backward baseball cap on his head, but unlike Beck, Grey's eyes aren't glazed over and bloodshot.

He pulls the door shut, and then his eyes all over me,

taking in every inch of my body and face. "You look nice." When his gaze lingers on my chest, I have an urge to cross my arms, remembering what Piper said about me being flat-chested. He drags his eyes off me and notes the vacated back deck. "Why are you sitting out here alone?"

"Ari was out here with me a few minutes ago, but he had to go home." I lay my phone down on the table and cross my legs. "I was inside dancing, but it got too hot."

His brow teases upward. "You dance?"

"What can I say? Apparently, I'm a closet DJ and dancer."

"Really?" He seems particularly interested in my declaration. "Do I get to see these dancing skills?"

"Sure." I rise to my feet, preparing to go inside, but he moves away from the door, takes out a phone from his back pocket, and swipes his finger across the screen.

"You got a phone?" I ask, tucking my hands under my legs.

He nods, glancing up at me. "My mom gave it to me when I got home from the session. She called it a congrats-you-are-no-longer-a-criminal present." He taps his finger across a small crack in the screen. "It's used, but it works." He shrugs. "The house finally sold, so she says she can afford to turn the service back on."

"That's good," I say. "You seem sad about it, though."

"I'm not sad. I'm just . . ." He sits down in the chair across from mine, setting his phone down on the table beside mine. "I know it's a good thing, because we can't afford the house anymore, but it was the house I grew up in, and a lot of my memories with my dad happened in there. I kind of feel like I'm losing him all over again."

I reach forward and thread my fingers through his. "I know it's hard, but those memories belong to you, not the house, and you can always think about him whenever you feel like it."

He studies me like I'm a complex puzzle he's trying to solve. "You really are an amazing person. You always make me feel better even when everything's so shitty."

"Grey, you know I'm not an amazing person. You heard what I admitted when we were running through the forest. I wasn't lying. I don't steal because I'm poor. I steal because I'm messed up." I start to pull away, but he tightens his hold on my hand, trapping it against his knee.

"I don't want to make you uncomfortable, and you don't have to answer, but I just want to know . . . Why do you do it?"

My chest tightens. "You really want to know?"

He nods. "But only if you feel comfortable telling me."

"You'll hate me," I whisper.

He swiftly shakes his head. "I could never hate you, Luna."

I don't believe him, but I want to tell the truth and get this off my chest.

"It's just this thing I started doing . . . to get control, I guess."

"Control?" He looks lost.

I sigh and tell him about the first time I stole, how I felt this need to gain control over my life and how stealing briefly gave me that. I confess how many times I've done it, how badly I feel afterward, and how I wish I knew I could stop, but I'm not so sure I can.

"When was the last time you did it?" he asks, his voice giving nothing away about how he's feeling.

"That time you saw me at Benny's was technically the last time I ever put anything into my pockets." I tip my chin down and focus on picking at my nails because it's simpler than looking him in the eye. "It doesn't mean I haven't thought about doing it, though. The other night, my mom told me I have to cut my hair, even though I love my hair the way it is . . . I wanted to climb out my window, run to the store, and stuff as many things as I could into my pockets just so I could breathe again . . . And this morning, I was at the gas station . . . I almost put a candy bar into my pocket, but the cashier saw me and said all this stuff to me. It was so embarrassing."

He stays quiet for what feels like an eternity, and it takes me forever to work up the courage to look at him. I instantly lean back from the intensity in his eyes, unsure what the look means.

"I want to stop," I say, my voice barely above a whisper. "Every time I do it, I promise myself never again, but then something happens with my mom or dad, and this pressure builds inside my chest. It feels like I'm going to explode and say stuff that will make the situation worse. So I bottle it down and deal with it the only way I can."

"Have you ever told anyone how you feel?"

I shake my head. "You're the first person I've ever talked to about this. Even my friends don't know that I do it."

He reaches out and molds his hands around mine, bringing me the smallest amount of comfort. "Can you do me a favor? The next time something happens when you feel that pressure, can you talk to me first before you do anything?"

"You really want me to keep talking to you after what I just told you?"

"You think I'd stop liking you because you steal sometimes?" He shakes his head in disbelief. "Luna, I let my friends torture you for years. If anything, *you* shouldn't be sitting here, talking to *me*."

"You're not that guy anymore," I say. "You're nicer, and you care about people."

"But that doesn't mean I didn't do all those bad things.

Things you forgive me for, even though I don't deserve it," he says. I open my mouth to say he deserves forgiveness, but he cuts me off. "Just let me get this out before you say anything, okay?"

When I nod, he continues.

"What I did to you back in sophomore year . . ." He struggles for the right words. "I never should've turned you down like that. I acted like an asshole on purpose. I was showing off for my friends because, back then, I thought their opinions mattered. And when Logan spread those rumors about you, I should've stopped him. I should've been a better guy, like my dad thought I was, but I was a self-centered jerk." He pauses, taking a deep breath. "But I get it now. People have so much shit they're going through, and some are struggling just to get through the goddamn day. The last thing they need is for some arrogant prick to beat them down and make their life even more complicated." He turns my hand over, palm up, and sketches his fingers along my scars. "You have to deal with so much, and I wish I could've seen that." He looks up at me with shame written all over his face. "I'm so sorry."

"It's okay." My voice is thick with emotion.

I might have said I was okay throughout the years and didn't care who said what to me, but the truth is, hearing him apologize makes me realize just how hard it was to deal with all the teasing and ridicule.

"And I forgive you." I already forgave him, but it feels like he needs to hear me say it aloud.

"I'm going to make it up to you somehow," he whispers, his gaze skimming across my lips.

Yes, please, pretty please, make it up to me by kissing me.

He gives me exactly what I want, leaning forward and pressing his lips to mine. My skin hums from the contact, and I let out this uncontrollable, somewhat embarrassing gasp. He seems to like the noise, though, and groans in response, slipping his tongue into my mouth.

Oh. My. God. This is way better than just using lips.

My lips part as I angle my head back, giving his tongue access to fully explore my mouth. Every graze of his lips and brush of his tongue drives my body further into a mad frenzy. My mom may have told me kissing was a horrible thing and that I shouldn't do it more than I have to, but God, was she wrong. Really, really wrong. Kissing is amazing.

His hands glide down my arms and come to a rest on my waist. Gripping tightly, he pulls me toward him. I'm not sure what he's doing until he suddenly picks me up and sets me on his lap so I'm straddling him.

My eyes widen in shock, and for the briefest second, I hear that voice in the back of my head telling me what I'm doing is wrong. But I shove the voice aside with surprising ease and fall blindly into the kiss, letting his hands rove all over my body.

I'm still nervous, though. With each touch of his hands, I worry he can feel all my flaws, and my self-doubt starts to wear on me.

He finally pulls away, sucking on my bottom lip.

"You can tell me to stop whenever you get too uncomfortable," he says.

"I'm just a little nervous. I've never . . . done this before." My cheeks stupidly warm.

He grazes his knuckles across my cheekbone. "Do you want to stop? We can go dance, get something to drink—whatever you want."

"Whatever I want?" I muse over the foreign concept. "I like the sound of that."

He smiles at me as I slant forward, sealing my lips to his again, kissing him because it's what I want.

Confession

SEVENTEEN

> I hate getting into fights.
>
> Grey

LUNA AND I stay out on the porch, kissing for what feels like hours. I don't take things too far, even though I desperately want to. I can tell she's nervous, and the last thing I want to do is make her feel like I'm pressuring her to do something.

"You're so beautiful," I hear myself saying over and over again as my hand wanders up her leg, across her smooth skin. My mouth leaves her lips to make a path down her jawline. A shudder vibrates through her body as I sweep her hair over her shoulder and place a soft kiss against the hollow of her neck. "And I don't think you should cut your hair . . ." I murmur, sucking on her skin as my hand drifts down her arm.

"I don't want to, but I'm not sure how . . . I'm going to get out of it. She said, if I argued, I had to move out." She shivers again then winces as my fingers brush her wrist.

I remember the bruises I saw there earlier. Even though it kills me, I move back to look her in the eye.

"The bruises on your wrist . . . Where did they come from? Because I know they didn't come from a trampoline."

She stares down at the purplish-blue imprints on her skin. "I had an argument with my dad . . . He didn't mean to, though. It's not as bad as it seems."

I hook my finger under her chin and force her to look up at me. "Luna, I know it's hard, but have you ever thought about just moving out?"

"I've actually thought about it a lot. I mean, I'm eighteen, so I technically can, but I don't have a job, and my parents won't let me get one. I think, in this twisted way, they like that I have no money of my own. I have to work for Benny for a while, but I'm not getting paid. My parents set it up so it looks like I'm helping, but really, it's another punishment for me." She shrugs again, dejected. "I don't mind doing it. I just wish I could get a real job." Sighing, she leaves my lap to go stand near the railing. "I feel like I can't win either way. Either I break my parents' rules and get a job, which will instantly get me kicked out of the house, or I walk out and live on the streets."

"There's no one you could stay with for a while?" I get up and move beside her. "Just until you get on your feet?"

She lifts a shoulder, staring at a group of people passing a Frisbee. "Wynter offered to let me move into her pool house, and I kind of want to, but"—she rests her arms on the metal railing—"I'm afraid."

"Of your mom and dad?"

"Of them getting upset, of me being a burden to Wynter, of her finding out stuff about me that I've kept from her. I'm kind of a coward."

"You're not a coward." My tone comes out sharper than I intended, which causes her to glance up at me. "Not at all."

"Grey, I keep so many secrets from people because I'm afraid of what they might think of me. And I can barely stick up for myself." Her voice is heavy with doubt.

I completely disagree with her and feel this overwhelming need to prove it to her.

"Do you know what my father's last words were to me?" I turn away from her to hide my shame. "He told me I was a good son and that he was proud of the man I'd become. And you know what I did? I looked him straight in the eye and nodded. I didn't tell him that I wasn't the man he thought I was, that I was a horrible person who acted like he was better than everyone else. My dad was dying, and I lied to him. I let him believe I was the nice guy. That's a coward, Luna."

I wait for her to say something. When she doesn't, I concentrate on watching the Frisbee get tossed back and forth in an attempt to ignore the uncomfortable silence Luna and I have crashed into.

"Grey." Her voice sounds firm when she speaks again. "I don't think that makes you a coward. Your father was dying, and you let him believe he raised you to be a good guy, that he did what he was supposed to do as a father. There's nothing wrong with that. Besides, you took those words and made something out of them. You changed for your dad, so really, he was right. It just took you a while to make it happen."

I turn to her, feeling ten times lighter than I did a few minutes ago. "I don't know how you do it, but you always seem to see the good in everything . . . except for maybe yourself. I wish you could see that."

"I do sometimes . . . It's just hard when, every time I go home, I'm reminded of what a crappy person I am." She picks at the cracks in the railing. "There's one thing I can't always see the good in, though." When she smiles up at me, I'm thrown off by her sudden shift in attitude. "And that's losing at any game, whether it's backgammon or checkers. I never, ever think it's good to lose."

"I'm still not sure if I believe you're a sore loser," I tease. "I think I have to see it for myself."

"Beck's got a whole closet full of board games." A challenge dances in her eyes. "But I have to warn you first. When I lose a hand, always keep an eye out for objects that can be thrown. If you win a hand and you're smug about it, duck for cover because you're more than likely going to get pegged in the face with a game piece, card, or maybe even a die. And if at any time you think about cheating, be prepared to get a lecture on how cheating can lead to more severe crimes, like robbery."

"What statistics are those based on?"

"They're not based on any statistics, per se. I just like to get people thinking about who they are because it distracts them, and a distracted opponent is a weak one."

"Wow, you sound really vicious." I pretend to be horrified when really I think she's freaking adorable.

"But at least I'm warning you about my viciousness, right?" she states innocently. I have a feeling the innocent act is a ruse to throw me off my game.

"I guess so," I say, "but just so you know, none of this scares me. I'm not holding back my mad board-game skills, no matter how ugly things get."

She grins like that's exactly what she's hoping for. "Don't say I didn't warn you."

One hour later, I'm sitting on Beck's bed with cards surrounding me. After Luna lost her tenth hand of Blackjack, she proceeded to—and very spitefully, I might add—declare that I needed to play fifty-two card pick up before she tossed all the cards into the air.

Instead of picking the cards up, I relax back on my elbows and stretch out my legs. "You know what? I'm kind of turned on by this."

A flush creeps across her cheeks, a look I'm starting to really like. "It's not supposed to turn you on. It's supposed to get you as irritated as I am." She flicks a card at me then crosses her arms. "I really suck at Blackjack, don't I?"

"You kind of do, but that's okay. At least you throw the cards in the air with great accuracy. I mean, not everyone can get them so scattered." I glance at the cards all over the bed and on the floor. There are even a few on the dresser across the room. "Think about how long it's going to take me to pick all these up. But once I do, I kind of win the game, so it defeats your point."

She struggles not to smile. "Maybe I won't let you pick them up." The challenge rises in her eyes again.

A second goes by before I dive for the cards, picking up a handful. She leaps after me and ends up landing on my back. I laugh then easily stand up, carrying her piggy-back style as I bend down to pick up the cards from off the floor.

"Now you're just showing off," she says with her arms and legs wrapped around me.

"Maybe a little bit." I stack the cards in my hand. "Are you impressed?"

"Maybe a little bit," she admits.

"Just a little bit?" I set the cards down on the computer desk and grasp her legs. "I guess I'm going to have to take it up a notch, then."

Without warning, I spin around and around, and she busts up laughing, her arms tightening around me.

"Nope, still not impressed," she says through her laughter.

"Man, you're a tough crowd to please." I stop spinning, lift my arm, and in one swift movement, swing her around and drop her on the bed.

She lands on her back, bouncing against the mattress, still laughing.

"Okay, that was a little impressive."

I climb on top of her, putting a knee on each side of her hip. "You think so?"

She nods her head, her laughter dying as she gazes up at me.

I play with a strand of her hair, raveling it around my finger, slowly drawing her up to me. Her tongue slips out, wetting her lips, and I stop moving slowly and attack her with my mouth.

I lean over her, propping up on my elbows, and she grinds her hips against mine in response, gasping as her fingers fumble along my back.

I slow the kiss down, taking my time, but my hands are all over her, wanting, needing, wanting. Eventually, I slip off her jacket, and she tugs my shirt over my head. Then we move up the bed toward the pillows.

I pull on a string on the front of her dress, opening it up so I can place a kiss on her neck, her chest, kissing, tasting, savoring. I've never felt like this before, never wanted someone so badly without just taking them.

"I want to take things slow," I whisper between kisses. "I don't want to rush everything like I normally do . . . I want to . . . experience this . . ." God, I sound like a babbling idiot.

Thankfully, Luna doesn't think so.

"I get what you mean," she whispers against my lips.

I relax and go back to kissing and exploring her body. We only pull away when Luna's phone starts ringing from her jacket pocket.

At first, she ignores it, but when the damn thing won't shut up, she pulls away, grunting in frustration, which may be the sexiest sound I've ever heard.

"That might be my grandma," she grumbles, scooting out from under me.

I roll onto my back as she climbs off the bed and picks up her jacket. I feel fucking buzzed, even though I haven't even had one drink tonight.

"I should probably get home," Luna says as she sits on the edge of her bed, staring at her phone.

I sit up and slide over beside her. "It's not from your grandma, is it?"

She hands me the phone, and I read the message on the screen.

> Wynter: Hey, princess, it's way after midnight, which means your carriage has long turned into a sober, rejected, depressing pumpkin and really needs to get home. Meet me out front soon?

"My friends and I have this rule that we can't leave someone at a party by themselves," she explains, combing her fingers through her hair. "Ari already went home, and I'm guessing Willow bailed out, too, and Beck's probably passed out somewhere, which counts as him being MIA."

"I love how you guys always look out for each other." I give her back the phone. "I should probably get home, too. I don't have a pact with my friends, but I do have to go to work tomorrow. It'll be my first day, and I'm already nervous that I'll fuck up somehow. The last thing I need to do is fall asleep on the job. Benny does seem pretty cool, though. He might not even get upset if I take a two-minute power nap."

"You're working at Benny's tomorrow, too?"

"Yep." I grin, brushing strands of her hair out of her eyes. "I guess you'll have to put up with me for two days in a row."

"I think I can handle that. And"—she rubs her hand across her arm, erasing goose bumps—"maybe you can keep an eye on me. I'm a little worried about being in a store."

"Absolutely. In fact, maybe I should keep an eye on you twenty-four seven, no matter what you're doing, just in case." I wink at her.

She shakes her head, wrestling back a smile as she gets up and laces up the front of her dress.

I watch her fingers move, gradually covering up her skin, only looking away when she ties the end in a knot. Then I pick up my shirt and pull it on while she puts on her jacket.

As she's putting on her shoes, I wander around the room. Beck's room looks a lot like mine used to, with sports equipment everywhere, nice furniture, and a big-ass stereo system. It makes me miss my stuff, but what really makes me choke up is when I see the baseball I gave him balanced on top of a shelf.

I want to reach up and touch it one last time, but I'm afraid I won't be able to let it go if I do.

"What is it?" Luna asks, moving up beside me.

I bottle down the pain choking me. "It's just an old baseball."

"Is it . . . Is it yours?"

"It was."

"You gave it to Beck for money." It's not a question. She knows Beck well enough that she probably understands the deals he does more than anyone else.

"Yeah." I inhale and exhale as quietly as I can, making myself relax before I turn to her. "Ready to go?" I offer her my hand.

She looks up at the ball then at me before lacing her fingers with mine. "Sure."

We leave the room together, and it causes a few strange looks and stares.

"Let me take you home," I say as we push our way down the hallway, winding around people doing almost the same thing Luna and I just did in the bedroom.

"That sounds nice, but you can't drop me off at the door or anything," she replies, disheartened. "You'll have to pull up to the corner of my street."

"I'm okay with that." But I wish it wasn't like that. I wish she wasn't so trapped in her own home that she has to sneak out to pretty much do anything.

She sends Wynter a text, saying she's going to ride home with me. Wynter responds that Luna better message her the moment she gets home so she knows I didn't try to murder her.

"She thinks I could be a murderer?" I ask, slightly offended but mostly entertained.

She laughs, shaking her head. "Don't take it personally. She always says stuff like that. She says it's so we won't forget that bad stuff can happen. Really, I think it's because she spends way too much time watching crime movies."

I chuckle, pulling her to me, and brush my lips across her forehead. "I promise I'll get you home safely."

"I know you will," she replies without an ounce of doubt.

Everything seems to be going great—I'd even go as far as calling it the perfect night—until we reach the bottom of the stairway, and Logan blindsides us, blocking our way to the front door.

"Babe, take a look at this," Logan says with his arms crossed and wearing his famous my-shit-don't-stink smirk. "I think you might've been right. Herpes does make you lose your damn mind."

Piper ambles away from a group of her friends and toward us. "Whoa," she mutters, blinking her glazed-over eyes at Luna's and my interlocked fingers. "Am I hallucinating?"

Great. She's drunk, and a drunk Piper means a sloppy, even more annoying Piper. I've seen her wasted before. She likes to make scenes and throw tantrums to get attention.

My hand constricts on Luna's as I start to swing around Logan, but he sidesteps us, getting in my path.

"Back the fuck off," I warn.

"Back the fuck off," Piper mimics then erupts in a fit of giggles. "God, Grey, you're so uptight." The heels of her boots click against the floor as she stumbles closer to me. "Let me loosen you up, baby." Her fingers wander toward my chest, but I step back. "Why are you acting like I'm diseased or something? You're the one who's gross!" She teeters to the side, bumping into the banister. "You have herpes."

"Thanks for the health update." I sling my arm around Luna and tuck her against me. "Do yourself a favor; go drink some water and have someone take you home before you make more of an ass out of yourself."

"I'm not the one making an ass out of myself!" she shouts, her face reddening. "You're the one who traded this"—she runs her hands over her hips then narrows her eyes at Luna—"for that freak. Now that's making an ass out of yourself."

"I didn't trade; I upgraded." It's a low and stupid blow, but I've spent enough time with Piper to know how to kick her where it counts. She gets off on making people feel beneath her. Take that superiority away, and she's lost.

"That's bullshit!" she screams with her fists clenched at her sides. It's amazing how many people don't look in our direction, probably because they've witnessed Piper act like this at parties before. "And I'm going to prove to everyone that your little upgrade is nothing more than a freak loser. And you used to think she was." She sucks in a breath at the end and grins, going from hot to cold in two seconds flat. Then she spins around and staggers away with her chin held high, walking a crooked line all the way back to her friends.

I turn to Luna. "Let's get out of here."

Luna eagerly nods, and we step for the door, but Logan moves in front of her, and she ends up running into him and almost falls down.

"I just want to understand why he'd go for you over her," he says, coming at her again with his hand out. "Maybe it's what's under that dress. Is that it? Do you have a magic pu—"

I slam my hand against his chest and roughly shove him back. "I warned you not to fucking touch her."

Logan stumbles back and crashes into the door. His eyes blaze with rage as he growls and charges at me. "I'm so tired of your shit!"

I gently push Luna out of the way and put my hands out to stop him, but he grinds to a halt at the last second and sucker punches me in the jaw.

My ears ring as my teeth knock together. "Goddammit!"

Logan grins and raises his fist again.

This time, I duck and counter-punch him in the gut then uppercut his jaw. He grunts as the wind gets knocked out of him and collapses to his knees, cupping his chin. I inch toward him with my hands balled into fists, ready to strike again, but fingers fold around my arm.

"Just let it go," Luna says. "You're better than that."

I'm better than that?

I used to not be. I used to hit and fight with people whenever they pissed me off, but hearing those words come out of her lips—*you're better than that*—it makes me think I am. I'm better than what I used to be.

I realize I hate getting into fights, always have.

I lower my arm, and she tangles her fingers through mine. Then we leave the party without a second glance back and get into my car. Neither of us say anything as I back out of the driveway, maneuvering through the long line of cars, and out onto the road. Eventually, I have to say something, though.

"I'm sorry." I blow out a breath as I stop at a red light. "I feel like I just messed everything up."

She twists in her seat and brings her leg up, tucking it under her. "Are you kidding me? You were calm up until Logan decided to take the first swing, and you stood up for me when Piper was tearing me down."

"It feels like it wasn't enough."

"It's exactly what my friends would've done for me, and they're really great friends."

"Is that what we are?" I search her eyes through the darkness of the cab. "Friends?"

She shrugs. "Being friends means you trust the person, and I trust you."

"Okay, we can be friends." My disappointment shows in my voice.

"Or we can be more if you want," Luna says casually, staring out the window at the houses lining the street.

I line our palms together. "Up until that thing with Piper and Logan, tonight was one of the best nights of my life," I admit.

"Really?" she asks, completely shocked.

I nod. "I've never been so comfortable with someone. You make me feel like I can be myself, and that's enough."

"Tonight was pretty amazing for me, too," she says, smiling, but then her mouth sinks. "Is your jaw going to be all right? He hit you pretty hard."

"I'm sure it'll leave a bruise." My fingers skate across her wrist. "It'll heal in a few days, though."

She nods. "Maybe put some ice on it."

"I will."

As I drive forward, the heaviness Logan and Piper put on the night fades away. But the second I pull up to her street and park at the corner, a blanket of worry gets thrown over me again as she kisses me then gets out of the car, hurrying up to the side of her dark house. Knowing the people who live there hurt her makes it almost impossible to drive away.

I make another vow to myself, one I know my dad would be proud of.

I'll help Luna get out of that house, no matter what it takes.

Confession

EIGHTEEN

I almost stole again today.

Luna

Wynter: Oh, my God! Tell me everything!

THE TEXT COMES through at ten o'clock the next morning, a couple of hours before I'm supposed to be at Benny's.

It took me forever to fall asleep last night because I couldn't stop thinking about Grey: how incredible it was to kiss him, how much I want to kiss him again. The problem is, as long as I'm living in this house, I'll never be able to really date him. Like with my clothes, makeup, music, friends—everything really—Grey will only be able to be a part of my other life, the life outside the one I live in this house. The idea of keeping him a secret like that doesn't sit well with me.

I know what I have to do. I understand that. But it's acting on the knowledge that's the hard part.

I sit up on my bed and text Wynter the details—well, the ones I feel like sharing. I tell her about kissing Grey and how he stood up for me when Piper and Logan attacked me as we were trying to leave.

Wynter: God, she's always been such a bitch. Even when we were in kindergarten, she was the one stealing everyone's glue and crayons and blaming it on the shyest person in the class.

Me: That shyest person in the class was me. I was grounded for, like, two weeks when Ms. Mayfaring told my mom I was stealing everyone's stuff.

I pause, rereading my text, the words really sinking in.

My mom probably thought I was a klepto back then. No wonder she jumped to that conclusion when she found all that stuff under the floorboards.

Wynter: I think we should get her back for all the nasty stuff she's done.

Me: I think we should just leave her alone. You know she'll come after us if we do, and I hate dealing with drama.

Wynter: Fine, I'll let it go for now, but if she comes after you again, mama bear is gonna be pissed.

Me: All right, mama bear, but don't go looking for trouble, okay?

Wynter: Fine. But for the record, I hate her.

Me: I kind of do, too.

Wynter: Good girl. Now if we could just get you to realize what a bunch of asshats your parents are, then we'd be making real progress.

Me: I know they're asshats. I just don't know what to do

about their asshatness.

Wynter: Move in with me? The pool house was just remodeled and it's free rent.

Me: I don't want to live for free there. I'd want to pay my way.

Wynter: Holy shit!!! Does that mean you're actually considering it?

Me: Maybe. If you're being serious about it.

Wynter: Duh. I'm always serious.

Me: Liar.

Wynter: Okay, you might be right about that, but I do want you to move in with me.

Me: Let me see what I can do about a job, and then we'll talk.

Wynter: Deal. YAY!!! SO STOKED!

Chuckling, I erase the messages so my mom won't see them when she goes through my phone. I may be considering moving out, but the last thing I want is for her to find out before I get stuff set up. And after what happened with my dad . . .

I gulp as I stare at my bruised wrist, knowing it's going to be intense when I tell them I'm leaving.

I spend the next hour getting ready to go to Benny's. Knowing I'm going to see Grey, I probably primp more than

I normally would. Unsure of what to wear, I put on a pair of jeans and a fitted, grey T-shirt, and then cover myself up with my hoodie so I can get out of the house without my grandma scrutinizing me.

I check my email before I head out, and my heart misses a beat when I see I have a reply from Aunt Ashlynn.

Hey,

I'm so glad you responded to me. I was so worried you'd just delete the email . . . or that they'd get to it and delete it before you read it. I really want to meet you, too. I'm going to be in Fairs Hollow next Friday to do some stuff at the college, which is only a few hours away from Ridgefield. I was thinking of driving out there, and could we maybe meet somewhere and have lunch? Let me know. I hope you'll say yes, though. I really, really want to see you.

Ashlynn.

And P.S. to your weird but very entertaining question, my birthday is July 25th.

"It's her!" I shout then slap my hand over my mouth.

Moments later, my bedroom door flies open, and my grandma races in. "What on earth is all that yelling about?"

"I . . . um." I scratch at the side of my nose. "I thought I saw a bat, but it turned out just to be a moth."

She glares at me before walking out, muttering, "Stupid girl. Bats don't look like moths, and anyone who thinks so is an idiot. Great. All my grandkids are turning out to be morons."

Once she's gone, I type Aunt Ashlynn a quick reply that I'd love to meet her and to email me the restaurant's address. Then I skip out of the house and drive to Benny and Gale's Corner Store.

Grey is stacking shelves a few aisles from the front door when I walk inside. His jeans hang low on his waist, and every time he reaches up, his shirt lifts up, revealing a speck of skin. I don't get much time to appreciate the view of him, because Benny motions for me to come over.

"It's so nice of you to do this," he thanks me as he meets me at the front of the register. "If it's okay with you, I'd like you to work in the office. My wife's been on my case about shredding old receipts and stuff, but I haven't gotten around to it."

"Whatever you need help with, I'm your girl," I tell him, but I'm already nervous about being in a store.

He smiles then escorts me toward the back of the store. I try not to pay attention to anything on the shelves, but as we pass by the nail polish section, I'm forced to remember what I was doing here only a couple of weeks ago.

But you're not here for that now. You're here to try to make up for what you've done, and that has to be the start of something new, right?

That's what I try to convince myself, but I still feel guilty every time Benny smiles at me as he explains what boxes of papers need to be shredded. After he has given me the rundown, he leaves me alone to return to the counter, putting all of his trust in me, believing I'm a good person.

I'm going to be. I won't steal, no matter what.

Benny wasn't joking about not getting around to shredding papers. Two hours and five paper cuts later, I still have countless boxes to go through that are filled with papers and receipts dated all the way back to the 1970s.

"I can't believe he's kept all of these receipts for this long," I say as I lift the lid off another box.

"It's that bad, huh?" Grey's voice floats over my shoulder. He's leaning against the doorway with a backpack slung over his shoulder, gaping at the boxes and papers covering almost every inch of the small space.

Smiling, I set the lid down and turn around. "It's crazy. There are papers in here that are fifty years old."

"This looks just like my mom's office."

"Is she a pack rat?" I straighten my legs to stand up.

"She used to be," he says, rubbing his scruffy jawline dotted with a fresh bruise. "But she's been selling a lot of stuff lately, so the house is pretty empty except for her office. She uses it to hide all the clutter, I guess."

"When I was little, I used to sweep all the stuff on the kitchen floor under the fridge when my mom asked me to clean up." I weave around the boxes, making my way over to him.

"Why didn't you just use the dust pan?"

"I don't know. At the time, I probably thought it just took too much time to get the dustpan out. Now I wonder if I got a twisted sense of gratification when I hid all those crumbs where my mom couldn't see them, yet they were still there."

"You little rebel," he teases with a grin.

"I guess I kind of was, wasn't I?" I stop just short of him. "What are you doing back here? Or did you just sneak back to see me?"

"I'm actually getting ready to take my lunch break," he says. "And Benny told me to come back here and see if you needed a break, too. In fact, he seemed really insistent that you not only take a break with me, but that you go and eat lunch with me."

"He said those exact words to you?" I question.

"I might have embellished a little." He peeks out in the store before stepping into the room.

He keeps walking, even when he reaches me and forces me to back up until my back bumps into a shelf. Then his lips come down on mine, and he kisses me fervently as his fingers splay across the side of my neck. I tangle my fingers through his hair and devour him, pulling him closer.

"Come to lunch with me," he murmurs between kisses,

and I nod.

With one last tangle of our tongues, he pulls away, blinking dazedly.

"I wanted to do that the second you walked in the store, but I didn't think it'd be a good idea to fondle my girlfriend in front of the customers on my first day."

"Yeah, that's definitely more fifth day stuff," I joke, but inside, my heart is hammering.

Girlfriend? He just called me his girlfriend. I know we had that talk last night and everything, but I didn't expect him to just throw the title out there the next day.

"What's that smile for?" Grey asked.

"It's nothing." I try to change the subject. "How's your face feeling?"

"My face is fine. Now fess up. What's the smile for?" He pinches my side, tickling me.

"No way." I skitter to the side, hop over boxes, and barrel out of the room with him chasing after me.

The second we enter the store area, we play it cool and calmly walk up to the register. We tell Benny we're clocking out, and he waves at us, seeming distracted with banging the mouse against the counter. Grey takes the mouse from him and turns it on before giving it back to him.

"I did that the day he hired me," he says after we push out the front doors and step outside. "I showed him how to turn it on, but I think he forgets things pretty easily. I think it might just be because he's old, though. My grandma got that way right before she passed away."

"My grandma is totally the opposite," I tell him as we stroll down the sidewalk past the quaint secondhand shops, the bookstore, and the coffee house. "She remembers everything. And I mean, *everything*. If I so much as even change my earrings, she's like, 'Why'd you put those in when you had a perfectly good pair in already?'"

Grey glances left then right before he steps off the curb. "Is your grandma as intense as your parents?"

I nod. "She's pretty much like my mom, which I guess kind of makes sense since she raised her."

"But you're nothing like your parents, and they raised you." He reaches out to take my hand. "I don't really believe the whole, 'like mother, like daughter,' 'like father, like son' saying is true. I think kids sometimes end up like their parents, but sometimes, they take a totally different route in life."

When I take his offered hand, he veers right and heads toward the park in the center of the town square.

"I hope I can. I don't know what I'd do if I ever ended up like my parents. I hope, if I have kids, I treat them better."

"You will," he says simply. "You're too nice to ever become like them."

I smile at that and let him lead the way past the swings and to the back of the park where picnic tables are tucked beneath a canopy of trees.

"What are we doing back here?" I ask as he releases my hand.

He sets his backpack down on the table and drags the zipper open. "Eating lunch."

"But I didn't bring a lunch with me."

"I made you one."

"You made me lunch?" God, if Wynter heard this, she'd die. She's always telling me about her fantasy that, one day, she's going to meet a hot guy who takes care of her, treats her right, and cooks her dinner.

"It's not fancy or anything." He takes out two sandwiches, two bottles of orange juice, a bag of homemade chocolate chip cookies, and a bag of chips.

"How'd you know I was going to eat lunch with you?" I

ask, sitting down.

"I didn't know, just hoped." He sits down across from me. "And if you didn't, I'd just eat all the food myself."

"You could eat all this food?" I ask, gaping at the spread.

He grins proudly. "And then some."

He hands me a sandwich, and I dive in, watching as two kids push each other on the swing set while another one watches from the sidelines. It reminds me of the days when Beck, Wynter, and I would take turns pushing each other. Only, one of us would have to be the third wheel and sit on the swing, lamely rocking by ourselves.

"What's so funny?" Grey asks, flicking a bug away from the food.

"It's nothing." I pick up my sandwich and take a bite. "I was just thinking about Beck and Wynter and how we used to play at the park sometimes when we were kids. I'd have to lie to my mom and tell her I was going to church activities. It worked until the leader of the activities ratted me out."

"What happened when they found out?" He pops open the bag of chips.

"They wouldn't let me see my friends for a week straight." I lick a drop of mayo off my bottom lip and catch him watching me. "They even kept me home from school just so I couldn't see them there."

He scoops up a handful of chips from the bag. "If my parents punished me every time I snuck off with my friends, I'd be punished all the time." He grins as he pops a chip into his mouth. "Thankfully, I won't have that problem anymore."

"You still have friends, Grey."

"No, I don't. I don't think I ever really did."

"Well, mis amigos son tus amigos."

He blinks at me. "Come again?"

I giggle. "It means my friends are your friends."

"You're going to share your friends with me?" He seems entertained by the idea.

"Of course. Isn't that what good girlfriends do?" I smile then take a big bite out of my sandwich.

"I've never had a good girlfriend, so I have no idea." He opens the bag of cookies. "I'll take your word for it."

"Good. Consider yourself an official member of the misfits and rebels circle."

"You guys named yourselves?" he questions, crooking his brow.

"We did when we were younger," I say, reaching for the bag of chips. "We don't call ourselves that now."

"So which of you are the rebels and which ones are the misfits?"

"Beck and Wynter were the rebels. Willow and I wanted to be misfits. Ari wasn't around when we were going through that phase, so he never got a title, but if I had to give him one, I'd say he's a misfit."

He slides a chip into his mouth. "What about me?"

"Hm . . . I don't know." I set the sandwich down and assess him with my head tipped to the side. "After that punch you threw last night and with that whole bad-boy smile you do sometimes, I'm going to have to go with a rebel."

"Bad-boy smile?" He pretends to have no clue what I'm talking about. I know he does, though.

"That half-smile you sometimes do when you're trying to fluster people."

"Does it fluster you?" he wonders.

I roll my eyes. "You know it does."

He dazzles me with the smile, and I throw a chip at him, getting flustered.

He laughs as the chip pegs him in the forehead. "So vicious."

"Think about that the next time you try to play me for a sucker," I say, twisting the cap off the bottle of juice.

"I'd never play you for a sucker," he promises. "I just like teasing you because it gets you to smile, and I like it when you smile. It makes me feel like I'm doing something right."

"I like it when you make me smile. I don't get to do that a lot on the weekends, because I'm always trapped at my house for almost three days straight." I shrug off the depression crashing down on me. "When I move out, hopefully that'll change."

He stops mid-bite. "*When* you move out? As in, you're going to move out?"

I nod. "As soon as I get a job, I think I'm going to move into Wynter's pool house with her."

"Good. I'm glad. I hate the thought of you being in that house with all that verbal"—he looks down at my wrist—"and physical abuse."

"It's the first time he's hurt me like that," I feel the need to say.

"And it'll be his last," he presses, "because, if he does it again, I'll beat his ass. I don't care if the guy's old."

I hate fighting. I really do. But I like the idea that Grey likes me enough to want to protect me.

"I do have some good news in the midst of all this craziness. That email ended up being from my aunt Ashlynn."

"How'd you find out?"

"I asked her when her birth date is. I didn't even know it until last night, so it has to be her."

He grabs his unopened bottle of juice. "Are you going to meet her?"

"Yeah. Next Friday . . . I'm a little nervous but excited. I mean, I know I've only emailed her once and gotten two from her, but she seems nice."

"If she's anything like you, then I'm sure she is."

I smile at that.

"Totally off the subject," he says, balling up an empty sandwich bag. "But I have to take my sister out tonight, and I was thinking that maybe you could come with us. I know it's kind of lame, but it'll give us more time to hang out."

"I might be able to do that. My grandma's going to be around until tomorrow, so I could probably get away for a while." I smile as I finish off the sandwich, trying not to get too excited that I'm going out with Grey tonight. But I can't help it. My stomach is so bubbly it feels like a bouncy house.

We finish the rest of our lunch then clean up the garbage and head back to the store, holding hands. I feel like I'm walking onrainbows until I receive a message from my mother.

> *Mom: We're coming home early. Make sure to come home the moment you get off work.*

I frown as I read the text again.

"I think I might have to take a rain check for tonight. My parents are coming home earlier."

"That's okay," he says. "We'll have plenty of time to go out after you move out, right?"

"Yeah, you're right." I start to put my phone away, but another text buzzes through.

> *Mom: I don't want to have this conversation over the phone, but I feel like, if I don't say something now, you might be ruined by the time we get home. We know about the guy, Luna. Mary Pepersoon saw you two holding hands today when you were supposed to be at the store.*

My head whips up, and I scan the sea of faces, realizing how badly I've messed up by holding hands with Grey out in the open.

"Luna, what's wrong?" Grey asks with concern.

I wiggle my fingers from his grip and hug my arms around myself. "Someone saw us holding hands and reported it back to my mom." My thoughts sink to what they're going to do to me, and that pressure builds in my chest again, smothering the air from my lungs.

I glance at the nearest store, desperate to go in there and fill my pockets with temporary relief. Just one more time. That's all I need.

His expression fills with frustration. "That's such bullshit. It's nobody's damn business what we're doing." He snatches hold of my hand again and steers me in the direction of the store, but he goes past it, heading toward the diner.

"Where are we going?" I ask, jogging to keep up with his long strides.

"We have fifteen minutes left until break's over," he says determinedly. "That's enough time to fill out a couple of job applications."

"But how do you know who's hiring?"

"Because I spent days applying to every place that is, but people wouldn't even give me the time of the day because of that whole stupid shoplifting thing. You, however, should be able to get a job easily." I open my lips, but he cuts me off. "Yeah, I know. You shoplifted, too, but no one knows about it, and you don't need to tell them."

"But what if I try to steal something? Because I kind of want to now."

"Well, right now you're with me." He stops in front of the diner and cups my face between his hands. "And working here, I don't think you'll have that big of a problem. Besides, I think it might be easier to control your compulsion when your parents aren't controlling you."

He's right, and even if he isn't, I won't know until I try.

Squaring my shoulders, I open the door and take my first step toward freedom. Crossing my fingers, I pray I can ride out the storm at home until I get everything put together.

Confession

NINETEEN

> I agreed to go to the dance with Piper.
>
> Grey

AFTER WE LEAVE work Saturday night, I don't see Luna for the rest of the weekend. She does send me a couple of texts on Sunday to let me know she's alive and that no one has physically harmed her. I reply, asking her if they've verbally harmed her, to which she responded, *I can handle it.*

I can handle it? She can handle it? Her words echo in my head for the rest of the day while I work on packing up my stuff.

The buyers of our home threw in some bonus cash if we could be out in two weeks. Wanting the extra money, my mom agreed, so we've been running around the house like a bunch of chickens with our heads cut off, trying to put everything in order.

My mom forces us to take a break at dinnertime to go and see our new place, though.

"I know it's kind of small," she says to Mia and me as we roam around the three bedroom, two bathroom apartment. "But it's cheap and will really help us get on our feet again."

Mia grimaces as she pokes her head into one of the bedrooms. "There's barely enough space for my bed," she grumbles.

Fortunately, my mom is too busy looking at the cupboard space to hear her.

"I know it sucks," I say, reclining against the wall. "But right now, we just need to be grateful that we have a roof over our heads."

"Yeah, I know." She sighs as she slumps against the wall across from me. "And at least we'll have more money now, right?"

"Maybe a little." I tread with caution. "But I don't think things are ever going to be like they were when Dad was alive, and Mom needs us to be okay with that. She's under a lot of stress."

"I know, but it's hard. I miss how things were."

"Me, too. But I think things will get easier eventually."

"I hope so."

"So, what do you guys think?" our mom asks as she walks down the hallway toward us with a hopeful look on her face.

Mia and I exchange a look then turn to her and smile.

"I love it." Mia skips up to her and encloses her arms around Mom. "Thanks, Mom."

Mom pats Mia's head, confused. "For what?"

"For making sure we didn't end up homeless," Mia says, looking up at her.

Mom's eyes water, and then she reaches out and yanks me into their hug. "We're going to get through this. Things will get better."

"I know they will." I wrap my arms around them and hug them both. "Mom, you're doing a good job," I feel the need to say. "I know things are complicated and different, but that's not necessarily a bad thing. Sometimes, changes can turn into something good."

Maybe it's Luna's optimism wearing off on me, but I mean what I say. The last four or five months have been difficult and full of change, and not all of those changes have been great. Losing my dad was the hard, and watching my mom struggle breaks my heart. But changing myself—trying to be a better person—has been my good through the bad.

Yeah, there have been a lot of ups and downs happening at school, but compared to the stuff going on with my family, school drama has been the easy part. It has given me a chance to grow and move away from the life where I surrounded myself with people who made me unhappy.

I'm feeling pretty okay with life in general by the time my mom, sister, and I return home. But, as I'm getting ready to go to bed, I receive a text message.

Since my contacts didn't transfer over when I got my new phone, it takes me a moment to figure out who the message is from.

Unknown: U r taking me to the dance.

Just one simple sentence, but it carries weight.

Me: Who is this?

Unknown: The person who's going to destroy your girlfriend if you don't take me to the dance.

Me: Piper?

Unknown: Duh. Who else would this be?

My jaw ticks.

Me: Why can't u just get Logan to take u to the dance? U two seem pretty into each other.

Piper: Jealous?

Me: U wish.

Piper: Don't pretend like u don't miss me. I might not be some sweet, little, innocent freak, but I do have my perks, something u used to take advantage of every time we were alone.

Me: Things change. I don't want that anymore.

Piper: Yeah, right. Every guy wants only that.

Me: Every guy who's a jerk does.

Piper: Whatever. I was just messaging you so we could make plans for when you're going to pick me up and make our pre-dance plans. We better do something amazing. No stupid dinner or anything cheap like that.

Me: I'm not going to the dance with u. Let. It. Go.

Piper: Oh, Grey, you were always kind of stupid, weren't u? I mean, u never even realized I was fucking Logan behind your back pretty much the entire time we were going out.

Okay, that stings a little, but I quickly shake it off.

Me: Good for u two. I'm glad u found each other.

Piper: Whatever. I know u care, just like u care if I tell the entire school about your girlfriend's dirty, little secret. I gotta say, I didn't think she had it in her.

Me: What r u talking about?

Piper: I heard u and Luna talking on Beck's deck the other night about how she feels like she has to steal because her parents are so mean. She really needs to be more careful when she tells her sob story.

Me: U better not do anything to her, Piper, or I swear to God I'll end you.

Piper: Like u could. U know as well as I do that I have everyone at the school so damn afraid of me they'll do whatever I tell them. So, if I tell them to break Luna apart, they'll do it because they'll be too afraid to go against everyone else. And I think the store owners would love to hear about the sweet, little, church girl who's been ripping them off, too.

My heart thrashes in my chest as I sink onto my bed and grip the living daylights out of my phone. "Fuck. This is all my fault." Piper wouldn't be going after Luna if she wasn't pissed off at me.

Me: What do u want?

Piper: U know what I want, Grey. I've spelled it out for you enough.

I flex my fingers, trying to control my temper.

Me: So, if I take you to the dance, u will leave Luna alone?

Piper: U have my word.

Me: Ur word means jack shit.

Piper: Guess you'll just have to trust me that I'm being honest this time. Oh, and I expect u to wear a pale pink tie and cummerbund just like we talk about.

Me: I still don't get why u r doing this. If u were screwing around with Logan, then clearly u never really cared about me.

Piper: I'm doing this because I can and because u broke up with me. I hate when I don't get my way, but worse, I hate when people think they're better than me when they're not. U were never a good boyfriend, but I stuck it out with you because you were hot and popular. I should've been the one to break up with you.

Rage waves through me, and I chuck the phone across the room.

"Goddammit!" I get up and pace the room. "What the hell am I going to do?"

Deep down, I know exactly what I'll end up doing. I'll take Piper to the dance because suffering through one night with her is worth protecting Luna from months of torture.

I TELL PIPER I'll take her to the dance the next morning, and she agrees to keep Luna out of this stupid fight going on between the two of us. The worst part is still ahead of me, though, because I have to tell Luna that not only does the most vindictive person in our high school know her secret, but I'm going to take her to the dance.

It feels like sophomore year all over again as I head for the grassy area in front of the school where Luna and her friends hang out during the mornings and afternoons.

Luna texted me a few minutes ago, saying she'd be there. I wanted to reply that I couldn't wait to see her, but I felt too nervous and guilty. My guilt only grows when she smiles at me.

"I was starting to wonder if you got my message," she says, looking happy to see me.

I stop just short of her, drinking her in. She's wearing a pair of red shorts and a black tank top that matches her boots. The outfit shows off her long legs and the freckles on her shoulders, freckles that I kissed the other night.

I finally drag my eyes off her, but then instantly shift my weight when I notice Willow, Ari, and Wynter scrutinizing me.

"I did. I was going to text you back, but I was driving," I tell her.

"Oh." Luna pats the spot next to her, and I drop my bag onto the ground then pause before I sit down.

"Mind if I sit with you guys?" I ask the other three.

Wynter trades a questioning look with Willow who casts a curious glance at Ari.

Ari shrugs, like *why are you guys looking at me?* "Sure. The more, the merrier."

I sit down behind Luna and slide a leg on each side of her, earning a look of approval from Wynter. I play with Luna's hair, tangling my fingers through it as she and her friends talk about what they're going to do at lunch.

"I can leave campus," Luna says to Wynter, relaxing back against my chest, "but I need to be careful that no one sees me."

Wynter slides her legs out from under her to stretch them out. "I can't wait until you don't have to hide anymore."

"Me, too," Luna agrees. "It's going to be soon."

Wynter smiles then turns to Willow and starts telling her that she should move in with them, too.

I circle my arms around her and put my lips beside Luna's ear. "Soon, huh?"

She bobs her head up and down. "I got the job at the diner. I start this weekend, which gives me the entire week to finish helping Benny shred his crazy amount of papers."

"What did your parents say about it?"

"They don't know yet, and with what happened over the weekend, I'm not going to tell them."

I trace circles on her shoulder. "What happened?"

She tips up her chin, meeting my gaze. "They told me they were shipping me off to an all girls' boarding school."

"What?"

"It's not going to happen. They're sending me away in a couple of weeks, which gives me a couple of weeks to move out." She anxiously chews on her lip. "I'm scared, though, that they'll somehow find out what I'm doing before I get out."

"You could always just come stay with me until you're ready to move in with Wynter," I offer, pulling her more tightly against me.

She laughs a little. "While I appreciate the offer, I don't think you're ready to handle me twenty-four seven, and I'd never want to impose on your family like that."

"You wouldn't be imposing. My mom would probably be happy that I was helping you out. She's actually the one who encouraged me to give you that long-ass apology I gave you the other night."

"You talk to your mom about me?"

"I talk to her about a lot of stuff, including you. She wants to meet you sometime."

"I'd really like that," she says with a trace of nerves. "I just hope she likes me."

"How could she not?" I brush my finger down the brim of her nose.

"I don't know. If you told her everything about me, she might not."

"She understands people make mistakes. She has me as a son, doesn't she?" Sighing, I move my arms from around her and scoot back. "I really need to talk to you about something. But not out here in the open." I stand up and offer her my hand. "Walk with me to my car?"

Nodding, she places her hand in mine, and I lift her to her feet. Right as we're about to walk off, though, all hell breaks loose.

It starts when Beck joins the circle, sitting down between Wynter and Willow. "Hello, my lovely comrades. What a fine day we're having. Don't you all agree?"

"Beck, are you high already?" Luna hisses under her breath, glaring at him.

He presses his hand to his chest, feigning hurt. "Luna, I'm insulted you think, just because I'm happy, I'm high." He drapes an arm around Willow's shoulder, grinning. "The only thing I'm high on is life."

Wynter snorts a laugh, while Willow looks like a skittish animal, ready to flee.

"You're so high," Wynter says to Beck.

Beck shoots Wynter the nastiest look I've ever seen, but the look fades as Willow ducks out from Beck's arm, grabs her stuff, and jumps to her feet.

"I have to go." She dashes toward the school.

"What was that about?" Wynter mutters, watching her friend run away from their circle.

Beck stares after her. "I think I fucked up," he says then stands up and chases after Willow.

"I knew the dancing thing was going to cause drama," Ari mumbles, shaking his head.

"They'll get over it. They always do," Luna tries to reassure him, but I can feel the tension in her fingers as she turns to me. "Ready?"

I nod. Then we walk back across the grass toward the parking lot. We remain quiet, and I know she has to be worried something is wrong; I can see it on her face. I want to assure her everything is fine, but I can't get the lie to leave my lips.

After we get into my car, I just spit it out. "Piper texted me last night."

She bites her nails, which I'm starting to notice is a nervous habit of hers. "Okay . . . ? I'm not sure what to say to that."

"You don't need to say anything." I take her hand and rip off the Band-Aid, telling her what happened.

She shakes her head a thousand times after I finish telling her but doesn't utter a word.

"Please say something," I beg her, desperate for her to tell me that everything will be okay, that she will forgive me for getting her into this mess.

"No," is all she says.

"No, what?" I tighten my hold on her, afraid she's going to bolt.

"No, you're not going to do this," she says with fierce determination.

I've never seen Luna look so angry before, and it startles me a little.

"I know this is really bad, but I have to do it. If I don't, then Piper will—"

"Screw Piper and her threats," she cuts me off, scooting across the seat until our knees are touching. "I've spent my whole life putting up with people like Piper, and I'm getting really tired of it. I don't want to be a coward anymore. I want to face this, just like I'm going to do with my parents."

"But what if she tells everyone?"

"Then she tells everyone. Words can only affect you if you let them, and I've let words affect me for too long. I've let them control me, make me afraid, make me question what kind of person I am, and I don't want to feel that way anymore."

"I don't want you to, either." I cup her cheek, caressing her skin with my fingertips. "But what if she tells the store owners?"

A soft breath trembles from her lips. "I'll deal with that if it happens, but Piper doesn't have any proof that I actually stole anything, so the store owners can't do anything to me other than look at me differently. And I guess that can be my penance for making the choices I did."

I love her self-confidence, but I'm still unsure if *I* want to see her go through this.

"Are you sure you want to do this?" I ask. "Because a dance is just one night, but Piper could drag this thing on for months."

"Even if you did go to the dance with her, it still doesn't guarantee she won't say anything to anyone." She mulls over something, sucking her lip between her teeth. "Grey, I only want you to go to the dance with Piper if you want to. Don't do it to protect me."

"I didn't even want to go to the dance with her when I was dating her." My fingers slip through her hair and spread across the back of her head. Her eyelashes flutter as I draw her toward me. "I kind of had my sights set on someone else."

"You did?" she asks, slightly breathless.

"I did, but I'm not going to ask her right now. I want

to ask her the right way and make a big deal out of it so she can have time to think about her answer."

"I think she might say yes." Her chest heaves as our lips brush.

"I sure hope so." I kiss her again and again, tasting her lips. "Are you sure you want to stand up to Piper?"

Her breath dusts across my lips as she exhales. "I should've done it a long time."

"No matter what happens, I'll be here for you." I move in for another kiss but stop. "You know that, right? I'm not going anywhere."

She nods. "I know, and I'm glad. It makes it a bit easier, knowing I won't be in this alone."

"You definitely won't be alone," I say then kiss her.

We spend the rest of the morning making out in my car until the bell rings. As we pull away, readjusting our crooked clothes, I get my phone out to text Piper that the deal is off.

"Are you sure you want to do this?" I double-check.

She fixes the strap of her shirt then takes my phone, types a message, and hits send.

"There. Now there's no going back." She returns my phone to me, trying to appear confident, but I can see the sea of concern in her eyes.

I'm worried, too. With how quickly Piper spread the rumor about me, I wouldn't be surprised if people are whispering about Luna's kleptomania before first class even starts. She'll probably drag me through the gutter more, too.

I wish she would only come after me. Piper's drama may be annoying, but I haven't been mocked throughout high school like Luna has, and I don't have to go home to parents who rip me apart.

If this is what Luna wants to do, though, then I have to

let her. The last thing she needs is more people telling her what to do. All I can do now is hold her hand and be there for her the entire way through. I can be the guy my father knew I always could be.

Confession

TWENTY

Being on my own is scary.

Luna

THE REST OF the week passes by excruciatingly slow, mostly because I'm so excited for Friday to get here so I can meet my aunt.

My parents have been focused on packing my stuff and seem really upbeat about the idea of me leaving. Of course, they're telling everyone I was awarded a scholarship to some prestigious private school up in Washington, and that's why I'll be moving away. They spend every dinner pointing out all the stuff I've done wrong and why I've ended up in the position I'm in.

I endure it the best I can, counting down the days until I move out it. My soon-to-be freedom is my motivation to keep my kleptomania under control, and it's working pretty well. I don't sleep very well, though, because I'm too worried my plans will be revealed somehow.

Getting through school is complicated, too. Piper made good on her word. Within an hour after learning Grey was no longer playing her game, she told the school my secret and decided to embellish, adding that Grey and I slept with each other at the party. So, not only am I a thief, but I'm also a slut.

Logan takes every opportunity to remind me of this while Piper sits back and watches the drama unfold. Then again, life could be worse. I could be going through this alone.

"I'm getting so tired of this," Wynter says to me on Friday morning when we walk up to my locker and find a bunch of "Living with STDs" brochures taped to it.

She rips the brochures off, marches over to the trashcan, and tosses them in there. On her way back to me, people whisper and stare, and it makes something snap inside her.

"Stare all you want, but you're the idiots!" she shouts, turning in a circle in the middle of the hallway. "You're the ones who are going along with this, but you know what? Sooner or later, she's going to come after you."

When the whispers and stares increase to laughter and gawking, Wynter fumes, returning to my side.

"I'm going to put a stop to this." She leans against the locker beside me with her thinking face on.

"Just let it go." I collect my English book and iPod before I close my locker. "Eventually, it will blow over."

"You're too much of an optimist," she mutters, putting a braid in her hair. "If anything, things will get worse."

"So they get worse." I shut my locker and hug my books to my chest as we start toward class. "I have you guys, and that's all that really matters."

"Yeah, I guess." Her lips thin as she pinches them together. I can see the wheels turning in her head, her thoughts heading to who knows where. "I need to go somewhere before class. I'll see you at lunch."

"Wynter, leave it alone!" I beg as she strides away from

me with her chin held high.

She raises her hand up and waves at me before turning down one of the side hallways.

I sigh and begrudgingly go to class, crossing my fingers that she doesn't do something that will add fuel to the fire.

BY THE TIME the lunch bell rings, I notice two things. One, this thing going on between Beck and Willow isn't simply going to blow over. The two of them still can't look each other in the eye, which makes the vibe in our circle awkward. And two, Wynter has definitely done something to Piper.

I first noticed something was off during third period, a class I have with Piper. Usually, whenever she walks in, she seizes the chance to whisper as loudly as she can to her friends, "There's the thief slut. Everyone keep an eye on your purses." Then her friends snicker and clutch their bags as if I'm going to get up and try to steal it from them.

Today, however, nothing. No whispering. No snickering. Piper doesn't even look at me. It's as if I've become invisible or something. The same thing happens with Logan during fourth period. He doesn't even so much as cast a glance in my direction.

By the time the lunch bell rings, I know something is going on.

"What did you do?" I ask Wynter the second she sits down with her lunch.

"You'll have to be more specific," Willow says, grabbing an apple and a soda from her bag. "I've done a lot of things in my life."

I narrow my eyes at her. "I know you said something to Piper. She hasn't said anything to me since you walked off this morning. Even Logan has left me alone."

"Hey." Grey sits down beside me, leaning in to give me a kiss on the cheek. When he catches sight of my face, though, he pauses. "What happened?"

"Ask Wynter." I glare at her. "I told you not to get involved in this. Now she's going to come after you."

Wynter waves it off, biting into her apple. "I'll be fine. I'm tough, Lu. You know that."

"But I don't want you to have to be tough," I say. "Not because of me."

"It won't be because of you." She pops the tab on her soda can. "You didn't make me do anything."

"What exactly did you do?" Grey asks, massaging my shoulders.

Wynter takes a sip of her soda, shrugging. "Something that should've been done a long time ago." She balances the can between her outstretched legs as we wait for her to explain further. "Look, all I did was talk to a few people and see if any of them had any dirt on Piper. Turns out, Beth, one of my friends from the volleyball team, has an uncle who is a plastic surgeon out in Fair Hollow. Apparently, right before Piper moved here, she lost some weight and really matured in the"—she points at her chest—"department, but only because she went and got a bunch of plastic surgery done." Wynter relaxes back on her hands and slips off her sandals. "Now, normally, that wouldn't be a big deal, but since Piper is so fixated on how people look, I didn't think she'd take it too well if people knew her little caterpillar to butterfly transformation was bullshit. It also helps that Beth knows how to get some of her before photos."

While I'm glad to have a break from Piper, I still feel guilty that this will probably eventually backfire on Wynter.

"I really wish you would've talked to me first before

you did anything."

She kneels up and moves over in front of me. "I love you, Luna. You're like the sister I never had, and when I made a promise to you in third grade that no one would ever hurt you, I meant it." She targets her gaze on Grey. "Remember that when you so much as think about doing anything that will hurt her."

Grey slings his arm around me. "Good thing I'm planning on never hurting her."

"Good boy," Wynter says then hugs me. "Now, let this go and start packing your stuff. We might have all the drama settled at school, but we need to get you out of that house."

I nod, and then we pull away, shifting the conversation to much lighter things, like the dance. Ari and Wynter decide they'll go together as friends while Beck works and works to get Willow to smile and agree to go with him. At first, I don't think he's going to be able to pull it off, but I should know better than to ever question Beck's ability to charm people. After doing a little dance and song performance in the middle of our circle with half the school watching, Willow finally cracks a smile.

"Fine, I'll go with you," she says, laughing. "Just no more singing."

"Sounds like the perfect deal." Beck grins as he plops down on the grass beside her.

"But just as friends, right?" Willow asks, twisting a strand of hair around her finger.

"Of course," Beck replies with a nod.

I'm still not exactly sure what happened between the two of them at the party. Willow insists it was just the sexy dancing that made things uncomfortable, but I wonder if something else happened after Ari and I took off.

If that's the case, Willow seems pretty dead set on keeping it a secret.

"I'LL BE AT the store if you need me," Grey tells me as we stand in front of the restaurant where I'm supposed to meet my aunt. He has his hands resting on my hips and worry creasing his face. "Maybe I should wait until she shows up, just to make sure everything is okay."

"I'll be fine." I stand on my tiptoes to give him a kiss. Even after a week straight of kissing him, it still turns my stomach into butterflies and my legs into goo. "And if you stick around, you'll be late for work."

"I can be a few minutes late."

"No, you can't." I step back and point a stern finger toward the end of the block. "Now go."

His lips quirk up. "I think your bossy side might turn me on more than the sore loser side."

I lightheartedly swat his arm, and he laughs, reluctantly heading away from me.

I watch him walk away for a moment before I muster up some bravery and open the door to the restaurant. I take a seat in a corner booth and order a Coke while I wait for my aunt to show up, worrying that I won't be able to spot her when she walks in. Although I've seen photos of her, she's almost fifteen years older now. She could've changed a lot over that amount of time.

All my concerns vanish when the door dings, and a woman in her thirties walks in with similar features as my mom and freckles on her nose just like mine. She recognizes me, too, and rushes toward me with joy radiating from her eyes.

"I'm so glad I finally get to see you after all these years," she says as she reaches the table I'm at.

"Me, too. I've wanted to meet you forever." I get up and give her a hug. As I put my arms around her, I become painfully aware of just how little my parents hug me and how most of the hugs I've received over the years have been from my friends and now Grey.

My aunt pulls away to get a good look at me. "You look so beautiful and happy." Worry suddenly masks her expression. "Does Mom know you're here?"

I shake my head. "She wasn't at the house when I left. She's at a church meeting, and she should be there until at least seven, so we have a couple of hours."

"How are things with her?" she asks as we take a seat across from each other in the booth.

"I don't know . . . Everything's fine, I guess." I reach for a saltshaker and spin it in my hands, feeling restless.

She shucks off her jacket and sets it aside. "That doesn't sound very convincing."

I sigh and start telling her what has been going on while she has been gone. I tell her about my strict home life, how hard things have been sometimes, how I never feel like I am good enough for them, and how part of me doesn't want to be good enough for them because, whenever I try, it feels like I'm not being true to myself. Then I tell her about my friends and how, when I'm with them, I feel at peace with who I am.

I talk for over an hour, and by the time I'm done, I feel so much lighter.

She collects the mug in front of her, takes a sip, and then smiles thoughtfully as she puts the cup down. "You sound just like me. I always felt like the walls were closing in every time I was in that house, but when I was at school or hanging out with my friends, it was like I could finally breathe."

"That's how I feel. It took me forever to act like myself in front of other people, though. I kept a lot of stuff from my friends for a while, afraid they wouldn't like me if they knew." I tear open a sugar packet and dump it into my coffee.

"It took me until I was about sixteen," she says. "Up until then, I spent every waking hour trying to do exactly what was expected of me. Of course, nothing was ever good enough, and I eventually got tired of trying, said to hell with it, and did what I wanted."

"Do you ever regret it?"

"Nah. I mean, I regret some of the stuff I did, but I don't regret getting kicked out." She cradles the mug in her hands. "Leaving that house was probably one of the best things that ever happened to me."

I stir my coffee with a spoon, mixing the sugar. "Can I ask . . . ? Do you mind if I ask why you got kicked out?"

Her brows spring upward. "They never told you?"

I shake my head. "I was always told you just did a bunch of bad things and that your mom kicked you out."

"I did do some bad things. That part is true." She sets the cup aside and rests her arms on the table. "I guess where it all really started was with the fire, though."

I turn my hands over on the table, palms facing up, showing my scars. "The one that put these on me."

Sadness creeps into her expression as she slides her hands across the table and places them over my palms. "I didn't know it left scars."

"They're not that bad. Hardly anyone notices them." Lie, but I don't feel as guilty as I typically do, because it helps erase some of the guilt in her eyes.

"Still, you never should've had them at all." Her tone is tight.

"Do you know how the fire started? Because I was

always told that it was intentional, but that was about it."

"Yeah, Mom started it."

"My mom started it?" My eyes become round like saucers.

"Burning my clothes," she adds. "Mom and Dad hated the clothes that I started wearing, so they threw them into the fireplace. One thing led to another, and the fire got out of control and spread throughout the house. They panicked and ran out of the house, shouting that it was all my fault. They were probably a little bit right. I did test their patience a lot. I was just glad I got you out of the house without us getting hurt. That's what they can't see—that their crazy punishments lead to so much damage. Even their verbal abuse isn't harmless. It made me hate myself for a very long time until I realized that maybe it was just them, that they had expectations that no person could ever live up to."

Two things crash down on me in that moment and knock the wind out of me. One, I realize why I always felt like I knew my rescuer, because it was her. She saved me from that fire. She might be the reason I'm alive today. And two, she keeps saying Mom and Dad like my parents are hers.

"Ashlynn, what are you to me?" I ask. "I mean, you're my aunt, right? Because that's what I've been told for pretty much my whole life."

"No, I'm your sister." Her shock slowly simmers to rage. "Those assholes. I can't believe they'd lie to you about something like that. I should've tried to get in touch with you earlier, but I thought, until you were eighteen, there was no way I'd be able to see you without getting the cops called on me."

"They threatened to call the cops on you if you tried to see me?" That's why she stayed away all this time.

She nods, her eyes wild with fury. "They said they'd

report me for stalking if I so much as ever came within ten feet of any of you. I should've said fuck it, though. I never should've left you alone with them, not after the fire."

I have so many questions, so many things I want to say, but before I can get the words out, our mom storms up to our table.

Untamed anger burns in her eyes as she grabs my arm and yanks on me, stabbing her nails into my flesh. "Luna Harvey, get your butt out to the car right now. I couldn't believe it when I drove by. At first, I thought I was seeing things because I thought there was no way my daughter would betray me like this."

I wrench my arm away from her and scoot back into the booth. "I'm not going anywhere."

Her anger blazes as she pounds her fist against the table, knocking a glass of water over. "You do not say no to me, young lady. Now get in that car before I make you. And say good-bye to Aunt Ashlynn, because you're never seeing her again."

"You mean my *sister* Ashlynn." My words carry a punch, and I can see the impact as my mother tenses.

"You can't make her do anything," Ashlynn says calmly. "She's eighteen years old, and she can decide when she's going to leave, where she's going to go, and who she's going to see."

Mom points an unsteady finger at Ashlynn. "You stay out of this. You're not a part of this family anymore."

"I might not be part of your family, but I can be part of hers." Ashlynn looks at me. "I'll be a part of her life as long as she lets me."

"That's not going to happen," Mom snaps. "Luna knows the rules. She knows she'll be kicked out if she continues to see you."

"I want to continue seeing her." My voice sounds small,

but at least I get the words out. "And I'm going to. She's my sister."

"She's not your sister." She targets her rage on me. "She gave up the privilege when she started the fire."

"You mean the fire she saved me from." I carry her gaze, even though I'm scared to death. But she needs to see that I know, see who I am and what choice I'm making.

"Her bad choices are what started the fire." Our mom places her hands on the table, leans toward me, and lowers her voice. "If you don't get up right this second, we're done. You can never come home, and you will never speak to your father or me again. You already embarrassed this family enough."

I hide my shaky hands beneath the table. "I'm staying here."

Mom breathes in and out before pushing away from the table. "Fine. You've made your choice. I hope you can live with your poor decision." She glances around the restaurant, suddenly aware that every customer is staring at her. She takes a moment to fix her hair then lifts her chin and turns her back on us.

I have a feeling I may not see her for a while, and I hate to admit it, but I'm sad things turned out this way. I'm sad she can't love me unless I'm the perfect daughter.

"Are you all right?" Ashlynn asks after my—our—mom is gone.

I nod, swallowing the lump in my throat as I clean up the spilled water with a napkin. "That was a long time coming."

"It's still hard, though. But it'll get easier. You'll be able to find yourself now, become your own person, set your own standards that don't revolve around them, the church, or Grandma and Grandpa. And one day, you'll look back at this and know you made the right choice." She offers me a comforting smile then flags down the waitress to order some tea to calm me down.

I hope she's right. I hope, when I look back at this moment in my life, I can see myself as more than the afraid, lost girl I feel like right now.

"What are you going to do?" she asks after the waitress leaves to put in our orders. "Do you have somewhere to live? Because I'm getting a place in Fair Hollow. I actually just got a teaching job there. If you need to, you can stay with me."

"Thanks for the offer, but I want to finish school here. I have a friend I was planning on moving in with, anyway. That wasn't supposed to happen for another week, but I'm sure she won't care if it's sooner." I feel so tired, like I'm about to crash. "I want to see you again, though. You're the only family I have left."

"I'll visit every weekend, and you can come and visit me," she says. "I'm not going anywhere. I'm not going to let you go through this alone."

Alone.

No, I'm not alone at all. I have a lot of people who care about me.

Two hours later, my sister drops me off at Wynter's house. I hate parting ways with her already, but she says she needs to get back to Fair Hollow because she has a flight to catch early in the morning. But saying good-bye is easier after she promises to drive out next weekend to see me.

"And I want to hear more about these friends of yours," she says as she parks the car in front of Wynter's house. "And Grey. It sounds like you really like him."

"I do." I unclip my seatbelt. "He actually knows more about me than a lot of people."

"I'm glad you have people in your life," she says. "I always worried that you'd be stuck alone in that house with Mom and Dad, and they'd wear you down."

"It felt like they did sometimes," I admit. "But my friends were always my light in the dark tunnel if that makes any sense."

"It makes perfect sense." She leans over the console to hug me good-bye.

I get out of the car and head for the pool house around back. As I hike up the driveway, I message Grey to tell him where I am. He doesn't respond, probably too busy working. Still, I feel this overpowering need to talk to him and tell him everything, and I hope I get to see him soon so I can.

When Wynter throws the door open, she greets me with a giant hug.

"I'm so sorry," she says, squeezing the air out of me. "I can't believe they lied to you about that. I mean, who does that?"

"Psychotic control freaks," I say through a yawn.

She pulls away, motioning for me to get my ass inside. "Man, you must be taking this hard if you're using words like psychotic and freaks."

I shrug and flop down on the bed. "I've given up on trying to hide what my parents are. They may want to, but after today, I think half the town is going to change their opinion on how put-together the Harveys are."

She lies down on the bed beside me. "It was that bad, huh?"

I tuck a pillow under my head. "She yelled in front of everyone. Seeing me there with my sister . . . I think it made her snap."

"That's her own damn fault."

"I know."

She gets up to turn the fan on then returns to the bed. "I'm glad you're here, though. We'll have fun living together."

"Are you sure your parents don't care that I live here for

a while?"

"I'm positive. Now stop worrying and take a nap while I start packing up my clothes and stuff," she says, pushing up onto her elbows. "You look so exhausted, Lu."

"I am exhausted." It's been an exhausting day, an exhausting year, an exhausting life. The crazy part is that it feels like I'm just getting started, like this is the actual starting point to *my* life.

And it's time for me to start living it how I want to.

Starting with a nap.

Confession

TWENTY-ONE

> *I like spooning in the dark.*
> *Luna*

WHEN I WAKE up again, the room is dark, and a solid chest is pressed up against my back. At first, I think it's Wynter, but how awkward would that be if my best friend was spooning me? Then I catch the faintest scent of cologne and soap, and a smile takes over my face as I roll over and nuzzle closer to Grey.

"You're awake," he murmurs, his lips moving against my forehead.

"Yeah." I rest my head against the crook of his neck. "How'd you get in here?"

"Wynter let me in," he murmurs, "after she made me promise I wouldn't wake you up with anything sexual."

Thank God it's dark, because my cheeks flame hot. "She has no filter."

"It's fine," he says, stroking his finger up and down my arm. "It gave me a little self-control. If she hadn't said it, who knows what I would've done when I walked in and saw you lying in bed with your shirt up."

I bite down on my lip, smiling. "You're such a liar. I didn't flash you when I was asleep."

"You totally were," he teases. "Nice bra, by the way."

"Grey, that's not funny." I pinch his side, and he laughs. "Did I really flash you?"

"No, I was just teasing you." His laughter settles down. "You actually looked pretty peaceful when I walked. And completely out of it."

"I haven't been sleeping very well," I admit. "I've been stressed out that my parents would find out I was moving out before I actually got out, and then they'd . . . Well, I'm glad I didn't have to find out what would've happened."

"They'll never be able to hurt you again." He slips his arms around to my back and urges me closer. "You're safe now."

"I know . . . It's just a lot to take in." I can hear his heart beating steadily in his chest as silence sets in.

The longer it remains quiet, the closer I get to dozing off again. Grey seems to have the same idea because, within minutes, his breathing turns soft.

"Are you spending the night?" I ask softly.

"If that's okay with you. Wynter told me I could," he murmurs. "But if you're not comfortable with it, then I can go."

"No, stay," I say with zero hesitation.

"I'm glad you said that," he whispers, kissing my lips. "Promise you'll tell me everything that happened in the morning. I want to hear more about what happened with your sister, but I want you to get some sleep."

"I promise I'll tell you everything." I roll over and pull his arm over my side, aligning my back to his chest again.

He chuckles, his breath dusting the back of my head. "You like the spooning thing, huh?"

I nod, realizing how comfortable I am, how much I like

this. "I really do."

The truth is, I don't know much about what I like. I know I love my friends. That one has always been a given. I like music a lot, and one day, I may want to do something with that, but I'm still not sure what. I like to dress fashionable without showing too much skin. I like my hair long. And I definitely like Grey. I like spooning with him, talking with him, fighting over a game with him.

That might sound like a lot, but really, it feels like I have so much more to discover about myself. Am I scared? Heck, yes. I'm scared out of my damn mind. I never thought I'd be on my own before I got out of high school.

For the first time in my life, it feels like I can breathe, like the walls aren't caving in on me, and all I'm doing is lying in bed with my boyfriend. There's no helpless feeling stirring inside me, no compulsion to steal and take control. Will things be that way forever? I have no idea what the future holds for me, but one thing is for sure.

It's my future.

And I'm going to live it to the fullest.

Confession

TWEENTY-TWO

I get giddy over dancing with my boyfriend.

Luna

Two weeks later . . .

"OH, MY GOD! You look so beautiful," my sister beams at me as she takes in the navy blue dress I'm wearing. It goes to my knees and elongates in the back, and it makes me feel elegant. I topped off the look with strappy, velvet heels and wore my hair down because Grey loves to run his fingers through it.

"Thanks for helping me pick out the dress," I say to her as I look at my reflection in the mirror.

For the first time in my life, I actually look happy, free, and like myself.

"I'm glad I could help." She starts cleaning up the make-up products she brought over. "I was so worried that Mom and Dad were going to somehow separate us again."

"That'll never happen," I assure her.

The sad truth is, I haven't heard from our mom or dad since the fight. They've cut all ties with me. I tried to call them a couple of times, but after the third attempt, they changed their phone number. I wish I could say it didn't bother me, but it does. At the end of the day, they are still my parents, and I'm still their daughter. I wish that could've been enough, but you can't force people to change. They have to want to, and as of now, my parents care more about their beliefs than having a relationship with their daughters.

"I can't believe I'm wearing a dress to this," Willow grumbles as she walks into the pool house.

I eye over her strappy, red and black dress that flows to her knees. "You look really beautiful."

"Thanks, but I still hate dresses." She sinks down in a chair. "So, how long do you think we're going to have to wait for Wynter to finish getting ready? My bet is at least another hour."

"Will you chill out!" Wynter shouts from the bathroom. "I'll be out in a minute!"

While we wait, I introduce Willow to my sister. The two of them talk for a bit, and then Willow asks me about the wall.

I take great pride in the wall. In fact, I think it might be my most prized possession as of now. Wynter and I painted it after eating way too many bags of M&Ms and drinking an entire six pack of soda within an hour.

"What? You don't like it?" I slant my head to the side, examining my handiwork.

"No, I like it." Willow moves up beside me, fussing with a strap on her dress. "It kind of makes me feel out of control. Like I could spin forever, yet at the same time, it kind of works as a whole."

"That's kind of the point." I trace my fingers along the psychedelic purple and black lines. "It kind of reminds me of us. We're all different, but when we're together, we just sort of work."

"Aw, Lu, that's so sweet." She tears up a little, which is super weird for Willow.

"Oh, my God! You don't need to cry about it," Wynter says as she whisks out of the bathroom, dressed to impress in her floor length, shimmering white dress that matches the diamonds in her ears. "I said I'd be ready in a few minutes."

"She wasn't crying over that," I tell Wynter. "She was crying over the wall."

"Oh." Wynter looks guilty. "Sorry, Wills."

"It's okay," Willow says, fiddling with a stud in her ear, "just as long as you do one thing for me."

Wynter picks up her clutch from the bed. "And what's that?"

She grasps the black and silver pendant of her necklace. "Stop bugging me about what happened with Beck."

"I'll stop bugging you when you admit that you guys did more than just dirty dancing." Wynter sits down on the unmade bed to slip on her heels.

Willow crosses her arms. "How many times do I have to tell you nothing happened?"

"You can tell me a million times, but I'll never believe it." Wynter gathers her dress, stands up, and admires her reflection in the mirror. "You two have been acting so awkward around each other."

"We have not," Willow fires back.

"Liar." Wynter shuffles for the door.

The two of them walk out, bickering, but hush when we reach the pool where the guys are waiting for us, dressed in tuxedos.

The sun is sparkling in the sky, and the air smells better than it has in a long time.

"You guys look so adorable," Wynter gushes, taking in Ari, Beck, and Grey. "Like little teddy bears."

Beck mutters something under his breath, and Ari

shakes his head, but Grey ignores her. His gaze is fixed on me as he stands up and meets me in front of the hot tub.

"You look beautiful." He places his hands on my waist, hauls me into him, and seals his lips to mine.

"So do you," I say when we come up for air. "Or handsome, anyway. I'm not sure guys like to be called beautiful."

He chuckles. "You can call me whatever you want when you look like that." With our fingers entwined, we return to the group. "My mom made me promise that we'd stop by later so she can take some photos."

"My sister's going to take some now," I say, resting my head against his shoulder.

He steals another glance at my dress. "Yeah, but I think my mom just wants to see you in your dress."

I find myself smiling. I met Grey's mom and sister a week ago. They may just be the sweetest family I've ever met. They care about each other, and for some crazy reason, they seem okay with letting me be a small part of their family. They have to know that I was kicked out, though, since half the town knows. But Grey assures me they don't care, and they like me.

His mom even helped him decorate the pool house with hundreds of lilies when he properly asked me to the dance. Wynter gushed over it for days, and I don't blame her. It was kind of a magical day and helped erase the bad memory of when I asked Grey to the dance years ago. Plus, the bed still smells like flowers, which helps me fall asleep each night.

After taking a ton of photos, I say good-bye to my sister, and then the six of us head for the limo Beck rented. It's parked in the driveway next to Grey's car. He has been working with his uncle to fix it up, and while it still has a very rustic look to it, it's not as dinged up as it was a few weeks ago. He has mentioned a couple of times that he might sell it when it's finished. I feel bad that he may have to get rid of something his father gave him, but hopefully, the present I'm going to give him tonight will make it easier.

Before I climb into the limo, I snag Beck's sleeve and steer us away from the group, ignoring everyone's questioning stares.

"Did you bring it?" I ask when we're far enough away from everyone.

Beck hitches his thumb over his shoulder, pointing at the limo. "I put it in the front seat so you can get it whenever you're ready to give it to him."

"Thank you!" I loop my arms around him and hug him before skipping back to the group.

"What was that about?" Grey asks as I duck into the limo.

"I just needed to ask him something," I say as I slide into the seat beside him.

I can tell he wants to say more, but he doesn't press. Grey never pushes me to tell him stuff when he senses I don't want to. Almost always, though, I end up telling him.

As we drive toward the school, we sip on champagne while Beck and Wynter argue about where we're going afterward.

"My place has the bigger television," Wynter says. "We should go to my house."

"Why the hell would we watch TV?" Beck retorts. "Do you know how lame that is?"

"About as lame as watching sports every stinking day," Wynter quips with a sassy bob of her head.

Beck's head bobs back as he heaves a sigh. "It's going to be a long night if she keeps going like this."

Thankfully for Beck's sake, Wynter gets distracted from arguing with him the moment we pull up to the school. We pile out of the limo one by one, and then everyone heads for the entrance. I catch Grey's arm and tow him around to the front of the limo.

"What are you up to?" Grey asks as I open the passenger side door.

"Hello, good sir." I smile at the driver as I lean in to grab the box Beck left there for me. The driver gives me a bored look as I back up and shut the door. "This is for you," I say, presenting the box to Grey.

He lifts the lid open and sucks in a huge breath of air. "Luna . . . I can't take this. It's too much."

"You have to take it," I insist. "Otherwise, I'll have to keep it, and I don't have much use for signed baseballs."

He shakes his head several times before looking up at me. "Where did get the money to pay for this?"

"I didn't pay for it," I explain. "Beck owed me." Which is the truth. "And he was happy to give it to me." Okay, the last part may be a lie.

I may have had to remind Beck that a) he didn't really need the money from the baseball, b) that giving me the baseball would show me what a good friend he is, and c) I reminded him of the time he wrecked my mom's car when he was racing it around at lunch time—when he had his driver's permit, I might add—and ended up running into a fire hydrant and denting the front end. To cover our asses, I lied to my mother and said someone ran into it while it was parked at the school and then took off without leaving a note. The last one really won him over, I think.

"Have you ever considered being a lawyer?" Beck said after I got him to agree to give me the baseball.

"No way. I'd never be able to talk in front of people like that."

"True. Plus, it'd be a waste of your awesome DJ skills."

"You're never going to give up on that idea, are you?"

He shook his head. "I need you to become a big time

DJ so you can get me into all the cool clubs."

I rolled my eyes but smiled. "I'll see what I can do."

"It doesn't feel right just taking it," Grey mutters, staring at the box.

I can tell he's torn, that he wants to take the baseball but feels bad about it.

"Please take it," I beg. "It'll make me so happy."

I know the happy thing will win him over. Grey always wants to make me happy.

He finally nods, puts the box in the limo, backs me against the rear end of the limo, and then his mouth collides against mine. He kisses me for a while, taking his time, before finally lifting me on top of the trunk. I fasten my legs around him, pull him closer, and grind against him. He groans and bites my lip as his hand travels up the front of my dress. Somehow, I completely forget where I am until I hear laughter from nearby.

We pull away, breathless, our eyes glazed.

"Thank you," he says, helping me down off the trunk. "That gift . . . It means a lot to me."

"I'm glad I could give it to you," I tell him. "Just promise me you'll keep it."

"I will," he promises. "But I'm going to make it up to you one day. Somehow, no matter what it takes, even if I have to do it years from now."

After a few more kisses, we head for the gym and join Ari, Beck, Willow, and Wynter, who are already rocking out on the dance floor. The music is loud and cheesy, and the matching blue and gold banners and streamers placed sporadically around the room look awful with the disco ball flashing from the ceiling. But the fact that I'm here with my friends and Grey, wearing a dress I picked out, makes me appreciate every single part of this.

Grey doesn't ask if I want to dance; he just steers me

toward my friends, knowing I'll want to dance with them. He has also learned from the few parties we've gone to together that he has to dance like there's no tomorrow whenever he's with me.

The six of us form a circle and begin doing our thing. Beck, being Beck, gets in the center and does his best break dance moves. For the most part, everyone is relaxed and enjoying themselves, but every once in a while, I cast a glance in Piper and Logan's direction.

Ever since Wynter threatened her, things have been fairly quiet—well, at least toward us. The two of them have found a new victim to torment—Dalton, a sweet, quiet guy who works with Ari. Tonight, Dalton is here with his friends, and Piper and Logan have made it their mission to make sure he has a terrible time. Logan keeps tripping him every chance he gets while Piper does her best to laugh as hard as she can.

"I can't believe I used to be friends with those assholes," Grey says as we grind against each other to the sensual beat of the song.

"*Used to* being the key words," I say, swaying my hips. "You're not like that anymore."

"I know. I just wish I could get them to stop." Grey grits his teeth as Logan bashes his shoulder into Dalton and knocks him flat on the ground.

Wynter suddenly untangles herself from Ari and marches over to Piper and Logan. Grey catches on to what she's doing and heads after her. While she yells at Piper and Logan, Grey helps Dalton to his feet. Piper rolls her eyes at Wynter, and Logan laughs in her face. Wynter flips them the middle finger, turns her back on them, and grabs Dalton's hand. Then she drags him toward us with Grey trailing behind her.

"Hey, everyone, this is Ari's friend Dalton," she says,

flicking her wrist at him. "And tonight, he's going to dance with us."

Dalton's eyes practically pop out of his head. "I am?"

"You are." Wynter twirls around and starts using him as a grinding pole.

Dalton looks like he has no clue what to do with Wynter's boldness, but after a song or two, he does manage to put his hands on her waist.

Grey slips an arm around me. "Wynter's got a big set of balls on her."

I let out a very unattractive snort. "I guess that's one way to describe her colorful personality."

As the fast, poppy song switches to a slow one, Grey and I align our bodies until there's no room left between us.

"I'm glad you came with me tonight," Grey murmurs, gently combing his fingers through my hair. "I was actually kind of worried you wouldn't."

I rest my head on his shoulder and play with his bowtie. "That's a silly thing to worry about. Of course I'd say yes."

"I wouldn't have blamed you if you turned me down," he says. "It's what I deserve."

"Nah, you've made up for those days and then some."

"You really think so?"

"No, I know so." My fingers trail from his bowtie to the buttons on his shirt. "People deserve second chances if they really want them, Grey."

"You think everyone deserves a second chance? To be forgiven?" he asks. "Even your parents?"

"I don't think everyone deserves one. I mean, if my mom came up to me tomorrow and offered me some half-ass apology, then no, I wouldn't forgive her. It takes time, effort, trust." I settle my hand above where his heart beats. "You, though . . . I could tell you wanted to change, and it wasn't something that you just decided. You knew you had to earn my trust, and you did that by helping me when I most needed it, by being a person I could open up to. By making me feel safe when I needed it. You didn't judge me. You didn't make me feel bad for the stuff I did. You let me just be me."

"I like letting you be you." He pulls me closer. "And I'm also glad you forgave me so I got a chance to see the real you."

"Me, too," I agree, knowing he almost didn't get to see the real me.

I almost let my fear and my parents' words stop me from showing anyone my true self. Thankfully, that didn't happen, or I would've missed out on this amazing moment, dancing with my boyfriend and feeling giddy about it. I would've missed out on getting to know my sister, working at the diner, and earning my own money.

And I probably would've missed out on a lot more stuff, because every day, new memories are made. Sometimes, they're epic. Sometimes, they're small. But each one means something. Each one has helped me figure out a part of myself, who I am in this world.

And, good or bad, I'm glad I get to experience each one.

COMING SOON

Rules of a Rebel & a Shy Girl (Rebels & Misfits, Book 2)

ABOUT THE AUTHOR

JESSICA SORENSEN IS a *New York Times* and *USA Today* bestselling author who lives in the snowy mountains of Wyoming. When she's not writing, she spends her time reading and hanging out with her family.

Connect with me online

jessicasorensen.com
and on
Facebook and Twitter

Other books by
JESSICA SORENSEN:

Isabella Anders Series:
The Year I Became Isabella Anders
The Year of Falling In Love (Coming Soon)

The Coincidence Series:
The Coincidence of Callie and Kayden
The Redemption of Callie and Kayden
The Destiny of Violet and Luke
The Probability of Violet and Luke
The Certainty of Violet and Luke
The Resolution of Callie and Kayden
Seth & Greyson

The Secret Series:
The Prelude of Ella and Micha
The Secret of Ella and Micha
The Forever of Ella and Micha
The Temptation of Lila and Ethan
The Ever After of Ella and Micha
Lila and Ethan: Forever and Always
Ella and Micha: Infinitely and Always

The Shattered Promises Series:
Shattered Promises

Fractured Souls
Unbroken
Broken Visions
Scattered Ashes

Breaking Nova Series:
Breaking Nova
Saving Quinton
Delilah: The Making of Red
Nova and Quinton: No Regrets
Tristan: Finding Hope
Wreck Me
Ruin Me

The Fallen Star Series (YA):
The Fallen Star
The Underworld
The Vision
The Promise

The Fallen Souls Series (spin off from The Fallen Star):
The Lost Soul
The Evanescence

The Darkness Falls Series:
Darkness Falls
Darkness Breaks
Darkness Fades

The Death Collectors Series (NA and YA):
Ember X and Ember
Cinder X and Cinder
Spark X and Cinder

The Sins Series:
Seduction & Temptation
Sins & Secrets

Unbeautiful Series:
Unbeautiful
Untamed

Unraveling Series:
Unraveling You
Raveling You
Awakening You
Inspiring You

Standalones
The Forgotten Girl

Printed in Great Britain
by Amazon